SIDEWALK DANCE

Also by Fletcher Michael

Glass Bottle Season
Vulture

Praise for *Sidewalk Dance*

"*Sidewalk Dance* is a life-affirming, raucous romp through a hyper-contemporary vision of New York City. Fish is a foolish, lost, yet eminently lovable picaro on a quest for meaning that Fletcher Michael comically & gracefully shows us is doomed. Because as Fish (possibly?) learns, maybe the truest thing is to shun laurels & aplomb & rectitude and just BE."

—Harold Rogers, author of *Tropicália*

"*Sidewalk Dance* follows Fish, a confused young man overly bewitched by the mythology of the New York artist. Determined to become a tortured playwright, Fish doesn't bother to read or attend plays. Instead, he focuses his efforts on looking the part with booze and drugs, and on resisting the gravitational pull of a committed relationship or a respectable career. At the root of Fish's delusion is deeply buried trauma that he's failed to confront. He might make us cringe at times, but we can all relate to Fish's quixotic search, as he tilts at authenticity amidst the city's condemned galleries and dive bars."

—Tyler McMahon, author of *One Potato*

"Rollicking, debaucherous, yet heartfelt, *Sidewalk Dance* goes all in, a take-no-prisoners bildungsroman that rattles with all the havoc and zeal of being (or at least coming across as) a viable artist in modern New York. Readers shall shimmy."

—Jakob Guanzon, National Book Award longlisted author of *Abundance*

SIDEWALK DANCE

A NOVEL

FLETCHER MICHAEL

+ KEYLIGHT
BOOKS
AN IMPRINT
OF TURNER
PUBLISHING

KEYLIGHT BOOKS
AN IMPRINT OF TURNER PUBLISHING COMPANY
Nashville, Tennessee
www.turnerpublishing.com

Sidewalk Dance

This is a work of fiction. All the characters and events portrayed in this book are either products of the author's imagination or are used fictitiously.

Cover design by Faceout Studios
Book design by William Ruoto

Library of Congress Cataloging-in-Publication Data
Names: Michael, Fletcher, author.
Title: Sidewalk dance / by Fletcher Michael.
Description: First edition. | Nashville, Tennessee: Turner Publishing Company, 2024.
Identifiers: LCCN 2023053176 (print) | LCCN 2023053177 (ebook) | ISBN 9781684420568 (hardcover) | ISBN 9781684420575 (paperback) | ISBN 9781684420582 (epub)
Subjects: LCGFT: Novels.
Classification: LCC PS3613.I34255 S53 2024 (print) | LCC PS3613.I34255 (ebook) | DDC 813/.6—dc23/eng/20231116
LC record available at https://lccn.loc.gov/2023053176
LC ebook record available at https://lccn.loc.gov/2023053177

Printed in the United States of America

1 2 3 4 5 6 7 8 9 10

For Drake and Sydell.

With such siblings, I never

sidewalk dance alone.

New York is stirring, insupportable, agitated, ungovernable, demonic. No single individual can judge it adequately. Not even Walt Whitman could today embrace it emotionally; the attempt might capsize him. Those who want to contemplate the phenomenon are well advised to assume a contemplative position elsewhere. Those who wish to feel its depth had better be careful.

—Saul Bellow, *It All Adds Up*

Conception

Chapter 1

In the beginning, Fish had thought it might end up being one of his *good* bad ideas. The kind that would lead to an anecdote of some kind that he could reminisce about on his deathbed and think, *sure, I made some mistakes . . . But that was one hell of a ride.* Now that his neck was sore and a bruise the shape and hue of a rotten apple tattooed his right ass cheek, he wasn't so sure.

Fish blamed Partiboy. If Partiboy hadn't shown up, maybe he'd still be living the story rather than nursing a poorly mixed Paloma while he scheduled an X-ray with the nearest urgent care clinic that popped up in his Google Maps search.

God, he hated Partiboy. Well, that wasn't entirely true, actually. Partiboy was, very often, an awesome companion. But when Partiboy was not awesome, he was *really* not awesome. Partiboy had gotten Fish arrested once, fired from a job another time, and banned from a bar yet another time. The three swooping cracks that traversed Fish's iPhone screen like veins were the result of Partiboy's antics on three separate occasions. But, to be fair to Partiboy, he'd also gotten Fish laid a few times, and for all the infamous evenings he'd delivered, he'd also gifted a few great ones.

Partiboy had kept his distance for the first few encounters that Fish had had with Madame Meticulous. That wasn't her name, but it was the moniker she'd been bestowed. Fish was pretty sure Bennett had come up with the nickname; it sounded like the kind of wisecrack that would slip from his perpetually sly grin.

They referred to her as Madame Meticulous because of the circumstances under which they had met her. This would've been about a month ago, a late-August zephyr frolicking down the avenues and leaving an aftertaste of summer's swelter in its wake. Madame Meticulous was a sculptor, and her work was to be featured in an exhibition at the gallery where Fish and Bennett worked.

Like many of the art types Fish delivered up to the gallery in the cavernous freight elevator, Madame Meticulous's looks could be described as noirish. She was a hipsterly, Tumblr hot, more than mainstream, Instagram hot. She was more intriguing, more appealing, more striking in her boxy tweed pants and chunky rubber-soled boots and clinging belly shirt than she was sexy. She was rail thin—and Fish had thought maybe even anorexic. Everything about her was tapered, sleek, and ever so slightly seductive, like a white ermine. She looked to be only a few years older than Fish—maybe thirty or so. She'd been anxious, thinking aloud as she talked through the potential boons and pitfalls of placing such and such piece here, in this light, rather than there, in that light, and was it always so frigid in here?

Her error was in asking too many questions, making too many requests. That is, her ostensible fault was being a petite white woman with an uncompromising sense of her own artistic vision. A more forgiving onlooker might have considered her a genius (Fish was still working to undo the profound influence that shows like *Entourage* had dealt to his male psyche). Or maybe Fish and Bennett had grown a little cynical about these art types, who seemed to feel the need to craft their personas as tweezeringly as they did their works. Or perhaps they were just jealous that she was yet another person who had achieved the artistic career that had, so far, eluded them both and for which they both pined.

There was no doubting her talent when the exhibition was finally staged—bulky humanoid statuettes bent in languid positions and bathed in buttery pools of light that revealed subtle concaves and shallow pits harboring shadows like tide pools. Still, as soon as Bennett had referred to her as Madame Meticulous in a brash whisper punctuated by a satisfied rip from his Juul, the name had stuck. It was too fun to say—the alliteration bounced pleasantly off their lips—and they couldn't help but repeat it again and again. She wasn't even French. All that Fish knew of her background was that she was half-Jewish (the fundamental preoccupation of her exhibition being something about conflicted identity that Fish hadn't really understood) and split her time between New York and San Francisco—*bicoastal*, she'd called it, scrubbing the word clean of irony before releasing it from her perfect teeth.

Fish massaged his neck. Fucking Partiboy. Always ruining everything. The first couple dates with Madame Meticulous had been good. Really good, even. They had enough in common that conversation never lagged and enough differences to keep the pauses in those conversations intriguing. She had initiated. After the second time Madame Meticulous invited him to a group bowling outing, Fish, having difficulty picturing her petite hands picking up a bowling ball, let alone hurl it down a polished alley, figured she might actually be trying to arrange a rendezvous that was romantic in nature. He took the hint and suggested a dinner date instead. However, a brief exchange of texts revealed that Madame Meticulous had far too many dietary restrictions to make a dinner outing any kind of casual affair. Between the gluten-free thing and the pescatarian thing, really only sushi was allowed, it seemed. In the end, they had agreed to meet at a cocktail bar in Williamsburg.

It was one of those bars that didn't have a menu. Instead, one just revealed to the conscientiously cool bartender (who had finger tattoos and slashes shaved into her eyebrows) what flavors and alcohols they enjoyed. Then, after a flurry of precise movements deployed with the tactical efficiency and unflappable calm of a SEAL Team Six member, the bartender would deliver some frothing or tinctured beverage in a bizarre glass with a sizable chunk of hand-chiseled ice clunking expensively against the bottom of the vessel. Despite himself, Fish enjoyed the drink. When the time came, he played the gentleman and ponied up seventy-four dollars that he didn't have, waving off Madame Meticulous's meek protestations as he slid his credit card across the bar. They'd had two drinks each.

From the bar they'd walked to Domino Park, where the city skyline had practically begged them to make out in public—an outward display of the kind that Fish, given his conservative upbringing, tended to avoid. A short while later, and after Madame Meticulous's assertions that this was something she almost never did on a first date, they were in her apartment, an elegant studio in a doorman building on North Tenth Street, overlooking the East River. Again, in keeping with his genetically ordained propriety, Fish defaulted to playing it cool; a mannered appreciation of the apartment and its tall mirrors and drooping emerald houseplants that translated, he hoped, a sentiment that existed in the sliver of space between studiously unimpressed and mildly curious. But he was duly flabbergasted by her living accommodations—especially considering that this was one of two coasts on which she'd signed a lease. *How much money did sculptors make, anyway?* he wondered.

At the time, Fish was living in an illegally lofted four-bedroom apartment in Bushwick. He'd secured the month-to-month sublet after a rushed, frantic Craigslist search several months earlier, when he'd first moved to the city. His roommates were all musicians and a drum kit—which was played, it seemed, only after midnight—occupied the majority of the cramped living room. One of the roommates was dating some semifamous actress from a Netflix show that Fish hadn't seen. Strange abstract art pieces painted by friends covered the peeling walls and the shelves were crammed with vinyl records, paperback novels, and succulent plants in small clay pots. It was not until he'd stood in Madame Meticulous's apartment, gazing at the constellation of yellow rectangles across the river and surreptitiously stroking the waxy leaf of a dwarf banana plant to determine if it was real (it was) that Fish thought seriously about moving.

Before joining her on the luxurious bed, Fish had been struck by how preposterously large the king-sized mattress was relative to her size. Perhaps because of this discrepancy, Fish was surprised to find that Madame was a rather assertive lover, detailing her preferences and no-no's in gasping breaths as their lips and hands roved exploratively over each other's now supine, now arching bodies. Though he thoroughly enjoyed the act itself, Fish had never been comfortable talking about sex, and thus was happy—and more than a little turned on—for Madame Meticulous to take the lead. With each article of clothing flung or dropped from the bed, it seemed as though the anxious knot that held her compact body together and clipped her motions and speech into staccato bursts was slowly loosened until it went slack.

After they'd caught their breath and sighed with that specific relief that follows the unstated end to which all dates are either leading or not, Fish and Madame had gotten to talking. She'd been raised in Berkeley, California, the daughter of a cardiologist and a tenured professor of anthropology. Then she'd talked a bit of trauma pertaining to her parents' divorce. She had a few faint scars on the inner bank of her left thigh—slim pink lines etched at fastidious intervals like railroad tracks—which she didn't bring up and Fish didn't ask about. When she asked, Fish said he didn't have any trauma—it was a word that, for him, meant something physical, like an amputation.

But within the hour he was telling her all about his brother and everything that had happened there. It all just came pouring out. He managed to hide the swollen blockage in his voice with a hollow laugh and willed a stinging tear back into its duct. He wasn't even sure how they'd gotten to talking about all that. Madame caressed his shoulders and suggested therapy and Fish said he'd tried it once, back in Connecticut, before he'd moved to the city. After describing how safe the space was for Fish to reveal his feelings, the therapist—a gray-bearded man with Coke-bottle glasses and a body that was nearly indistinguishable from the lumpy armchair on which he sat—had spent the majority of the session complaining about how overspecialization at an early age had ruined youth sports (Fish had felt safe enough to disclose that he'd played lacrosse in college). Fish guessed the therapists were better in San Francisco. For Madame's therapy, she had stared at flashing lights and recalled traumatic things from her childhood, apparently.

Partiboy, to his credit, had kept his distance on date number two as well. It would've been entirely like him to impose his presence on an otherwise low-key occasion. The night after the expensive cocktail bar, Madame had answered the door in a red lingerie outfit she'd purchased that day in SoHo, she'd later explained. Apparently, the shops in Williamsburg were too trendy for Madame's tastes. Fish had nodded agreeably, somewhat transfixed, and mumbled some lame joke about how few bras he'd seen worn by the L-train's female-identifying passengers, while David Byrne's now crooning, now humming voice issued softly from wall-mounted speakers.

Date number three had gone somewhat badly, but that hadn't been Partiboy's fault. Fish and Madame Meticulous had met up at a bar in East Williamsburg and she'd introduced him to a group of her friends. One of them, described by Madame Meticulous as "Instagram famous"—the ring leader, as Fish quickly deduced—led them purposefully from one bar to the next. Fish wasn't on Instagram, though he knew that fame of any kind required, in New York, a certain level of obsequiousness from those who happened into its orbit. Approaching the woman, who had a Polaroid camera tattooed on her right shoulder blade, Fish had complimented her on her Instagram fame.

"I hate that," she'd replied, smirking a little and returning her attention to the lime wedge she'd been mutilating with her cocktail straw.

"Oh?" said Fish. He wished Partiboy had been there. Partiboy would've had the perfect response to a thing like that.

As they'd left the bar, Madame Meticulous, in a burst of tequila-induced exuberance (she drank only mezcal tequila, as a rule), had jumped down off the stoop and sprained her ankle. Almost immediately, her Bambi-like joint had swollen to the size of a lacrosse ball. Fish piggybacked her all the way back to her apartment, only to find that she'd locked herself out. She was embarrassed by the turn of events, Fish could tell, though she tried to disguise it with self-deprecating remarks and a strenuously upbeat tremor in her voice. For three hours they'd waited for a locksmith, chatting and making out with their backs going sore against her door. At four in the morning, the locksmith finally arrived, disturbing the Sunday sleep-ins of Madame's hallway neighbors with the mechanical whirrings and brutal clunks of his tools. Once they'd finally made it inside the apartment, she'd iced her ankle with a frozen packet of cauliflower rice until the swelling went down.

On date number four, however, Partiboy had interjected. He had a rare talent for announcing himself at the crux of things, emerging just when things were starting to feel ever so slightly concrete beneath Fish's feet. At work that day, Fish's boss—an eccentric man named Marcel who considered himself, despite all evidence to the contrary, to be on the fringes of the Warhol-Basquiat-era pop art scene—had decided that, this being a Friday, they'd close the gallery for the remainder of the day, open some wine, and have themselves a three-day weekend. This announcement was more calculated than inspired, as his husband Stanley (who hated when Marcel drank) was upstate attending to his ailing father. Bennett had called in sick. Around eleven in the morning, Marcel had boiled two pounds of pasta and sloshed a full bottle of Rao's spaghetti sauce over the steaming noodles. This much was enough of an excuse to open a bottle of pinot noir, which was soon followed by a bottle of zinfandel and then, around three in the afternoon, a bottle of cheap vodka that had been resting dormant behind a row of rusting paint cans on a shelf in Marcel's painting studio for as long as Fish had worked there.

That's when Partiboy showed up. Fish hadn't noticed him until he went to the bathroom, sometime between the first and second joint he and Marcel had smoked on the roof while slurring their timeworn philosophies about the ostentatious grandeur of the new Hudson Yards development's ruination of Manhattan's West Side. They'd been watching as a compact orange elevator slowly ascended the face of a glassy skyscraper, depositing a pallet of cinder blocks and a handful of neckless workers in neon vests and hard hats half-way up the building to where the glass stopped and the skeleton of steel beams began before making its slow descent back down to the ground for another load. After splashing cold tap water over his face in an attempt to revive himself to the startlingly early hour of his intoxication, Fish had noticed Partiboy. He was right there, in the mirror, staring back at him with his cantankerous grin.

What the fuck are you so happy about? Fish asked.

Partiboy just wants to party, boy, Partiboy said.

Have it your way.

Fish dried his hands on his pants and left the gallery without saying goodbye to Marcel. Klein, a ride-or-die bro with whom he'd played lacrosse back in college, had texted Fish, imploring him to put on a funky outfit and join him at this rave in Bushwick. *Gonna be lit*, the text read, punctuated with the sunglasses emoji in place of a period. Partiboy stole Fish's phone and agreed to come.

Has Madame Meticulous texted? Fish asked, weakly grasping at his phone in Partiboy's hand.

Partiboy yanked the phone out of his reach.

Partiboy just wants to party, boy, he said.

Partiboy was terribly unoriginal like that. But very persuasive, too.

Fish bought a pair of black denim overalls—he was pretty sure they were women's—from a thrift shop in Bushwick and yanked them over his limbs before heading to the concert. He'd lost a bit of weight since moving to New York and so, though a little snug over his thighs, the overalls fit well enough for a one-night excursion. And they'd only cost fifteen dollars. The late-summer humidity rendered a T-shirt beneath the overalls superfluous, and Fish was more than a little vain about the way the straps clipped snuggly over his bare back and shoulders. Partiboy very much approved and soon enough they were in an Uber heading to the concert venue (a dark and cavernous warehouse space called Brooklyn Mirage).

Partiboy just wants to party, boy, Partiboy kept saying.

Would you shut up? Fish said, though he was smiling, too.

At the concert—it was some EDM group that Fish had never heard of—Klein greeted him with a knucklebump and a melted bar of mushroom chocolates that he'd purchased from a smoke shop in the West Village. All the smoke shops sold them these days—this was during that year-ish period before the police cracked down on black-market sales of the hallucinogenic chocolates. Fish took a few chomps from the gooey bar, clumsily wiping the dark rind it left on his lips with the back of his hand.

Before the shrooms hit, a skinny dude wearing a linen shirt with the buttons undone to his belly button offered them a few bumps of coke. Klein complied happily (he worked in finance and reveled in the Hollywood-ized aspects of the job) and plugged one nostril while taking an expert snort with the other. Partiboy thrust Fish's nose down onto the tip of the brass key on which a brief hillock of white powder was waiting. Though he'd been offered many times, Fish had never tried cocaine before. But since moving to the city, he'd made a habit of doing a good many things he'd never done before. Mimicking Klein's nostril-plugging technique, Fish inhaled sharply and felt the powder punch into the back of his throat. At first, it felt a little like when one took an overeager bite of tiramisu, the cocoa powder speckling the back of the throat in a way that surprised the biter enough to warrant a hacking cough.

Partiboy just wants to party, boy, Partiboy sang.

I know. That's kinda your whole thing, you know? You ever worry that it's your only thing, Partiboy? You ever worry about that? Fish demanded.

"Who the fuck are you talking to?" Klein hollered over the roar of the kicking bass as the cold, chemical flavor dripped slowly and pleasantly down the back of Fish's throat. The crowd came into exquisite focus. Girls wearing costume fairy wings swayed atop their NBA jersey–clad boyfriend's shoulders and dudes with gauges straining at their earlobes bobbed and thrusted to the beat of the music, their eyes closed and their mouths hanging slightly ajar. Fish felt the throbbing bass hits cascading into his chest like cannon blasts into a beachhead and yielded himself to the strobing light show emanating from the stage.

That's when Madame Meticulous had texted him. She wanted to know what he was up to, and if he happened to be in Brooklyn.

Partiboy, what do you think? Fish asked, shouting to be heard over the pounding chords.

Partiboy just wants to party, boy, Partiboy replied, smirking conspiratorially.

How did I know you'd say that? Fish grumbled through an irrepressible smile.

Fish was late to date number four with Madame Meticulous, and for that he blamed Partiboy. Partiboy had suggested that they have one more drink at the concert before cutting loose and rendezvousing with Madame in Bushwick. Fish had agreed, just as he'd always agreed to Partiboy's nonsensical plans, and after they'd chugged a few overpriced beers from a bar cart at the concert venue, he was blinking against the startlingly bright sunshine and pumping his legs on a Citi Bike. Partiboy smiled placidly as he perched himself on the bike's handlebars, and Fish had almost crashed, his vision occluded by his companion's swaying form.

By the time Fish had reached his apartment building, Madame Meticulous was already on the roof, where they'd agreed to meet. He wasn't sure how long she'd been there or how she'd gotten into the building—it was likely that one of the building's pit bull–owning, mohawk-having residents had let her in on their way out to the street to smoke a hand-rolled cigarette—but Fish greeted her with a gregarious hug all the same.

"Hey!" Fish shouted, his ears still deafened from the concert.

"Nice overalls," Madame said, smiling. She sipped a concoction of mezcal tequila and grapefruit juice from a Nalgene water bottle. Madame Meticulous cared deeply about the environment.

"Thanks. Fifteen dollars," Fish replied, tugging at one of the overall straps. Or had it been Partiboy who'd said that? That sounded like a Partiboy line. Completely ignoring insinuations of guilt? That was Partiboy all the way. Fish always felt a little bit of guilt—even sometimes the guilt of *not* feeling guilty—which was pretty much the most Catholic thing about him.

"How's your ankle?" Fish asked.

He'd just noticed the crutches tucked under Madame's slim arms and a strappy boot thing adorning her foot. Her other foot sported an unblemished Vans sneaker.

"Bad sprain," Madame Meticulous said. "I'm seeing a specialist tomorrow to find out if it's broken."

"Ouch," Fish said.

Careful not to upset her balance, he stepped close to her and she wove herself into his chest. They made out for a little while, right there on the empty roof. The Manhattan skyline to the west was truncated by a summer fog, making the skyscrapers look as though they were puncturing the heavens.

"Do you want to go back to my place?" Madame suggested.

Partiboy just wants to party, boy.

"My apartment's right downstairs if you want to . . ." Fish half suggested.

"Mmm . . . Maybe we could go to my place, though? I have no roommates whereas you have . . . three? And you've mentioned something about a ladder, no?" Madame replied diplomatically.

It was true; to get into his bed required an ascent up a rickety, wobbling ladder. It was a tricky climb to maneuver, even with both ankles intact.

"Four. But Jeremy's on tour and Aaron's staying with his girlfriend tonight. But okay, yeah, good point. I'll carry you," Fish said, lifting her into his arms as he spoke. The effort of cradling Madame Meticulous in his arms made him feel, suddenly, very fucked up.

Partiboy just wants to party, boy.

"Are you sure you're okay to . . . Wait, stop, can you handle these stairs?"

But Madame's concerns were too late. As soon as Fish attempted the first step, his foot miscalculated, and they'd tumbled down into a pile of limbs on the landing. Partiboy was laughing his ass off.

"Oh, shit, are you okay?" Fish asked, getting to his feet. "Fuck, I'm so sorry."

He twisted and stretched, feeling for broken bones. So far everything felt groovy, though he knew he'd be sore in some places come morning. He reached out his hand toward Madame Meticulous, but she refused to look at him. She remained on the ground, silent. Fish looked at Partiboy. Partiboy was stifling his laughter, holding a hand over his mouth as he walked down the stairs. Despite how often he caused them, Partiboy hated awkward situations. It was often the case, as now, that he'd remove himself from such encounters, leaving Fish to deal with the aftermath alone.

So, the fourth date ended pretty much like that. Madame Meticulous crumpled, with her arms clasped over her knees and silently fuming at the bottom of the stairs, and Fish waiting for someone to tell him what to do. Madame ordered herself an Uber, scoffed at Fish's offer to pay for it, and haughtily slammed the door closed without a word. Fish watched as the car accelerated up Knickerbocker Avenue. Maybe it was the drugs or the beers he'd chugged or the spaghetti brunch he'd eaten, but Fish felt sick.

Partiboy just wants to party, boy. Partiboy just wants to party, boy. Partiboy just wants to party, boy.

Fish supposed the next night qualified as a fifth date. *But is it a date if it's completely devoid of romantic intention?* he pondered.

Partiboy was into it. He showed up when Fish had downed his third Paloma at a Williamsburg dive, killing time until the meeting Madame Meticulous had arranged would commence.

What the fuck are you doing here? he asked Partiboy. *Wait, wait. Never mind. Don't fucking say it . . .*

Partiboy remained silent, though his eyes glinted mischievously from the graffiti-coated mirror in the bar's bathroom.

Madame Meticulous pretty much ended things that night. She talked through the trauma of her experience on those stairs, detailed the finer points of Fish's less-than-caring text messages following the incident, and said she had already scheduled several emergency appointments with her therapist. Fish nodded in the right places, and picked his moment for a sincere apology and kid-gloved resistance to a few accusations he found to be a little unfair. It was Partiboy's fault, he knew. All of it. But Madame did not know Partiboy like he did. Partiboy had good intentions, believe it or not. It was the only reason Fish put up with Partiboy in the first place. Partiboy wanted Fish to live the kind of life he might one day reminisce upon. Too bad for anyone who imposed on his designs.

Sometimes Fish thought about cutting off Partiboy for good. They hadn't known each other all that long—just a few years, really. After brushing shoulders on several memorable (for better and for worse) occasions throughout college and a little while after, they'd only become close when Fish had moved to New York. Sometimes he thought about yielding himself to Partiboy entirely. God, Partiboy would love that. He thought about sending Madame Meticulous a well-crafted apology text, but by the time the thought struck him, he was too drunk to well-craft anything more than the soggy snake he'd sculpted from a damp cocktail napkin. Fish knew it was over. The descent down that staircase had been more than the physical descent of a handful of concrete steps. The small part of him that he liked to think of as poetic gleaned that much.

Fish felt bad. He knew he'd fucked up a good thing, Partiboy or not. Every time a Talking Heads song played from his shuffled Spotify playlist, he felt a twinge of guilt in his stomach. Madame Meticulous had exposed him to the band, and now she haunted the tracks' cascading lyrics and bopping rhythms. Would he still feel bad on his deathbed, Fish wondered, the memory of his disastrous fourth date with Madame Meticulous interrupting the steady stream of colorful exploits on which Partiboy had guided him? Maybe. He could ask Partiboy, though Fish had a feeling he knew what Partiboy would say about all that.

Chapter 2

Fish was maneuvering a U-Haul truck up FDR Drive when Madame Meticulous called. He sent the call to voicemail and returned his focus to the road. Honking cars flew past his window, occasionally offering their middle finger as they passed. Fish was not a great driver, and the mania of piloting a twelve-foot box truck through rush hour traffic was threatening to trigger a nervous breakdown. Klein sat in the passenger seat, engrossed in his phone, toggling between the Google Maps directions that he was half-heartedly relaying to Fish and a YouTube recording of a Barstool Sports podcast. Constricting the steering wheel with fingers that had taken on a noxious shade of white, Fish maintained a painfully slow speed of ten miles per hour under the limit. Each clunk from the cargo bay made him jump, and he felt trickles of sweat careening down his flanks. His neck and back still felt a little sore, especially now that he'd spent the last six miles bracing himself for disaster in the rigid seat of the moving van. Nothing was broken though, according to the doctor who'd glanced rather quickly at his scans.

He and Klein had scored a deal on a two-bedroom way uptown in Spanish Harlem. Their mutual need for a new living situation had aligned towards the end of the summer, Fish having tired of his roommates' late-night jam sessions and Klein having recently been dumped by his live-in girlfriend (a friend of a friend had texted her a screenshot of Klein's active Hinge profile). Just when it seemed that Manhattan's real estate gods had forsaken their plea for a lease beginning October first, the firmament had opened to reveal the second-floor walk-up with high ceilings and plenty of natural light on the corner of One Hundred Seventeenth Street and First Avenue, and they'd received it like a theophany.

The realtor was a girl named Lexi and she looked to be about twenty years old. Fish and Klein had taken to referring to her as Lexi Spanish Harlem. For reasons they hadn't overthought, the conjoining of the Manhattan neighborhood to her name seemed to accurately describe her appeal.

What was it about the adjective Spanish *that carried inherent sexual weight?* Fish wondered. *Was it the stereotype of the country's seductive flamenco dancing?* Images of dark haired, dark eyed people sipping dark red wine and making out to rapid-fire castanet percussives passed lazily through Fish's mind.

Lexi Spanish Harlem had a monarch butterfly tattooed on her neck, right over her jugular vein, and she wore large sunglasses atop her head, pinning her scarlet-dyed hair behind her ears. These facts, along with her ratchet coquettish demeanor and her insistence that she was not to be contacted after 5:00 p.m., explaining that she worked three jobs, had left Klein and Fish to conclude—with the excitement of two suburban boys tickled by the lascivious thrills of metropolitan life—that she might be a stripper. Months later this theory would be disproven; Klein discovered her TikTok account, which appeared to function as an extension of her OnlyFans account, which, after further digging on Klein's part (motivated, he explained, by curiosity and nothing more), was the landing page for Lexi's thriving self-employment as an escort. "Y'all are fucking for free??!! In this economy?!?!" read the subtitle to her most popular video.

After a brief text exchange and a hastily coordinated tour, the apartment was theirs. Upon signing the lease and exchanging exuberant high fives and back slaps, they strolled through their new neighborhood to Red Rooster Harlem. By the end of the meal, fried chicken grease glossing their lips and martinis blurring their vision, they summoned a final reserve of energy for the walk back to the subway station. Though their stomachs had never felt heavier, they ambled down Malcolm X Boulevard with a buoyant hiccup cushioning their footfalls.

The apartment wasn't necessarily as close to the downtown action as they'd hoped but still, it was Manhattan. The borough of boroughs. They'd found it on Craigslist after giving up on StreetEasy listings. Nine times they'd toured a would-be dream apartment—albeit slightly out of Fish's budget, if not Klein's, who was armed with the fat salary of a recently promoted financier—and nine times they'd lost out on the place after spending more than a little money on application fees and untold hours gathering and scanning reams of documents providing evidence of their financial stability (most of it lies, in Fish's case) into PDFs and emailing them to faceless realtors who'd promised them they were in the running to ink their names on the lease.

It had been Fish who'd recommended they switch their attention to Craigslist, like a beleaguered hunter suggesting that some further valley might be replete with the game that had been hunted to extinction in their usual haunts. New Yorkers more or less trusted the sleek images and comprehensible industry lingo of StreetEasy, whereas trust for Craigslist—a site that had not updated its interface since its advent in the 2000s—remained a murkier corner of the internet. But Fish admired Craigslist. Every job he'd ever landed had been found through the site. Both cars he'd bought (and subsequently crashed) had been purchased via Craigslist. One time he'd even bought a bike on Craigslist—a squeaky fixed-speed for a hundred bucks—from his doppelgänger. When they'd met in front of a Thai restaurant in Newport, Rhode Island, the seller had looked eerily like Fish; lanky, slightly unshaven, wavy hair tucked sloppily behind over-large ears, darkish complexion, and an unhurried gait complete with the rolling shoulders of an ex-athlete. Fish had gleaned over the years that while some aspects of Craigslist had been corrupted by the lonely, the perverted, and the desperate, much of Craigslist still functioned as a portal of commerce for privileged white bros like himself who shared a whimsical appreciation of life's smaller opportunities for adventure. It was tantamount to snagging a fluttering contact tab from a thumbtacked flier on a job board hung askew in a pour-over coffee shop, long after the advent of the internet had rendered such modes of communication and commerce laughable to all but those who viewed the world as an essentially absurd playground of sorts.

Fish lurched the U-Haul to a halt in the bike lane in front of their new apartment building, a shabby tenement with an establishment called Pretty Girls Salon occupying the first floor. It took a moment for relief to seep in, replacing the anxiety that had seized his veins for the entirety of the drive from Brooklyn. A few of their new neighbors held the door open for him and Klein as they ferried furniture from the truck up to the apartment. Fish fought to recall some of the Spanish he'd learned in high school, but all he could manage was a shy "gracias." The neighbors smiled and replied in accented English, asking sincerely about their names and where they were from and welcoming them to the neighborhood. A herd of bike messengers tinkled their bells and yelled bilingual obscenities as they whizzed past the truck.

"So does this make us, like, gentrifiers?" Klein asked.

The question was on Fish's mind, too. They'd passed cheerful signs announcing the opening of a new Chipotle location on One Hundred Sixteenth Street, right next to a shabby little taco restaurant that had probably been serving the neighborhood for years. Someone had spray-painted the words "WHITE POISON" in big dripping letters over the street-facing windows of the new Chipotle. Fish and Klein drank Modelo beers, their legs dangling off their new fire escape. Mariachi music blared from a boxy radio perched on the stoop, and an elderly couple danced slowly to the rhythm, sipping Tecate beers as they swayed against one another. Fish waited for the sound of a passing ambulance to peter out down First Avenue before responding.

"Yeah dude, pretty sure it does," Fish replied, surveying the street below his feet.

A skinny guy wearing nothing but a pair of baggy basketball shorts was passed out on the sidewalk, and a squat family of six patrolled a stroller around his slumped form. Across the street was a gas station and a local-chain supermarket, and up the block was a twenty-four-hour laundromat—one of Lexi Spanish Harlem's selling points. Fish was excited to learn his new neighborhood—to determine his go-to spots for coffee, cigarettes, groceries, late-night snacks, and happy hours. Maybe there was a gym close by. He loved how One Hundred Sixteenth Street, from around Lexington Avenue all the way to York Ave and East End, became a sort of parade at the end of the day. As residents returned home from work or school, the sidewalks were subsumed by all manner of sensory delights; Bad Bunny lyrics poured from open car windows, blue corn tortillas sizzled in pork fat, children bickered and laughed in Spanglish, straining under their oversized backpacks, strollers clunked over curbs, sirens whined, shoeless folks rattled coins in wilted Burger King cups, basketballs thudded against the pavement, and the impending sunset washed the blocks in a salamander orange. Exiting the subway station at such a time, one could reasonably conclude that they'd missed their stop and arrived in a foreign city. But a glance to the south revealed that iconic skyline, its dutiful eyes trained on each and every one of the idiosyncratic neighborhoods that characterized the borough like shepherds surveying their flock.

Fish was halfway up the first flight of stairs when his phone started buzzing in his pocket again. He set the AC unit—which he'd just discovered on a stoop two blocks away—down on the landing, sweat veiling his face and soaking his T-shirt. It was the first day of October, but the night air was still thick with city humidity. Everyone kept telling him it would cool off soon, but he wasn't about to pass up a free AC unit, regardless of the season. When he saw that it was Madame Meticulous calling again, Fish sat down on the steps to catch his breath before answering. He didn't want to sound sweaty if it turned out to be a booty call.

Partiboy just wants to party, boy.

It wasn't a booty call. Madame Meticulous's light, tinny voice was saying hi, and that she hoped she wasn't interrupting anything, and that she had just paid a visit to a gynecologist after the radiologist had flagged something during her ankle scan. When Fish didn't respond, Madame Meticulous took a small, sharp breath, and said she was pregnant. The air disappeared from Fish's lungs. He felt as though he'd just attempted to take a nonexistent but nevertheless expected final step on a stairwell. The sweat that had been beading his skin seemed to creep back up into the pores from which it had been dispensed.

And yet, Madame Meticulous delivered this information as though she were reading it off a teleprompter. It sounded rehearsed. Maybe she'd been practicing in a mirror.

That would've been just like her, Fish thought, imagining her with a pen and paper, scrutinizing every syllable until she was happy with the final product. He couldn't form words, his synapses somehow firing from one thought to the next while his brain went completely blank. The only concrete thought that he could manage to shape into a question in his mind was also the most insensitive thing to ask a person who'd just revealed their pregnancy. He kept his mouth shut—or, that is, silent and agog.

Fish knew it was a dick move not to want a kid. *But what the fuck, man?* he asked Partiboy, and the world. *I just blew my own life up! How can I be expected to bring a kid into my mess? I'm twenty-six years old, for fuck's sake!* Madame Meticulous had just turned thirty, he recalled. *Unless . . .* But it was not his place to bring that up, he knew.

At some point Madame Meticulous must have hung up. Fish sat on the stairs for he wasn't sure how long. Eventually Klein hollered to him from the top of the stairs, puncturing his stupor. Gathering the blockish AC unit into his arms, he trudged the rest of the way up the stairs. The door was propped open with Klein's massive tub of protein powder—a staple accoutrement of any bro's apartment. Fish kicked it aside and set the AC down on the futon. Madame Meticulous's disclosure was particularly ill-timed, as Fish's on-and-off (mostly off, as of late) college girlfriend, Becca, was shortly due to arrive in the city for a medical residency interview. Somewhat ironically, she was planning on becoming a gynecologist.

• • •

F ish had taken the week off of work to move, sacrificing the five hundred dollars he would have earned otherwise. He didn't care. Bennett could cover the limited duties of the rarely visited gallery, and Fish didn't much like working, anyway. As of late, he'd taken to seeing himself as the kind of fellow that might die young and whose works—whatever they might be—would be appreciated decades after his death. *I'm like a phoenix in that way*, he mused to

Partiboy in his less self-conscious (that is, drunker) moments. But not the phoenix that rises from the ashes. Rather, the ashes themselves, swelling and burning with *potential* rebirth. He was the embers that would, ultimately, succeed his physical demise in the form of some kind of artistic legacy. Or else (and here was the more likely outcome, he admitted to himself with a somewhat satisfied smirk) these embers might never resuscitate. The end would be the end, dust to dust, and that would be that.

Before moving to New York, Fish had been living in Connecticut. Not in New Canaan, the affluent suburb in which he'd been born and raised and where everyone had called him by his full name, Fisher, but in New Haven. He had been studying to become a lawyer. Yale Law School. To Fish (the moniker he'd adopted upon moving to New York), it all felt like a separate lifetime, though it had only been a few months ago.

He'd been accepted off the waitlist, thanks in large part to a recommendation letter from a judge of the Southern District with whom his father was a cigar-smoking buddy. In the culture from which Fish had emerged, law school was simply the only logical progression available to one who had graduated from a non–Ivy League school with a degree in English literature. *What else am I gonna do, teach?* Fish had sighed, filling out the application forms. *Party's over, Partiboy.* As boring and wrong as it had all felt at the time, it had also felt steadily, safely, familiarly *right*. Like a freshly hatched sea turtle making its plodding way, by instinct, toward the moonlit waves of the ocean.

But he'd burned out faster than a hastily carved apple pipe on a New England winter night. For all the half-assed effort he'd put into those applications, his heart wasn't in the law game. After just a semester and a half in New Haven, Fish, like thousands before him, succumbed to the magnetic pull of New York City and its promise of excitement. And so he dropped out of the prestigious program to which he'd barely been accepted in the first place. He envisioned himself penning offbeat avant-garde plays in coffee shops, wearing peacoats, shoving long strands of unkempt hair out of his eyes and sipping espressos in the wee hours among the city's performative derelicts rather than memorizing torts in libraries insulated with leather-bound tomes amidst the regularly shorn, loafer-wearing future politicians that made up his cohort. He wanted to be the kind of guy that read paperbacks in ill-lit dive bars, the kind of guy who beat out absurd but brilliant (and thus obscure) one-act plays on a typewriter late, late at night with a glass of Fernet-Branca, the kind of guy who walked the streets of Manhattan late at night without any particular destination but simply to ruminate away from his typewriter for a little while. It was a vision of himself that he'd been nursing in secret, though he rarely admitted it even to himself. *Why shouldn't I write plays?* he'd asked Partiboy at the time. *I've got things to say, haven't I?* Partiboy was supportive, in his way.

Once his abrupt departure from New Haven had become a subject of gossip among his former classmates, a few had reached out with texts, feigning disappointment in seeing him withdraw, urging him to reconsider, telling him that, if he simply applied himself, he could make a great lawyer. But he was no longer interested. Landing the job (which he'd found on Craigslist) at a quirky art gallery in Hell's Kitchen confirmed for Fish the path that his life was about to take. The job itself, which he'd finagled by bullshitting an art history minor on his resume, paid even less than his meager law student stipend.

"But don't you worry that your life will be thrown off track?" his classmate, Phoebe Johansen, had inquired. Riding a buzz from the second round of Old Fashioneds they'd ordered, Fish had let slip his half-baked plans to quit the program and move to New York.

Phoebe had nodded sagely, taking a sip of her drink before posing her question. *Off-track from what, exactly?* Fish had wondered.

What he really wanted was to be free. Free from the responsibilities and suppositions that had dictated his life to that point. Private Catholic middle school, with the adjoining church where he'd been baptized and confirmed and served as an altar boy, obeying the haughty commands of the ancient Benedictine monks. Private boarding school, where he'd served as head boy and captain of the lacrosse and debate teams. Private fencing lessons, private viola lessons (god, did he hate the latter, and the stringent Korean woman who made him repeat scales until his fingers developed calluses as thick as watch bands). Private liberal arts college, where he'd played lacrosse and majored in English literature—his greatest rebellion to date, refusing to pursue economics as his parents had hoped. And then on to the pretentious law school. At least, he'd found it pretentious.

The other day, walking the Brooklyn promenade, he'd heard a tall, chubby white guy pronounce this statement:

"If you want your kid to be athletic, I'll give you my seed."

Not one iota of irony in his tone. Fish hated to think that he was ever like that guy. For all the etiquette and Catholic guilt that had been hammered into his psyche throughout his childhood, he suspected that he himself might have been a douchebag, too, on more than a few occasions. But he'd always glommed onto and stored away little snippets of conversation like that, for as long as he could remember. He thrilled at the idiosyncratic ways in which humans conversed with one another. That's why he wanted to write plays; they were composed mostly of dialogue, as far as he knew. Not that he'd ever written a play. He just imagined short exchanges in his head that, he thought, sounded pretty damn believable. Maybe even masterful. He thought maybe he'd stumbled into his *thing*.

Upon quitting law school, Fish admitted to himself that he wanted to be like Walt Whitman. He wanted to celebrate himself and sing himself for a spell. He wanted to loaf and invite his soul for a change. Absorbing all to himself and for this song, etc. Something like that. He'd SparkNoted more than half of what his syllabi had required him to read in college, but Whitman had stuck with him. *That old dandy was on to something, Partiboy, I'll tell ya.*

All this to say, Fish wanted to yield to Partiboy for a change. He'd kept him at arm's length throughout college—and even throughout most of his intercollegiate year as a paralegal in Stamford. But now he was ready to allow Partiboy to take the reins. To see what life might be like in the passenger seat, for a while. Maybe forever. The day he'd walked out of Yale's campus, he felt as though he'd just removed one of those weight vests the strength and conditioning coach would strap to his torso during team lift sessions back in college.

But Madame Meticulous was determined to fuck it all up, it seemed. Here Fish was, trying to cut himself loose from the puppetry strings that had guided him through life, and then WHAM, Madame Meticulous comes in with consequences for his actions. He'd worn a condom each time they'd been intimate. Except once, actually, now that he thought about it. She'd said she was willing to be exclusive, and he'd said, "I'm down if you are."

Partiboy just wants to party, boy.

That was before their disastrous tumble down the stairs, of course. Fish wasn't even entirely positive that he *could* get a girl pregnant. His left testicle had fallen victim to an errant lacrosse ball. It was an away game, junior year, and he'd forgotten his cup back in the locker room. Some freshman phenom midfielder on the rival team sniped his crotch from twelve yards outside the crease. The pain had been blinding. It had nearly ruined his season. Becca, stroking his head in the hospital afterwards, had said he would probably still be able to have kids. She'd been pre-med at the time, and the late nights she'd spent in the campus library had paid off spectacularly—she was less than a year away from graduating from Drexel University College of Medicine, in Philadelphia. A short train ride away. But back then, his concern for his fecundity had been largely hypothetical, a far-off thing that he *might* want, *maybe, probably,* some vague day in the future. Now, as he pondered the reality of his fertility, he half wished the freshman phenom had pulverized his other nut, too.

• • •

At times, the A train looked as though it was gliding atop the water, moving just fast enough to keep from sinking. Fish had been grasping the rail since they'd changed trains at Union Square. He switched hands when his palm began to ache on the stiff metallic bar, and he bounced up and down on his toes to keep his ankles from going numb. Klein had bought an assortment of bagels from Tal's, and they'd devoured them before the train even left Manhattan. A brown paper bag that smelled of gravlax and chives was all that remained of their breakfast. Fish used his tongue to prod at a sesame seed stuck between his teeth.

The subway charged further and further south through Brooklyn, and people in bathing suits filled the train car. They smelled of sunscreen and toted umbrellas and picnic blankets, dark sunglasses perched atop their heads. Though they smiled, there was a palpable tension that pressurized the subway car with each new set of rubber flip-flops that stepped onto the train. Fish felt it, too. The ride to Rockaway Beach was longer than he'd expected, as though New York felt compelled to prove the supreme reach of its public transit system, stretching so deep into the outer boroughs that it could, yes, it *could* take you from a Chinatown wet market to a sun-soaked idyll all in the same day. All for two dollars and seventy-five cents. Still, the quixotic beachgoers glancing warily out the windows seemed as though they might remain skeptical about the existence of the beach until they saw it with their own eyes.

Klein had a new girlfriend. Her name was Carmen. The beach trip had been her idea. Klein and Fish had never even heard of Rockaway Beach, a fact which had flabbergasted Carmen. She had been born and raised in New York's Yorkville neighborhood, where, as an only child, she still lived in her parents' condo. Her parents, now retired, spent most of the year in Montauk, so she had the sleek three-bedroom overlooking Carl Schurz Park essentially to herself. She had an appealing New York attitude and a slight Spanish accent (her mother, who was much younger than her father, was Colombian) that became especially pronounced when she was drunk. She routinely contested Klein's bloviating manner, not in a rude way but with the confidence of a person who knew their own mind. Fish had never seen Klein so infatuated. He laughed—genuinely, Fish observed—at all her jokes and held her hand everywhere they went. Seeing them together, it was hard for Fish to comprehend that this was the same Klein who had, very seriously, made it his senior year mission to have a threesome (he'd come close once or twice but had never landed the plane on that one). After their first date, Klein had deleted his Hinge, Bumble, and Tinder profiles, determined not to repeat his mistakes. He'd met Carmen at a rooftop bar a few weeks ago, and they'd been inseparable ever since. They both worked crazy hours, which suited them, cherishing their weekends and occasional late weeknight dinners together while very seriously pursuing their respective careers for sixty to eighty hours per week, exchanging memes and *hahahas* via text whenever they got a second's reprieve to check their phones. She worked in advertising and wore strange shimmery outfits that Fish could tell were expensive. Like Klein (and Fish, for that matter), she had been raised in the kind of home that had a special set of silverware used only at Christmas dinner and Easter brunch. Her ears were clustered with an assortment of small hoops that, jumbled together, looked like shower curtain rings. A small faded tattoo of a heart was inked on her wrist. Fish wondered who, if anyone, it was for.

Sunshine flooded through the windows and drenched the interior of the train car, settling into yellow puddles on the floor. Carmen freed her hand from Klein's palm and wiped it off on the purple beach towel draped over Fish's shoulders. Though it was now early fall, summer's heat had yet to relent. Skinny archipelagos of rock buttressed the tracks, but they could see only blue-green water shimmering and churning beneath the train.

"Hitting the beach in October," mused Klein, shaking his head. "Fucking climate change, am I right?"

Eventually, the train arrived at its final stop, and the trio joined the crowd of people shuffling up the steps of the subway station, emerging into a new, preposterous world. All around them, smiling New Yorkers whipped their heads and contorted their necks in bewilderment. Beach houses with sagging white porches replaced the towering gray buildings of the city. Sand coated the sidewalks in lieu of black city grime. Seagulls sailed overhead, replacing the pigeons that were so often underfoot.

"Isn't this great?" Carmen hooted.

"How have we never done this before?" Fish responded, gazing toward the glimmering ocean.

"I can't believe we're still in New York," Klein said.

Only the crowds were the same. But the people looked different here. The Manhattanites and Brooklynites and Queensites seemed unsure, like newborn foals testing their knobby knees. They didn't charge around corners in heavy boots and thick jackets shoulder first because there were no corners, only each other, sand, and water. There was space up the beach a ways but the people seemed more comfortable grouped together, the bodily compactness of the city a familiarity they clung to.

"Beer! Getcha beer here! Hot day, folks, hot hot hot day! If you don't drink beer, you're gonna die!"

A tall man with a shaved head walked with two large rectangular coolers held at his sides. Sweat streamed down his chiseled torso.

"Is that legal?" Klein asked.

Carmen shrugged. "It's New York legal, you know?"

"What do you mean?" Fish asked.

"It's like, there's so much bigger stuff to worry about, you know? Like bomb threats at Penn Station and shit. Like, look at that cop over there, the one with the ice cream cone? This isn't some small town where the cops have to, like, go looking for people to get in trouble, you know? This is New York! There's plenty of, like, *real* crime to keep them busy. He doesn't care about people drinking beer at the beach. It's a New York thing. Everyone is sort of, like, in on the game, you know?"

Klein and Fish nodded reverently, watching the beer salesman driving his knees against the sand and working his way up the beach, his hoarse voice carrying up the shoreline. They had gotten into the habit of deferring to Carmen on all matters concerning the idiosyncrasies of New York. She knew all the subway lines by heart, had been to all the noteworthy restaurants more than once, had seen all the famous Broadway shows, could converse in flawless Spanish with the bodega clerks, knew the best spots for avoiding or watching the parades, and (sexiest of all, in Fish's opinion) she could hail a cab from three blocks away with a steam-engine whistle—two fingers held to her mouth and played like a trumpet.

Sweat trickled down Fish's sideburns and curved along his jaw. He drank a nip of Tito's vodka—his third—that had gone warm in the bottom of Carmen's beach bag. A boy with flowing red hair wearing an eggshell-white speedo hula hooped near the water, staying just out of reach of the lapping waves. A group of teenagers blasted A$AP Rocky from a Bluetooth speaker and lazily passed a Frisbee back and forth. A woman with her legs covered in intricate tattoos smoked a cigarette and held a mirror under her chin. Two male bodybuilders held hands as they strolled along the beach, their bulbous shoulders bumping against each other as they stepped to avoid shells and rocks.

The ride back to the city felt longer, though the tension was gone, since they'd smoked a joint together as they watched the sun set. As the train clacked along the tracks, Carmen napped with her head tilted against Klein's shoulder. Around them, their fellow passengers were sunburned, their hair crusty with salt, a film of sand clinging to their feet and ankles. It was dark by the time they got back to Harlem. Fish poured a glass of wine and collapsed onto the futon while Carmen took a shower and Klein went to pick up his laundry from the laundromat up the block. Fish dozed off listening to Carmen's true crime podcast, which echoed softly from behind the bathroom door.

· · ·

Fish's on-and-off girlfriend (the determination was currently ambiguous, Becca living a few hours away and all) arrived via train on a Friday evening. They met up at Penn Station. She'd taken the last train from Philly.

"How's the fam?" Fish asked.

"They're . . . the same," she replied, wrapping him in a familiar hug.

They went straight to a dive bar called Rudy's on Ninth Avenue. It was one of those Manhattan dives that offer a beer and a shot for ten bucks. Without the ample lawyer payday lingering enticingly, comfortingly on the horizon, Fish had been forced to become the economical sort.

"Are you eating enough? You look thin. And your hair is getting long," Becca said, grabbing at the dark locks that fell over the nape of his neck.

"Too expensive to get a haircut here," he replied.

His first lie of the weekend. He liked how his hair looked, grown in and unkempt, as though he was too consumed by his creative pursuits to bother with cutting it. He had yet to write anything, but he could feel a real showstopper coming on.

That night, at his new apartment, cardboard boxes, beer bottles, and empty Chinese food cartons littering the living room floor, Becca tried to initiate sex. Fish withdrew, citing exhaustion.

"From what?" Becca asked.

"Work," he said.

The second lie.

"Sitting in that gallery all day? How is that exhausting?" Becca scoffed.

Then they'd had a familiar fight, one they'd been having since freshman year of college, when they'd first started dating. About Fish's ambitions, his long-term plans, his commitment to the relationship. A text from Madame Meticulous illuminated the screen of his phone. Fish flipped the phone upside down on the night table.

First Trimester

Chapter 3

Fish had forgotten his keys, though he knew Marcel and Stanley kept a spare tucked in the folds of canvas behind the portrait of Rocky and Monty that loomed in the stairwell. He ducked into the garage, taking refuge from the autumn storm. Rain fell in fat splashes, soaking the streets. A few of the mechanics gave him icy nods from behind their protective masks. The chemical smell of car paint and exhaust fumes caught in his throat. Pushing through the battered metal door, he halted his foot just before it landed on the first step of the neon orange stairwell. Marcel must have repainted it recently—it had been lavender just last week, and fire engine red the week before. Fish touched the tip of his finger to the cool metal railing. It came away clean. Multicolored streaks and dribblets had made a Pollock of his shoes for all the times he'd failed to check first. Ascending to the third floor, he fished his hand behind the portrait and closed his fingers around the angular grooves of the key.

As he stepped inside the door of the gallery, Rocky and Monty—so named after Rock Hudson and Montgomery Clift—trotted towards him, their paws thudding gently against the polished floor. They curled through his legs as he set his bag down onto the sagging plywood desk, rubbing their whiskers against his shins. The two cats—a brother and sister duo, rescued from a shelter and transported to the gallery in a limo hired by Marcel and Stanley—followed Fish knowingly into the kitchen. He pried open a hockey puck–sized tin of cat chow and plunked a few spoonfuls of the ole-aginous brown matter onto teacup saucers. The cats plunged their snouts into the chunky mounds as soon as he set the plates on the floor, their sharp teeth gnashing quietly. Fish held his breath against the cat food's cloying odor until he could wash his hands with cheap lemon dish soap, inhaling the pleasant citric scent that mingled with the warm steam rising up from the sink.

After he'd poured himself a coffee and burned his tongue on an overeager first sip, Fish tugged his phone out of his pocket. The red notification bubble indicating the text from Madame Meticulous, which he'd neglected to read for the past two days, beckoned him like a zit begging to be popped. He tapped the icon and the message sprawled across the screen:

Fish, can we talk? Maybe coffee sometime this week? I know this is a lot . . .

With a double tap and a swipe, the message was gone. Fish thrust the phone back into his pocket.

Walking back toward the desk, he heard Marcel's voice hit a pan-icked tenor from somewhere below, echoing up the elevator shaft. Fish heaved the old elevator doors apart. It took the full weight of his body to lurch them closed again once he was inside. According to Marcel, it was the oldest operating elevator in Manhattan. Fish had once gotten stuck inside the damn thing. Stanley had come to the rescue, prying at the doors with a crowbar and apologizing profusely. This time, however, the doors met with a heavy medieval clunk and Fish made sure to latch them closed with the rusted iron clasp. Toggling the crank, Fish piloted the elevator down to Thirty-Ninth Street, watching the ancient pulley rotating unhurriedly in the shadows above him as he descended.

By the time he unclasped the doors and heaved the two iron walls away from each other, Marcel's voice was approaching a frantic decibel.

"They're knocking us down!"

"No, they won't," chided Stanley, stepping into the elevator. "Morning, Fish. Thanks for opening up."

"No problem," he replied.

Fish was almost always the first one into the gallery, but Stanley always thanked him for it as though some exception had been made, like he'd done them some favor. The truth was that Fish was far more excited by the gallery than Marcel and Stanley. He'd been working for them for just a few months while they'd spent the last thirty years trying to turn a profit on the space, to little avail besides a few noteworthy bookings per year that afforded them their rent-controlled Hell's Kitchen one-bedroom. At some point, the novelty of the grand space had worn off for them, replaced by the frustrations of operating a business. Stanley wanted to retire, maybe move to some little town up the Hudson. But Marcel was adamant that he'd die while painting in the unused elevator control room that sat atop the building's roof and functioned as his private studio.

"They are! Eminent domain!" cried Marcel. "The city is coming a-knocking, and we're toast, Stanley, I'm telling you. What, do you think the city government just sends out those notices for fun? They're tearing us down! Every old brick building in Hell's Kitchen like ours is getting the boot. Just look at those massive glass dildos they're tickling the sky with! The Hudson Yards project. What a load of crap, right? Like Manhattan needs a few more skyscraping condo complexes and office buildings. What are those drones going to do when they're not working, huh? Admire their own buildings? No! Let them peruse an art gallery! How about that?"

"Who doesn't love an art gallery?" Stanley said, nudging Fish and rolling his eyes dramatically. "It sure is a lucrative business."

"And do you see this?" Marcel flung an indignant arm in the direction of Tenth Avenue. Vendor carts coated in grime and fry grease littered the sidewalk and spilled out into the street. A turbaned man smoked a cigarette and hosed down the garage where the vessels would be kept until the Times Square vendors claimed their pretzel and kebab carts for the day.

"It's fine. Would you get in the elevator?" Stanley said, already pulling the elevator doors closed. A river of rainwater coursed down the banks of Thirty-Ninth Street. Marcel's trench coat was freckled with dark droplets.

"It's not fine! The street cleaner won't be able to get by. Look how dirty our street is! It's bad for business, Stanley, you know that. I've called 311, I've emailed the district councilor, and nothing ever happens. Nothing! Ever!"

"Marcel!" Stanley hissed.

Marcel stepped into the elevator and Fish yanked the doors closed. They could hear machines whirring and tires screeching as they ascended past the auto body shop that occupied the building's first two floors. Fish released the crank and the elevator rumbled to a halt at the third floor. He pried open the doors. A patch of sun broke through the gray shield of clouds and filled the gallery with pale light, limning the paintings that covered the walls. Through the floor-length windows that faced westward over the Hudson River, the new skyscrapers caught the emerging sun's fire, orange streaks glinting off their sharp blue edges.

"Have you fed the kitties?" Stanley asked.

"Yep, they're all set," Fish said.

Stanley said okay, but he looked a little disappointed. He loved feeding the cats.

Fish followed Marcel to the kitchen while Stanley bent to stroke Rocky, who had padded across the gleaming floor to greet him. Marcel collapsed onto a plush purple love seat and Fish poured beans into the coffee press.

Fish took his coffee black, but into Marcel's mug he dumped a healthy splash of cream and two spoonfuls of sugar. He pressed a steaming mug, also black, into Stanley's expectant hands. Stanley mouthed a *thank you* and gave Fish a conspiratorial glance that seemed to say *good luck with that*, rolling his eyes in Marcel's direction. The rain subsided to a soft mist and the cats followed Stanley through the French doors and out to the terrace, watching with mild curiosity as he set about pruning his hydrangeas. Holding the ceramic mug of coffee seemed to calm Marcel; the simple act of clutching something fragile and filled with hot liquid forced him to remain seated, to keep his gesticulations—which were often erratic—to a moderate orbit around the mug.

"They're knocking the building down, you know that, right?" Marcel rapped his fingernails against the side of the mug as he spoke.

"You always say that."

"I'm telling you," Marcel continued. "They're knocking us down and there's not a thing we can do about it."

Fish shrugged and sipped his coffee. The cats wandered back indoors. Rocky leaped onto the couch and traversed the cushions, settling into a comma shape on Marcel's lap. Monty was basking in a pool of sunlight by the window. Marcel stroked Rocky's flank absently, staring out the window at nothing in particular.

"You look hungover. Fun last night?" Marcel asked, a wry grin creasing his spray-tanned face.

It hadn't been long before Fish came to be treated more like a nephew than an employee by Marcel and Stanley. After bearing witness to a few of Stanley's tantrums and weathering more than a few of Marcel's drunken tirades, it seemed they'd deemed him sturdy enough to provide support for both their business and their relationship, the division of which was blurry to Fish, even a few months into the job.

"Ah, yeah. Went out with some friends," Fish lied.

"Oh god, on a Sunday night? Oh, to be young and good looking again. I was a model once, you know? Have I shown you the picture? Oh, but go out on Thursday nights. On Friday and Saturday, you have to deal with the bridge-and-tunnel crowd. You're a New Yorker, don't forget. Oh, but have fun, Fish. Drink it in. Drink this city from the hose. Now is the time to be doing that. So long as you know when to stop. But where'd you go? And if you say Kips Bay— like you did last time, do you remember that?—I'll absolutely die."

Marcel punctuated his diatribe with an emphatic swig of his coffee, nearly emptying the mug.

"East Village. Just a low-key night, really," Fish said.

This part was not a lie. He had gone out to the East Village last night, riding a Citi Bike down Second Avenue all the way from Harlem until he'd found an appropriately empty dive bar. His intention had been to write. He'd brought a notebook and a pen and everything, both items purchased from a Duane Reade drugstore he'd stopped at along the way. He had a vague notion about writing a play about his hometown and his pals back in Connecticut, maybe something about the time he'd gotten fired from a bartending gig at the Greenwich Polo Club. He'd stolen (accidentally stolen, to hear his side of the story, which the world would, in due time) a bottle of Veuve Clicquot that had been earmarked for his boss's wife.

Partiboy just wants to party, boy.

But after three gin and tonics, the page remained blank, save for the squiggly line where he'd tested out the pen.

"I'm tired of this arrangement," Marcel announced, scanning the walls of the gallery. "In fact, I think it's dreadful. I say we hang a new exhibition."

Fish nodded and looked around the room with an expression that he hoped conveyed enthusiasm for the idea. He hated rearranging the paintings. Of course, as the gallery had few visitors (the trend, of late, given the incessant construction of the Hudson Yards development scuppering foot traffic for blocks in all directions), there was little else to do besides answer the two or three emails that popped up in the gallery's inbox each day. Still, hanging a new exhibition meant dealing with Marcel's demanding yet fickle temperament for several hours as he restlessly attempted to reposition the paintings in a way that would best display their value. The overwhelming majority of the paintings were his own.

"Careful with that one. It's priceless." he'd say, but to Fish's knowledge, none of Marcel's works had ever sold for much. Not that he'd ever say—or even insinuate—such a thing to Marcel. Preserving Marcel's fragile sense of self was, it turned out, the brunt of the job.

"Bennett can help you move the big stuff when he comes in later. He is coming in later, right?" Marcel asked, his eyebrow cocked.

"Yep, he should be," Fish said.

"I'm getting worried about him," Marcel grumbled.

"Oh?" Fish said, glancing away. He feigned surprise, but he was fairly concerned about Bennett, too.

Marcel shrugged.

"They're tearing us down, I'm telling you," he said, muttering almost entirely to himself. "Big ole wrecking ball . . ."

• • •

"Okay, but, like, how did he say it?" Bennett asked.

"I don't know, just, like, 'I'm getting worried about him,'" Fish said.

Together they heaved one of Marcel's larger pieces up onto two rusting nails protruding from the wall.

Bennett laughed and shrugged his slim shoulders. He ran a hand through his recently bleached hair (part of a character he planned to debut at an Upright Citizen's Brigade performance later this week), and let out a sigh of relief as the nails accepted the weight of the painting. They stashed the final painting—a colossal abstract piece depicting two birds bursting in color as they veered away from each other at the last instant—in the vestibule, resting it against the other paintings which Marcel had recently decided were unfit for the gallery walls.

"You want another coffee?" Bennett asked, his Vans already padding in the direction of the kitchen.

"I'm good. I'm already two deep." The bitter liquid ached in Fish's empty stomach.

"Me too, but I think I need it," Bennett said.

"Late night?"

"Hell yeah, dude. Went to House of Yes. Out in Bushwick, you know it?" he asked, pausing between sentences to rip at his Juul. The vapor poured from his nostrils in twin rivers.

"That's the place where you have to wear a costume to get in or something, right?" Fish asked.

Bennett proffered him the Juul and Fish accepted gratefully, taking a long drag. He'd never smoked prior to moving to New York. He'd dipped snuff a few times in the locker room after lacrosse games, but that had really just been because most of the other guys on the team were doing it, too. He'd never really cared for it. But then, after he'd quit the law program and scored the art gallery job, he'd met Bennett, who'd been smoking a pack a day since high school before his recent switch to the Juul. Bennett had worked at the gallery for almost a year. When the gallery was empty—as it often was—they'd kill time down on the street by talking shit about their bosses and splitting cigarettes while purportedly enticing the nonexistent foot traffic into viewing some art. Coffee and nicotine, all day. Fish had lost fifteen pounds since taking the job. Since moving to the city.

"Basically, yeah. Cool spot. You should check it out sometime," Bennett said. He stooped to stroke Monty's tabby fur as the coffee machine burbled rich, dark liquid into a waiting mug. A set of keys dangling from a carabiner on his belt loop clattered against his hip each time he moved.

• • •

The slim black rectangle blinked back at Fish, daring him to depress one of the keys under his fingertips instead of hovering over them like a nervous parent watching their child at swim camp. The West Village had seemed like the kind of place where he might get some writing done. Maybe even bang out a masterpiece. Or, at the very least, a promising debut with a flavor of the stuff that would burst to fruition in his third or fourth play and be reminisced upon in appreciative but condescending tones as his "early period" in graduate school seminars for eons to come.

But the café on Bleecker Street that he'd selected for the site of his creative outburst had disagreed with his muse. He'd been too distracted by the couples maneuvering strollers around the intentionally mismatched, wobbly wooden tables and chairs and the white dudes wearing running shorts and AirPods asking for oat milk lattes. *Where the fuck are all the artists?* Fish scanned the yuppie café patrons with mild contempt. *Where are the fellows in peacoats and the chicks with shaved heads smoking hand-rolled cigarettes over cooling espressos as they discussed all the ways in which Foucault had changed their life or how Noah Baumbach was, actually, if you thought about it, even more mainstream than Michael Bay?* Madame Meticulous was one such, but she was nowhere to be found. Fish hadn't heard from her—or reached out to her—since they'd last spoken at a coffee shop in Alphabet City, a few weeks ago now. When he tried to picture her elfin frame with a swollen belly protruding from her rabbit-narrow hips, he couldn't. And so, he didn't. He pushed the thought away, downward, into the embroiled furnace of suppressed emotions and prereleased passions that was supposed to be fueling his playwriting career.

When the pour-over coffee shop in the West Village proved to be a bust, he'd returned to Harlem, but not before purchasing—with a hundred dollar bill his grandmother had mailed him for his twenty-sixth birthday—a vintage typewriter from an antique shop on Christopher Street. Despite not having realized how heavy the instrument would be, he'd lugged it on the six train all the way back to Harlem with a proud smile on his face. Surely, he thought, for the kind of play he was to write, he would have to shun the modern world, return to the unadorned simplicity of words impressed on a blank page.

But the typewriter turned out to be a real motherfucker to use. It kept jamming each time he'd work up the chutzpah to transfer a word from his frontal lobe to the page, and ink stained his hands every time he had to unjam the ribbon. It hadn't helped that, after lugging the typewriter up to his cramped bedroom, he'd seen fit to refresh himself with a twelve pack of Modelo beer from the Mexican grocer that adjoined the apartment building. He'd purchased a bag of garlic plantain chips as well—a new obsession of his that had begun when he'd first moved to Spanish Harlem. The dark purple bags featured prominently in every bodega and deli for blocks in all directions. He'd tried to practice his Spanish with the cashier, a heavyset Mexican man with tattoos neatly inscribed along the edge of his face, dripping down from his sideburns and tracing the length of his jawline. But the words had stumbled clumsily from his mouth, reeking of the uncertainty he felt in uttering them. He felt compelled to advance some defense against his observable gentrifier visage, but the cashier had responded to Fish's garbled Spanish articulations in English—a total diss.

After several crushed Modelo beer cans littered the floor beneath his desk and the sun had long since dipped beneath the horizon, smothering Manhattan's northeastern corner in a bluish dark, Fish managed to craft the semblance of an idea for his debut play, and even a title. It would be called *Postlapsaria, Connecticut*, and it would be a metaphorical retelling of the genesis story through the prism of an affluent suburb of New York City, much like New Canaan, Connecticut, where he'd grown up. He imagined that the players would be suspended from winches of some kind until they would, ultimately, after metaphorically biting into whatever metaphorical representation of the apple from the Tree of Knowledge (*Maybe an apple pie*, he thought? *Just spitballing here . . . No bad ideas in brainstorming and all that*), succumb to gravity, finishing the play on their feet. Pretentious, he knew. But it was the best thing he'd come up with in three months of consternation on the subject, so he wasn't about to ditch it now just because he kind of hated the idea and hated more the fact that he also kind of thought it was genius. It was an idea, he felt, that might be worthy of being beaten out on a finicky old typewriter, becoming, ultimately, a better play for this struggle.

· · ·

To Fish, it didn't feel appropriate to think of the café rendezvous with Madame Meticulous as a date. Rather, it felt like a showdown. His psyche was still bruised from the last time they'd spoken in person. Despite Partiboy's crude interventions, Fish cared for Madame Meticulous. Or, at least, for the *idea* of Madame Meticulous. Successful sculptor was a sexy career, there was no denying that. And she seemed like the *type* of neurotic artsy chick that a would-be playwright like himself might get involved with. She was certainly a departure from the Ugg boot–clad girls he'd been attracted to in college. And the fact that she somehow made such solid, impenetrable forms out of marble and granite with her dainty hands made her all the more impressive—all the more alluring—to Fish. He could fit both her hands comfortably in a single palm. She was smart, too, regularly dropping references to philosophers whose names sounded familiar to him but whose theories had become jumbled in the B-minus caliber mental filing cabinet in which he'd hastily stored memories from his Philosophy 101 class. And she could talk circles around him in all things music and film (apparently, all of Fish's favorite directors were ripping off some dude named Wong Kar-wai and everyone that came after David Byrne was derivative). They didn't have the same sense of humor, though. He'd make some remark that he found funny, and she'd just kind of smile and nod and say "yeah" or, at her most evocative, "oh, that's funny." She had long copper hair that fell in curls to her tailbone, and she'd mentioned (bragged, he now wondered?) that she only weighed a hundred pounds—half of Fish's weight. Half of what he used to weigh, that is. Before the cigarettes. Back when he'd still been hitting the gym five days a week and chugging grainy protein shakes in the locker room afterwards. He couldn't recall the last time he'd eaten breakfast. And very few of his meals were eaten at regular times anymore. More like dollar pizza slices purchased and consumed as he walked home from the subway station or eagerly scarfed empanadas sold from a cart outside his apartment or surreptitious spoonfuls of Klein's peanut butter. Sometimes Klein brought home an extra sandwich from work. He worked at one of those places that catered lunch every day and had foosball and a beer draught in the office.

They'd arranged to meet at a little café in Alphabet City. Fish walked past the window once before entering, risking a quick glance as he passed. She was already there, punctual as ever, sitting primly in a corner booth. On his second lap around the block, he felt someone thread their arm through his, pulling him close. *Oh shit . . . Partiboy? Really? How in the fuck do you think this is the time or the place?* But it was too late. It was always already too late by the time Partiboy showed up. Because a maybe-not-so-small part of Fish *liked* when Partiboy showed up. It always felt like that moment when, halfway through some exam in school that he'd underprepared for, he'd accepted his fate and yielded to the inevitable. The liberating thrill of saying "fuck it" and bailing out.

Partiboy steered him down St. Mark's Place to the nearest corner store with bongs lined up like trophies in the window. There were dozens of them scattered throughout the East Village. Fish had recently read a Reddit post confirming Klein's claim that mushroom chocolates could be purchased at such establishments, and he'd been eager to put the Redditor's assertion to the test.

"Do you have any . . . magic chocolates?" he asked the bearded dude manning the cramped store's register.

The guy barely batted an eye, pausing the soccer game he'd been watching on his phone to pull a slim technicolor rectangle from a trash bag stashed under the counter. He handed it to Fish without fanfare, resuming the soccer game with a tap of his thumb. It sounded to Fish like the game's commentators were speaking Arabic, though he didn't know enough about that part of the world to be certain. His brother had taught him a few words in Farsi once, but Fish had since forgotten them.

"Forty bucks. Cash only," the guy said. He spoke with a thick

Brooklyn accent.

Partiboy was bouncing up and down on the balls of his feet. *Play it cool, Partiboy. Jesus!* But Fish was smiling, too.

Partiboy just wants to party, boy.

Fish chomped a few bites out of the bar before tucking it into the front pocket of his JanSport backpack, with which he'd recently replaced the leather messenger bag his father had given him as a congratulatory gift when he'd been accepted to Yale. It just didn't feel right to use it now, so the leather satchel gathered dust beneath his bed, hidden from view.

"Hi. Thanks for coming," Madame Meticulous said as he slid into the booth across from her. The ice which had crystallized around her words the last time they'd spoken seemed to have thawed.

"No problem," Fish said, dribbling Americano down his chin.

He imagined the relief he'd feel when this conversation was over and tried to recover that future feeling in the present. It didn't work.

"So, basically, all I wanted to tell you was that I'm seriously considering keeping the baby."

Madame Meticulous had breathed the whole sentence out in a single breath, staring right into his eyes. Fish thought for a second that the shrooms might be kicking in, that his mind was playing tricks on him. "I thought I ought to let you know," she added when Fish didn't respond.

"You're . . . You said you're going to have a baby?" he asked, struggling to find the words.

He raised the Americano to his lips as if to muzzle himself but realized he'd already drained the mug. Setting it back down on the table, he crossed his arms over his chest and tried to meet the serious stare that Madame was lasering through his face.

"Not *a* baby. *The* baby. But it will be *my* baby, okay? What I mean is . . . I don't expect anything from you *or* from . . . well, shit, I suppose that's the other thing we need to talk about," she said.

Her gaze dropped, but her coral-blue eyes quickly flashed back up to Fish's face. And then they sort of got bigger, but also sort of smaller. Her hair looked like it was swirling down over her shoulders in thick, Van Gogh–like strokes. Fish had to look away.

Oh, shit, he thought, as the psilocybin metabolized in his stomach. *Partiboy just wants to party, boy.* Fish rubbed his eyes and took a deep, steadying breath. His palms felt damp and warm. *Partiboy, not now, dude. Read the room*, Fish hissed. *Should I say something now, or keep looking contemplative? How long has it been since she said that thing about "my baby?" Do I even look contemplative right now? Fuck! Am I about to be a fucking dad?! Because obviously I can't abandon this chick and this baby, but it is her choice but by telling me about it, is she doing what she thinks is just the right thing to do, or is she subtly implying that maybe I should offer—at least offer—to be involved in some way? Am I about to be a fucking dad?!* His face felt like a swollen nectarine, and an inexplicable smile was muscling its way up through his cheeks.

The booth seemed to be undulating underneath him, as though the café had been loosed from its mooring and begun to float down a lazy river. *Partiboy just wants to party, boy.* So much for euphoria; he was fully bugging out. *Damnit, Partiboy. We mistimed it. We fully fucking mistimed it. Fuck.* Then Fish remembered that she'd mentioned they had something else to discuss.

"What's the other thing?" he asked.

Madame Meticulous took a small sip of her green tea. She didn't drink dairy or eat gluten because of some gastrointestinal stuff she'd explained to him in clinical terms one time after he'd DoorDashed her some cupcakes from Milk Bar the morning after their second date. She'd had to politely refuse them because they were made with wheat flour even though they were advertised as gluten free, which was the only reason why Fish had bought them for her in the first place.

"Well, there's another person . . . another guy. Who could be the father," she said, commanding her voice into confidence when shame threatened to wobble her tone. Still, she was blushing a little, and Fish felt tender towards her then.

"Okay, gotcha. But, wait, so . . . Okay, I think I . . . But so, you're saying, what you're saying is, I might not be the fa . . . the dad?" Fish stammered, his words chasing his thoughts.

The thought that *father* sounded older than *dad* crossed his mind. His brain felt as though it were sinking slowly into a whirling jacuzzi.

"Too soon to say," replied Madame Meticulous. "But these things happen, Fish. Condoms break. Birth control isn't perfect. And sometimes a woman who never thought she'd want to grow a human being inside of herself gets to thinking about it and decides—or almost decides—that maybe she didn't know herself quite as well as she thought."

She'd politely left out the other option, in which two horny people simply get fed up with using condoms. A mutual yielding to a momentary weakness, synthetic barriers—however thin—sacrificed at the altar of unimpeded sensation. Still, Fish had an earful for the hack pharmacists behind the pills that Madame Meticulous had trusted enough to ingest daily in order to prevent this exact scenario.

When she stood to leave, he noticed the strappy boot still clasped tightly around her petite ankle. He held the door open for her and she offered him a wan smile before clunking, with a heroic effort at grace, up the street.

Chapter 4

The grass of Tompkins Square Park smelled ripe and verdant, and each of Fish's footfalls seemed to land with the cushion of a new pair of running sneakers. A coterie of goth teens showed off their switchblades to one another in a tight huddle over a bench. Vacant-eyed pigeons pecked at an abandoned bagel. A sinewy, shirtless man with a shaved head and a thick beard performed an endless series of pull-ups on the jungle gym, hoisting himself up and down with the relentless exactitude of a factory piston. Sunshine embalmed Fish's veins, seeping through his skin like a lotion.

Everything felt just a little bit amusing to Fish, if he yielded himself to the feeling even slightly. He felt euphoric, though he wasn't entirely sure why. On the one hand, he felt a tremendous sense of relief that this whole thing might be some other poor sucker's problem. He tried to consider this possibility—however distant—as nobly as a gentleman should, but this proved impossible. He couldn't deny the relief. It was as though a guillotine blade had been careening toward his neck only to melt into cotton candy just as it touched down on his skin. But equally undeniable was the flattery he felt at the possibility that Madame Meticulous would be willing to carry *his* child. This notion painted the other poor sucker in an entirely different light. *Who was this guy, anyway? And what made him so great that Madame Meticulous would be willing to have his child, too?* But maybe

Madame Meticulous didn't care who the father was. She had been adamant on that whole "*my* baby" point, Fish recalled.

But there was also the possibility, equally if not *more* palpable than the others, that he was experiencing the thrill of having fucked up so epically. He'd committed the *essential* fuckup. An *historic* fuckup. And yet he was alive. He had done something entirely out of the ordinary, something his parents had never felt the need to caution him against because to commit such an act—such a *fuckup*—was so beyond the pale as to never need mentioning. The kind of fuckup that elicited eye rolls and *that'll-never-happen-to-me*s in eighth-grade sex-ed classrooms. It was precisely the kind of fuckup that a tortured New York playwright might be burdened with, fueling his art with an unspeakable inner turmoil of grievous sins committed. Caravaggio had killed a guy. *Must've been a pretty goddamn intense feeling, eh, Partiboy?* More intense than *creating* a life? He pondered on that for a spell until his thoughts oozed pleasantly down a different track. Fish allowed himself to revel in the possibility that he had gained a few grooves on his inner being that weren't there before. Or perhaps the euphoria was just the psychoactive agents disco dancing through his bloodstream. His ears opened and flared like the flowers in those time lapse videos, unfurling to embrace a warming sun. A giggle crouched at the back of his throat, tensed to leap from his mouth.

Partiboy just wants to party, boy. Partiboy was right there next to him, turning cartwheels on the grass.

You know what, Partiboy? Yeah. Fuck yeah. Let's party, boy.

Fish, for once, led the way to a margarita bar on the corner.

• • •

While he'd intended to open a tab, Fish hadn't intended to flay the damn thing open like a wriggling striped bass. Partiboy just kept ordering rounds. At some point Fish had texted Becca and Klein to come join the fun. He'd given Psycho B a call, too, but he was home in Boston for the week. Psycho B, whose real name was Brendan O'Connor, had also played on the lacrosse team at Quinnipiac. His appetite for a distinctly chaotic style of partying had earned him the nickname. Psycho B was known to pregame with a snorted line of crushed up Ritalin, which he'd chase with a protein shaker full of Svedka and Red Bull. One time, about a year ago, Fish had visited Psycho B in Boston. He and two other guys from Quinnipiac were living in Cambridge. All of the furniture in their living room was pushed up against the walls, leaving an ample space in the middle of the room. When Fish asked about it, Psycho B had explained that they had each purchased a VR headset and that, when all three of them wore the headsets at the same time, they kept crashing into stuff, so it was just easier this way. Though he was basically the most Boston kid Fish had ever met—Irish, elitist while somehow maintaining a blue-collar attitude, confrontational, overeducated, fiercely loyal to his friends and family, chip on his shoulder—Psycho B had recently decamped to New York. He'd been fired from his job and decided he needed a change of scenery.

"Boston's totally beat, dude. New York's where it's at now," he'd told Fish over the phone.

Somewhere between the sixth and seventh margarita, Klein and Becca showed up. Klein was wearing a shimmery gray suit, which tipped Fish off that this must have been a weekday. He'd been so consumed by his concerns about meeting up with Madame Meticulous that he hadn't shown up for work. Fortunately, Marcel and Stanley rarely knew what day it was either.

"What day is it?" Fish shouted in Becca's direction as she settled on the stool to his left. Klein took the stool on the right, signaling the bartender with a circular motion of his index finger meant to indicate another round.

"Are you serious? Fish, it's Tuesday," Becca said.

Her tone was haughty, but she was laughing. She'd had another residency interview in the city. Tomorrow morning she'd head back to Philadelphia.

Fish nodded as he drained his glass. Becca was wearing makeup, which she usually didn't. And her eyebrows had been freshly threaded, faint red patches lingering at the sharp edges of her brows. Fish went to kiss her on the cheek, but he lost his balance en route, nose-diving into her clavicle.

"Looks like somebody's had a very happy hour," she said, pushing him upright.

"I'll say," Fish slurred.

"Jesus, dude, save some tequila for us nine-to-fivers, would ya?" Klein hollered.

The bar was getting pretty crowded. It felt like they were back at Quinnipiac, laughing and shouting together in a bar on a spring day, graduation around the corner. Sometime after the ninth margarita, Fish found himself signing off on a form that legally asserted his sobriety. Salt from the rim of the margarita glass still clung to his lips, but if the piercing artist noticed, she didn't seem to mind.

Partiboy just wants to party, boy.

"Is there any chance that you can, you know, *not* do this?" Becca asked, sighing, already knowing the answer.

"Don't listen to her, man. Do you!" bellowed Klein before collapsing into a fit of laughter in the corner of the tattoo shop.

He was recording the procedure on his iPhone, alternating between filming the hoop penetrating Fish's ear and a selfie of his own cackling face. Fish had given him a few bites of mushroom chocolate. Becca had refrained, citing an upcoming board exam.

Partiboy just wants to party, boy.

It had been Becca who had originally convinced Fish to apply to law school. Not that she'd ever said anything about it outright. But when she'd been accepted to medical school, he'd thought something along the lines of, *welp, time to grow up, I guess.* He'd sent in his applications the very next day. If he was going to marry Becca, as he'd thought he would at the time—and still surmised fate would have it that he would, in time, once he got this *thing*, whatever it was, out of his system—he'd better score himself one of those *real jobs* everyone was always talking about. *Time to get serious.* Before landing the paralegal gig, he'd been contentedly stocking shelves at a liquor store in New Canaan, a source of growing concern to his parents, and, he suspected, to Becca, too.

The piercing didn't hurt as much as he'd expected it to. Or maybe he was just too drunk to feel it. A quick punch to the left lobe (the non-gay lobe, he'd been assured by Klein, not that Fish cared, exactly, but if other people were going to make presumptions, then, well . . .) and he had a small silver hoop dangling from his ear. Shakespeare had had such a hoop, according to the few extant portraits of English literature's elusive bad-boy don. As did Harrison Ford and Anthony Bourdain—two figures even more responsible for Fish's (secretly) long-held desire to bedazzle his second sense.

"Dude, that looks dope!" Klein yelled. His necktie was knotted around his head like Ralph Macchio in *The Karate Kid*.

"I don't hate it," Becca agreed, shrugging. She was a little drunk, too.

Obviously, Partiboy was into it.

Fish touched the tender lobe, feeling a dry crust of blood around the entry point, and then ran his index finger over the small metallic hoop. He felt satisfied. The disfigurement of his outward, physical self was beginning to reflect the torsion of his insides. Or so he told himself.

"Try not to touch it for a few days," cautioned the piercing artist, who looked like the type of person who touched all kinds of things that people warned her not to touch.

Becca cracked her back, twisting abruptly to the left, then to the right, as she often did when she was anxious. She'd been a hurdler in college—no surprise, given her long, lean legs, which Fish's eyes now lingered on for what was probably an ungentlemanly amount of time—and she'd always performed this same ritual before settling her feet into the starter blocks. The familiarity of the display touched a nostalgic organ in Fish's chest.

"Another round? Let's go to Doc Holliday's. It's cash only, though, so we may have to stop at an ATM," Klein suggested, making for the door.

Fish locked eyes with Becca, and they exchanged a wordless, knowing message.

"I think I should get this one out of here," she said, taking Fish by the hand.

He submitted, allowing Becca to pull him in the direction of the subway station. Klein shrugged knowingly and made a beeline for the piercing artist, who had returned to reading a battered paperback copy of *Pale Fire* behind the counter. She had a tattoo of a rattlesnake eating its own tail surrounding her neck like a choker.

• • •

Warm gusts cologned with exhaust leached out from the Lincoln Tunnel, pummeling Fish as he crossed the roof to the crumbling elevator control room that Marcel had converted into his painting studio. Fish paused before entering, glancing across the Hudson River, where Weehawken's skyline crouched obsequiously to New York's West Side. Despite the rushing wind, he could hear humming coming from the other side of the iron door. *He'll be upset when I tell him*, Fish thought. *Better to get it over with.* He yanked open the door and stepped inside.

"I've got another one for you," Marcel said.

He glanced over his shoulder as Fish entered but quickly returned to the joint he was hastily rolling with the help of a weary dollar bill. Thick oil paints smeared his shirt and hands. A faint streak of blue traversed his forehead.

"Marcel, I—" Fish began.

"Money doesn't last, but memories do," Marcel continued, cutting him off.

At some point, Marcel had taken it upon himself to be not only Fish's shepherd through New York City living, but through life and the beyond, too. He would regularly offer up little aphorisms—such as the one he had just delivered—once he'd phrased them in his head to his satisfaction, only then presenting them to Fish like individually wrapped gifts. He held his finger up to the sky as he spoke, reveling in the profound silence that followed his statement.

"I'll remember that, Marcel, thanks. Listen . . ."

"Can you bring the kitties up here? I'm lonely," Marcel whined. "Oh my god, your ear."

The paint that Marcel had been about to mix on a pallet ceased its stream from the small tube clutched in his hand. Fish debated using the rare silence to interject the news he had to share, but he knew, too, that Marcel would be able to focus on nothing else until the earring was addressed. He was also more than a little interested in what Marcel would have to say about this recently acquired ornamentation. Especially because, just yesterday, Stanley had requisitioned Fish's help in picking out a septum piercing on Amazon. At fifty-five, Stanley had never seen it as a necessity that he learn how to use the internet—or computers, for that matter. All the same, he maintained a childlike fascination with technology, and he seemed to enjoy having Fish summon the images up onto the screen before him, conjured, to Stanley, merely from the words he'd spoken aloud.

"Look, I can already fit a pencil through," Stanley had said, demonstrating with a gallery-branded pencil while seated at the desk next to Fish. It was barely nine in the morning and Fish was hungover. He'd almost thrown up, but his curiosity overcame his nausea.

"Whoa, when did you get it pierced?"

"Oh, I didn't. It happened over time. From drugs," Stanley had replied, as plainly as though he were discussing how packed his subway car had been that morning.

They'd settled on a modest steel band with unobtrusive baubles capping the ends. To Stanley's shock and delight, it would be delivered the very next day.

"What do you think?" Fish asked Marcel, smirking and blushing at the same time.

He wasn't even totally comfortable with the idea of being an "earring guy" himself just yet.

"Oh, you're gilding the lily," Marcel declared with a dismissive wave of his hand, returning to his self-portrait. "You're a young, handsome man. You have no need for adornments. Everyone under thirty is attractive, you know that, right? Well, you will, someday, if you don't now. Just don't ever get a tattoo."

The sour smell of pot hung in the musty air of the unventilated brick room. Joint roaches littered a picnic table that had been dragged (by Fish and Bennett, on a sweltering June day) to the center of the room, some only half-smoked. Marcel only liked the first few puffs, and only ever smoked a newly rolled joint. Sometimes Bennett and Fish would sneak up to the roof after the gallery closed for the day and relight some of the half-finished joints, trading tokes and laughing breathlessly at each other's respective imitations of

Marcel and Stanley. Spatters of dry paint covered every surface of the room in gummy, multicolored bumps. Paint brushes with withered bristles stuck up out of a tall pint glass and paintings in various stages of completion rested on rickety easels, further cramping the already-tight space.

"Sure, but Marcel, listen. The building inspector called. They're coming by for an inspection," Fish said, speaking quickly to slip the words through Marcel's mimed protestations.

"No!"

Marcel turned so quickly that he slashed a thick yellow streak across the self-portrait he'd been painting. Among the other jarring angles and bold colors, it didn't look entirely out of place. In fact, now, with his eyes wide, his brows plunging, and his mouth agape, his physical features looked almost as exaggerated and angular as those of the self-portrait.

"They'll be here tomorrow morning," Fish finished.

Marcel swiveled his head repeatedly back and forth as though he were punch drunk in the corner of a boxing ring and stared out of the broad picture window that overlooked the water towers and rooftops of Hell's Kitchen. The window was the room's only source of light. Most of the ancient panes were yellowed to waxy opaqueness and segmented by cracks from decades of New York winters.

"They're tearing us down," Marcel muttered, turning back to the portrait.

Fish heard the paintbrush lashing violently against the canvas as he made his exit, quietly closing the door behind him.

• • •

It was that night that Fish started writing. There was nothing particularly remarkable about the night his fingers finally managed to start beating the keys of the dilapidated typewriter. He was drunk on Modelo beers and sleepless from the six pieces of mushroom chocolate he'd inhaled towards the end of his shift at the gallery, anticipating a night out with a college buddy who was in the city for a work conference. Like Klein, College Buddy had been Fish's lacrosse teammate. Despite Fish's heroic pregaming efforts, the plans fell through. College Buddy ended up rekindling something with a chick that had nipped at the periphery of their friend group back in the day. She lived in the city, too, apparently. Too revved up for sleep and too overwhelmed by his streaming options to pass out to the dulcet tones of Klein's Netflix account, Fish had stumbled into his bedroom and—almost accidentally—begun pawing at the keys of his typewriter. It wasn't so much a three-act play as a diary entry, but the sentences were pouring out of him, arriving in his skull as quickly as he could impress a semblance of their felt significance into blocky ink letters. And maybe it could be a play, he thought to himself, watching as Wednesday became Thursday on his iPhone's lock screen. Fish was ecstatic. *There's some usable shit here, no?* Here's what he wrote:

> *I snapped a picture of myself in the bathroom mirror tonight. It was one of those pictures you take when you're hoping to remember something. I guess that's why anyone takes pictures of anything, though, right? But this is that rare varietal of bathroom selfie in which one snaps a picture of themselves in a mirror stained with chalky flecks of toothpaste with the intention of shaming themselves with said picture when viewed with sober eyes the next morning. Even staring at the picture now, tonight, drunk, with my (objectively) unfocused, sleep-deprived eyes, the picture registers the self-disgust that was the ultimate goal of its original capture. My pupils seem to have subsumed my irises and the sclera of my eyes that are normally white are*

stained a devilish hue of orange-red, as though a daub of ketchup has been hastily wiped from their surfaces. A neat swoop of purple skin slashes from the inland corner of my eye at a southeasterly angle through my face before flaring outward to my stubbled cheeks, where it peters out in a brief valley of parchment yellow skin. Smile and I can lift my face back upwards an inch, giving the impression of a dude having a good time. But yield to gravity even a little bit and the sleepless nights declare themselves on my skin in dry red patches at the corners of my mouth and nostrils and in the pits of my gaunt cheeks. How much weight am I losing, exactly? When I traipsed to the nearest bodega earlier, I was terribly conscious of my footfalls, to the point that I was walking as though attempting stilettos for the first time. But it's a good thing. All for the best. All an experience, right? I'm writing, aren't I? Converting debauchery into art in the way that all the greats had. Maybe Madame Meticulous was right. Maybe David Byrne was some kind of mystic. That's how she'd described him when shaming me for not having seen Stop Making Sense. I've watched the whole thing thrice now. I can't stop listening to the Talking Heads, despite the fact that each track bores a small but painful hole in my chest with the thought of Madame Meticulous limping defiantly up St. Mark's Place. Maybe that's why I'm still listening. Maybe all of this, every word that I'm haphazardly committing to the printer paper I filched from the gallery, is shit. But it's the first time I've been able to actually string together a few sentences that smack my corrupted senses as just a little bit original. Maybe this'll become some monologue for a bright but woe-is-me dope in a play I'll write someday. I'm barely thinking about the words now, just letting them flow through my fingers. Which means it's true, right? And truth in writing is a good thing, according to a thing Hemingway said or something. It all feels true, anyway, which seems like a good first step. Maybe I do have something to say, after all. Something originally my own and, simultaneously, universal to the human experience that has yet to be set down in ink. Here's something true: Just a few minutes ago, I threw up in the toilet.

Chapter 5

The day Fish was hired at the gallery, he'd been walking along the High Line with Becca. He'd just moved to New York—into the Bushwick sublet with the musicians. And although Becca had looked at him with an expression of disgust, skepticism, and worry at the threshold of the cluttered apartment, Fish had pressed on through the door, his battered suitcase in tow, with a smile on his face. It was precisely the kind of place a guy who'd recently pressed eject on his life should end up, he'd thought.

Becca was visiting for the week, helping him get settled. They'd been very much together at that point. So, that week, they'd done more than a few of the touristy first-time-New-Yorker-type things everyone had to do at least once. They'd marveled at the Statue of Liberty and lazed their way through the Metropolitan Museum of Art. They'd spent a solemn, dutiful half hour paying their respects at the 9/11 Memorial, Becca clutching Fish's hand the whole time. Her eyes welled up a little and she kept checking to see if his would, too.

Though New Canaan was less than an hour away, Fish had never spent much time in the city. There'd been a few school field trips here and there, one or two Broadway shows with his parents and his brother, a couple lacrosse tournaments at Fordham. And when he'd started law school, despite Yale's proximity to Manhattan, he'd been so busy with assignments that he'd hardly had a chance to leave New Haven. He'd been living with two other law students he'd met through Facebook. Even though his lease was for the entire year, he hadn't wanted to keep living there after he quit the law program. All his roommates ever talked about was law school stuff, anyway. He'd felt he needed a clean break. He'd hate to have been stuck being The Guy Who'd Quit Law School, which was surely what he would've become, he felt, had he kept living there.

Sipping a Modelo beer while seated on the bare mattress in Bushwick that he had yet to cover with the one set of sheets he owned, Fish reflected on the fact that he'd been more profoundly struck by the indomitable faces of the Egyptian sarcophagi resting in the Met than he had the 9/11 Memorial, which surprised him, given that his older brother had died in the war that had resulted from the tragedy that the memorial memorialized. The High Line was pleasant, though. He and Becca had been walking unhurriedly and uncynically among the morass of tourists shuffling along the elevated path when Fish's phone buzzed against his thigh. Herds of people filed in and out of Chelsea Market below their feet.

"Hi, is this Fisher?"

"Fish, yeah, hi."

Becca made a face at this mention of his new self-bestowed nickname, but he pretended not to notice.

"Hi! So, you applied to be the gallery assistant, right? Craigslist?"

"Oh, right! Yes, that was me, hi."

Twenty minutes later, Fish was standing in front of the large square elevator doors. They were black then; Marcel hadn't painted them blue yet. Actually, he'd painted them green before they'd become blue. Fish heard a metallic thud from inside the elevator shaft and Stanley's compact form appeared as the doors separated.

"Come on in! I'll take you up."

Fish knew he'd work there as soon as those doors opened on the third floor, revealing the slick white floors, the massive abstract expressionist paintings bursting with color (derivative of Basquiat and Keith Haring but falling way short of both), eclectic furniture salvaged from antique shops strewn at jaunty angles throughout the space (a plush purple love seat here, a Victorian armchair there), rusting water towers and soaring glass skyscrapers strung like a backdrop beyond the broad picture windows. Actually, Fish reminisced, he'd known he'd work at the gallery as soon as he'd stepped into that freight elevator, watching the dusty paintings pinned to the brick walls of the shaft slowly scroll past as the old elevator lurched steadily upward. It had been June, and a sticky haze had descended over the city like a cobweb. But the liberally air-conditioned gallery had been refreshingly chilly, an oasis distilling cool air on the fringes of the steaming city. Fish inhaled the paintings, the skyline, and the waxed white floors into his lungs. It was precisely the kind of place, he'd thought, under precisely the bohemian circumstances, that an aspiring playwright might land upon bailing on the phony mainstream life thing and going all in on the whole starving artist thing.

"You don't mind cats, do you?" As soon as Stanley said it, Rocky and Monty padded across the floor to sniff furtively at Fish's shoes. "They're named after Rock Hudson and Montgomery Clift," Stanley had giggled. "Are you a fan of golden age Hollywood? You're probably too young. And too straight. This is Rocky, and that's his sister, Monty—she's a girl, but we call her Monty anyway."

He pushed through a set of tall glass doors and led Fish out onto the tiled terrace. Potted plants lined the rails at the edge of the building. Stanley proceeded to take Fish around to each plant, telling him its name and what it needed in terms of water and light, occasionally holding petals up for Fish to smell. In one corner stood a massive statue of a man, his body composed of old car parts that Fish would later learn had been salvaged from the auto body shop downstairs. A mass of tangled wires, frayed at the ends and tangled into long rubber knots of various lengths, widths, and colors, cascaded off the sculpture's head in a manner suggesting dreadlocks. The piece was nearly a story tall and stood with its rigid back to the Javits Center.

"Oh, that's Marcel's robot sculpture. It's not finished yet. Neat, huh?"

The warm breeze carried the scent of manure. Fish hadn't asked about the smell that first day, but later he'd learned that the stench came from a skinny brick building across the street. It was where they kept the horses that labored for the Central Park carriage tours. A shabby strip club called Headquarters squatted in the building's shadow.

• • •

In July, buoyed by a sense of embarking on a fresh start with his new life in New York, Fish had taken up running. The route he'd devised took him, huffing and puffing and slowing to a walk every quarter mile or so, through Maria Hernandez Park. He would pound out a few laps on the concrete boundary that encircled the grassy quad on which old Asian women practiced what looked to Fish like tai chi. In the jungle gym area, a cluster of men with dreadlocks piled like beehives atop their heads had assembled an outdoor gym. A random assortment of equipment sat beneath the monkey bars and astride the slides. Their muscles were visible even through their thick sweatshirts, and they passed around a joint between sets on a rusting bench press rack. Young families chattered in rapid Spanish, the knee-high children flying kites, chasing after soccer balls, and blowing bubbles.

But by the time August rolled around, Fish had given up running. He told himself that it was too damn hot and that gym memberships were too damn expensive. It wasn't like he was gaining weight. Given his nascent nicotine addiction and the irregularity of his diet, he weighed less than he had in high school. He'd get back into running in the fall, though, he'd told himself. Once it got a little cooler. Maybe even join a gym, if he could manage to save a little money. *Definitely*, he thought to himself. *In the fall, things will be a little more settled. Everything's just a little . . . up in the air right now.*

• • •

The black Chevy Suburban nosed into the elevator slowly, careful not to catch its mirrors on the close walls. Once its tires crossed the threshold, a thud echoed up and down the cavernous shaft. The driver gave Fish a disconcerted glance from the window, but Fish just shrugged and motioned the SUV forward with his hand. The back windows were tinted like they always were for high-profile artists. Fish couldn't tell who was sitting in the back seat. He flattened himself against the wall to get past the car to the crank and pulled it down. The elevator lurched into motion and Fish watched through the metal screen above him as the rotating pulley turned the thick cable belt, hoisting the elevator upward.

"Hey, how old is this thing?" Following Fish's eyes, the driver arched his neck to watch the massive, slowly churning cog.

"Came with the building. Around 1940, I think."

"Shit. You always take cars up here?"

There was a faint twinge of fear in the driver's voice. He drummed his fingers against the steering wheel, watching the brick wall scroll past the windshield as they ascended.

"Yeah, all the time. This used to be a Checker cab company. Around World War II, Mercedes bought the building. This was where they retrofitted bulletproof siding onto military vehicles. They bricked over the whole building, even the windows, so that nobody could see what they were doing. There's still a garage on the first two floors. Hence the freight elevator."

Fish had given the spiel so many times that the words left his mouth on autopilot. He released the crank and the elevator trundled to a halt at the third floor. He heaved open the doors with a dramatic flourish that he liked to include when bringing up first-time clients. From outside, the nondescript brick building looked like any other relic of old New York, a crumbling homage to industry. Were it not for the elevator doors that Marcel had painted bright blue and stenciled "Temporary Contemporary Gallery" (so named for the imminent wrecking ball that would, according to Marcel, soon demolish the building) in orange lettering, the building would've looked like any of the other tired brick buildings that populated Hell's Kitchen. The pure white space of the emptied gallery expanded before the vehicle as the elevator doors pulled away from each other like a yawning mouth, shimmering in the morning light. *Stanley must have waxed the floors last night*, Fish thought.

"Well, shit," breathed the driver, exhaling slowly.

He took it all in for a moment before starting the car and driving as slowly as he could onto the gallery floor, as though it were a fresh blanket of snow he was hesitant to disturb. The driver, a short, rotund Greek man, stepped down from the car, stretched briefly, and opened the back door. A man in a drab olive flight suit spattered with paint stepped out. His bright blue eyes—which looked all the brighter peering out from under a riotous mane of white hair—darted about the gallery as he nodded a thanks to the driver. All that Bennett had told Fish about the artist was that he was a big deal in Los Angeles. He looked to Fish like the kind of guy who might, when feeling grateful, do prayer hands unironically.

The artist extended his hand. Fish took it, nodding hello.

"I was watching you. In the elevator there. You're a good-looking fella. Ever do any acting? Modeling? No?"

Because the esteemed artists who occasionally exhibited at the gallery typically flat-out ignored his presence, Fish hadn't been expecting the questions. The thick Australian accent also came as a surprise. It took him a moment to respond.

"No. I'm a playwright. Or, well, I'm trying to be a playwright."

"Not much money in that for a handsome fella, is there? Well, I suppose Sam Shepard did all right with it, didn't he?"

Fish made a mental note to Google Sam Shepard later on. When Fish offered an affable smile in lieu of a response, the artist continued.

"How much they payin' you here, eh? Not much, I'm guessin'. No offense, of course. If you're ever looking to make some fast cash, doing some handsome fella type work, you give me a call, yeah?"

The artist—who, Fish later discovered, was famous for his sprawling graffiti murals featuring graphically depicted male nudes—handed him a business card with a not-so-subtle wink.

"Thanks. I'll remember that," Fish mumbled, stuffing the card into his wallet between his subway pass and his expired Connecticut driver's license.

• • •

Bennett exhaled a warm white cloud and passed the Juul to Fish. "Have you told Marcel yet? He likes to know," he said. Speaking as he exhaled, the words came out as though thrust through a tuba.

"Not yet. I'll head up there now. Watch the door for the building inspector, yeah? Marcel's all worked up about it."

Bennett nodded and Fish left him on the terrace. Out of the

corner of his eye, Fish watched him take another long rip from the Juul. The exhaled cloud nearly obscured his small head entirely before an autumn breeze whipped it away.

Inside the gallery, the temperature was so warm as to be almost uncomfortable. Marcel and Stanley spared no expense on air conditioning in the summer or heating in the winter, cranking the thermostat as soon as the first chill of fall wove its way through the city. The entire gallery had been conceived around their comfort. Phone chargers sprung from every outlet. Couches, chairs, and ottomans clustered together like football players in a huddle. A French press coffee machine rested heavily on the kitchen counter. A small fridge tucked into one corner was always stocked with fresh fruits and cheeses and a chilled bottle of pinot grigio or rosé. Even Rocky and Monty were never far from the cat toys that Stanley bought in excess, enraging Marcel each time he sat on a stuffed mouse or heard a cat treat crush underfoot.

"Has the building inspector come yet?" Marcel asked, not looking up. "He's due any second, the bastard."

He used a dollar to roll a joint in his paint-stained fingers. Car horns bleated at intervals on the street below, trapped in the eternal traffic of the Lincoln Tunnel.

"Not yet. Some famous artist is here, though."

"Oh, what good are you?" he said, smiling as he twisted the tip of the joint. "The tiniest, most petty part of me is so jealous of famous artists you wouldn't believe it, Fish. Without even knowing his name, a minuscule part of me hates him. Almost as much as I hate Jeff Koons. And *that's* saying something."

Jeff Koons occupied a secret studio in the bowels of the body shop on the second floor of the building. His obscure outpost on the far reaches of Hell's Kitchen was deliberate. He used the long stalls—typically used to paint cars with little spray arms that poked out from the walls—to coat his iconic balloon dogs with their signature unblemished sheen. He was mass producing them, right there below where Fish and Marcel now stood. He had sold out big time, they'd both agreed. And Koons must've known it, too, otherwise he might have selected a chicer locale for pining away at the artist's eternal struggle. But still, his fame tormented Marcel from one floor below their feet.

A helicopter thundered past, off to land on one of the helipads that jutted into the Hudson. Fish picked at a rubbery crust of paint on the picnic table.

"They're gonna knock us down. Can you believe that?" Marcel's tone was suddenly serious. His gray eyes were piercing. They might once have been blue, but Fish couldn't tell now. Red veins and puffed eyelids obscured their color in a cloudy film.

"I don't think they will. Not soon, right?" Fish couldn't help but hear the desperation in his own voice. Only a few months in, and he already felt as though he was integral to the place, as necessary and unremarkably present as the bricks themselves.

Marcel scoffed and stood up, walking with purpose to the window. "They're looking for any excuse to tear us down. Old wires, dry rot, asbestos. Our contract is up at the end of May. Think it's a coincidence that we get a building inspection now? We're six months out from the end of the party. This is a warning shot, Fish, make no mistake."

"It could be," Fish suggested, adding a shrug that he hoped conferred a dose of calm. "Careful you don't trip on all that red string you're busting out, though."

Marcel rolled his eyes and turned back to the window. The thin hairs clinging to the outer rim of a growing bald spot at the crown of his head whipped about as he moved.

"See that? *That* one was built twelve years ago. *That* one they put up maybe a decade ago. These three over here came in the last five years." Marcel used the joint to point out the towering skyscrapers. "And now this."

He held the joint up to the cluster of sleek, metallic skyscrapers with their walls piercing skyward at aggressive angles. They stood around the shining copper sculpture known as "The Vessel" like homeless men around a trash fire, warming their steep steel walls and dark reflective glass on the colossal sculpture's undulating orange curves, which would fade to green over time as all copper does.

"It's going to be the death of us," he said finally.

"The Hudson Yards project?"

"Hudson Yards today. Hell's Kitchen tomorrow. They won't be happy until the whole city is high-rise office buildings and luxury condo complexes. Dark glass so we can't see inside, but reflective so we won't want to. They keep building them higher because they want to escape the street. But the street's where everything interesting happens, Fish. That's what they don't see."

Marcel passed Fish the joint, and he took a long drag.

• • •

That night, ochre leaves fluttering against his bedroom window, Fish got wasted on a bottle of cheap red wine and clobbered the keys of his typewriter.

What prompts the young capital-R Romantic to leave their square red house by the railroad tracks in a Frost-y, Lowell-y New England town to move to New York, that Siren song of promise and possibility, sadism and sanctity, truth and dare, I can't say for sure. It is not the same as the snow crab that pulls young Alaskan men with smooth chins out to arctic waters and rubberized orange suits only to return them a season later, bearded and with a billfold weighing their loose jeans down to one side so they have to keep hitching them up with their thumb and forefinger. The sustenance New York provides is different altogether. It is a Death Star tractor-beam—invisible but for the banshees that sing its presence visible. It is a ratty net cast by a sometimes benevolent fisherman. Anthony Bourdain is probably one such, in my case. Scorsese, Biggie Smalls, Greta Gerwig, F. Scott Fitzgerald, Jay-Z and Jay McInerney, and probably Jennifer Aniston, too. Whatever it was I had been looking for, I found, though I could not show it to you in my hands or point it out to you in the street or sketch it out with a pencil. I do not have a name for it. I have only the girl with pink hair reading Hebrew comic books on the J-train. I have the Haitian woman who plaits hair and reads palms for five dollars. And I have the oddly pleasant smell of pizza and street trash and city sunsets on summer nights when the rays pierce through the buildings and gild the avenues in gold. There must be some charge that the city gives off, has been giving off for generations, ever since the Dutch settled New Amsterdam, saturating the air with its beckoning call, churning out its apostles; actors, artists, writers, geniuses, chefs, titans of industry, activists, and alcoholics to carry its gospel to the world and further layering intrigue and hope into the city's aura until the lore, at some point, became inseparable from the city itself. To live here is to be interesting. And each day a new idealistic Sisyphus in skinny jeans arrives at Penn Station, dragging a heavy suitcase to atone for a boring youth spent on farmland or in the dull protection of a suburban cul-de-sac. They smile as the subway takes them to their expensive new home, a room scarcely larger than a restaurant booth. They plop down on an old mattress and a little plume of dust escapes out of the cracked window, rising up to join the hazy smoke clouds pouring, ever pouring forth from the city's torched, unknowable core. They smile and ignore the room's odd smell and the disconcerting clunk of pipes thrashing against their walls—for they have done IT! Or at least they have done SOMETHING, which is nearly as good. Anything to become a character in the ever-unfinished manuscript that is New York City. For it is death to be omitted from these pages.

Still no play. But damn, Fish mused, it sure sounded like something.

Chapter 6

By the time Thanksgiving had come and passed, construction from the Hudson Yards project had crept so close to West Thirty-Ninth Street that the gallery was closed to foot traffic while men in neon vests operating cruel looking machines tore up the road and erected scaffolding between Tenth and Eleventh Avenues. Fish and Bennett took turns going in to open the gallery for a few hours on weekends, though nobody ever showed up. Despite Marcel's tangential relation to Andy Warhol and Keith Haring in the '60s (he'd occasionally alluded to having slept with both of them), his abstract expressionist style had never attained much cachet. Relatively few people even knew about the gallery, hidden on the third floor of a former taxicab garage on the outskirts of Hell's Kitchen. All the chic galleries were several blocks away, in Chelsea. It didn't help that Marcel refused to pay for advertising, either. He claimed it was a strategy for making sure only purists, *real* appreciators of New York's underground art scene and *not* confused German vacationers or Croc-wearing tourists, laid their eyes on his work. So far, the method had done little but to prove that New York was severely lacking in whatever worthy clientele Marcel hoped to attract.

On one particularly dead morning, without a single person poking their head tentatively into the gallery, Marcel got frustrated and flipped the OPEN sign to CLOSED. Fish left Marcel muttering about the city's declining art taste. It was a sunny day, the air pleasantly crisp. Fish began walking in a direction he'd never taken before, heading south on Tenth Avenue and making turns by whim. He bypassed the minimalist art galleries of Chelsea and turned east, past the emotionless skyscrapers of Midtown where men and women in suits with sharp haircuts pushed through revolving glass doors. They strutted elbow first, holding their phones up to their ears and jabbering in quick bursts.

Gradually, Chinese characters began appearing on the awnings of tired shop fronts offering laundry services and foot massages. Or else they advertised their wares wordlessly: tantalizing ducks hung by their crooked necks in the window, arranged like suits in a closet, their brown crisped chests meeting in a neat row. By the time he'd reached Canal Street, the riotous color spectrum of Chinatown overwhelmed the block. Boys in school uniforms sipped casually at their bubble teas while scrolling through TikTok feeds. Fish fought to ignore the sweet smell of soup dumplings as he turned down Mott Street, reminding himself of the less-than-impressive balance in his checking account. *This city wants to be ingested just as bad as it wants to spit you out*, he reflected.

Money ought to have been a larger issue for Fish, given the reduction of his hours at the gallery. Lexi Spanish Harlem was supposed to swing by the apartment on the first of every month. But their door buzzer hadn't sounded on the first of November. Nor on the second, third, or fourth. Klein and Fish hadn't pursued the oversight, wary of compromising this unexpected gift by speaking it aloud. They theorized, giddily, that the leasing agency might be some kind of front, perhaps a laundering operation connected, somehow, to Lexi Spanish Harlem's escort service. The head honcho with whom they'd signed the lease *had* seemed sleazy enough to be, possibly, some kind of mid-level pimp. At the lease signing appointment, he had made a lewd comment about watching Lexi Spanish Harlem ascend stairs in booty shorts that had made Klein and Fish—who were no strangers to the casual misogyny of locker rooms—cringe and glance at the floor. While Klein could have easily afforded the November rent, Fish would've been screwed. Not really, of course. He could always make an awkward, pleading phone call to his parents. But this would have confirmed their most entrenched concerns about him, he knew. Fish kept walking.

In the East Village, skinny girls with buzz cuts tromped about in their studded boots and bearded men in beanies took photos with Polaroid cameras. NYU students clutching binders and Mac laptops to their chests shuffled along the sidewalks in small herds, sipping at their Starbucks lattes. A shirtless man leaning against a covered bus stop crooned out the same lyric on repeat, like a vinyl record caught on a loop. Fish recognized the song despite the man's wheezing articulation.

"Mona LI-sas and mad Hatters . . . Mona Li-sas and mad HATTERS!"

By the time Fish got to the Williamsburg Bridge, a small circle of sweat had formed between his spine and his backpack. The Governors Island ferry passed under his feet, and he watched it through the corrugated red metal screen of the bridge. An occasional jogger puffed past him, their cheeks red and their neon sweat-wicking shirts whipping behind them. When the subways streamed by, the sound was gloriously deafening, thundering through his chest. He paused in the middle of the bridge to drink in the Manhattan skyline on his right and Brooklyn's dignified, if not *as* striking, building-scape to his left. Manhattan looked as though it were about to sink into the East River, succumbing to the burdensome concrete and life it had heaped on top of itself over the years with reckless abandon, growing unchecked in height and population as though to test the laws of physics itself, ultimately refusing the river the satisfaction of swallowing up humanity's crowning metropolitan achievement.

The wind rifled through Fish's riotous hair. He hadn't gotten it cut since he'd started law school—a sharp, mature cut to prepare for his sharp, mature life. He hitched the waist of his jeans up with his thumb to keep them from slipping down past his narrow buttocks. He could remember when these jeans had been a little snug over his rump, back when he'd been squatting three days a week and cross-checking skimpy midfielders to the ground to keep them from scoring. He smiled. He liked that New York was leaving its mark on him, eating away at him. He felt himself tattering, his loose ends slowly knitting themselves into the fabric of the city, a single identity slipping into nondescription as it joined the faceless millions who made up the five boroughs.

Acting on an impulse, Fish pulled his iPhone from his pocket—a rose gold 6s that he'd inherited from Becca after she'd upgraded—and, because *Partiboy just wants to party, boy*, hurled it into the East River. He watched as it careened through the air and plopped insignificantly into the water.

Chapter 7

The building inspector finally showed up on a gloriously sunny Tuesday. Despite the brilliance of the sun, it was cool enough that Fish had slipped on a tattered crewneck sweatshirt that said PHILLIPS EXETER LACROSSE in neat black type over his heart. He was looking forward to improving the sweatshirt with a few deliberate splatters of paint once he got to the gallery, vandalizing it just enough to suggest that he worked in an arts-adjacent job. He'd ridden a Citi Bike to work, cutting through Central Park and taking the West Side Bike Path the rest of the way to Thirty-Ninth Street. The leaves on the trees curled in on themselves at the edges, yielding to hues of pumpkin orange and barn red.

When he arrived, he found Marcel stomping frantically around the gallery. Bennett was late, as he had been more and more frequently of late. This discovery disappointed Fish, as he'd been hoping for a surreptitious rip of Bennett's Juul to fuel his patience before engaging Marcel's tantrum. Fish briefly considered sneaking back outside to smoke one of the hand-rolled cigarettes tucked in the small pocket of his backpack. But the door clunked behind him, and his keys jangled from the carabiner on his belt loop, alerting Marcel to his presence. Marcel stormed in his direction, eyes roving. He launched into his diatribe from across the room.

"He's here, Fish. He's here! Out of the blue! Just showing up whenever he wants! Can you *believe* that? It's bad news, Fish.

Very, *very* bad news. Oh, and of course Stanley is upstate. Never here when there's a crisis . . . Oh, I can't talk to him. I'll get too angry . . . I *always* get too angry! You have to go. Go, Fish. He's checking the garage downstairs first. Make him like you, Fish. Be charming. We need a clean report. They're looking for any excuse to shut us down. Go!"

Only when he turned back to the staircase did Fish notice the half-empty bottle of wine dangling from Marcel's hand like a hunted duck. It was just past nine o'clock in the morning.

It was chilly in the auto body shop, cold gusts pouring in each time a car entered or exited the wide doorway. Amid the grinding noise of metal work and sputtering welding tools and coughing engines, Fish heard laughter. The building inspector wore a toothy grin under his kempt gray mustache. A yellow hard hat was perched atop his head, though he didn't look as though he'd spent much time around cinder blocks. His stomach spilled over his pleated khakis. He glanced at Fish out of the corner of his eye as he approached but continued talking to the body shop's foreman.

"You guys have some stones smoking cigarettes down here, you know that?"

His deep grating voice harmonized with the sounds of tools and engine gears. A few mechanics standing close by smiled sheepishly as they stubbed out their cigarettes with the toes of their boots on the greasy cement floor and wiped their hands on their filthy blue coveralls.

"How about the alarms, do I have to check those?" the inspector asked.

"No, no. They're fine," the foreman said, batting away the question with a loose flop of his hand.

The inspector gave the foreman—a Syrian man with a thick cloud of white hair floating atop his head—a wink.

"Sure, sure. I trust you."

The inspector made a little mark on his clipboard and tore off a piece of paper for the foreman.

"You fellas behave down here, all right?"

They laughed again and shook hands. This meeting was a formality, Fish knew. Marcel had once mentioned something about the mechanics having already signed a new lease on a new garage in Midtown East, a preemptive move for which the gallery did not, at the moment, have the funds.

The inspector fixed his eyes on Fish, looked him up and down, eying the crew neck sweatshirt, the earring, the shoulder-length hair, the paint-spattered canvas shoes. Already Fish knew that his interaction with the inspector would not be as genial as it had been for the mechanics. Despite their cosmopolitan origins, dubious legal worker status, and Mecca-facing prayer rugs tucked in the corners, the mechanics spoke the same language as the inspector. The world of cars and grease and tools and calloused hands was not unfamiliar to the inspector—or, at least, to the version of himself that he leaned into.

"So, I suppose you're from artsy-fartsy land upstairs. That right?"

"The Temporary Contemporary Gallery, yeah," Fish mumbled.

He hadn't thought he'd be so nervous. But now, facing the man who could, with a few strokes of his pen, slate the building for destruction in the first wave of demolition rather than some later wave, Fish couldn't help but see the rotund man as a personal threat. Though in the last few weeks he'd managed to cobble together a tortuous outline for the play that would eventually, he hoped, become *Postlapsaria, Connecticut*, as of this moment, his job at the gallery was the only thing he felt legitimated his dubious ties to the art world that he so desperately wanted to inhabit.

The inspector raised his thick owlish eyebrows and jotted something down on his clipboard. He hitched up his belt and adjusted himself in his slacks. "Well, let's take a look."

As Fish led him into the freight elevator, he saw a mechanic lighting up a cigarette in the corner, tossing the match into a pile of busted rubber tires.

The building inspector—Fish learned his name was Toomey—made a noise in his throat as the elevator rumbled to a halt at the third floor. Fish pretended not to notice, listening for the sound of Marcel's voice before opening the doors. He prayed that Marcel had taken his drunken vocal ruminations up to the studio, away from here.

"Not stalling, are we?" asked inspector Toomey.

Fish winced and turned back toward him, his hand still on the elevator crank. He heard a door slam and a muffled monologue, footsteps slapping against stairs. If he could just make sure that Marcel had left the gallery . . .

"Er, yeah . . . I wasn't sure . . . Do you need to check the elevator or anything?" Fish asked, feigning naivete.

A patronizing grin spread beneath the inspector's brushy mustache as though Fish had just asked him if the moon was really made of cheese.

"You know, the whole point of these drop-by inspections is to observe your procedures on a regular day. If we allowed you time to prepare for us, we wouldn't really get an accurate picture, would we?"

Fish paused a moment, looking for any trace of the grace that the inspector had extended to the downstairs tenants. The inspector sighed and adjusted himself in his pants again with a twitch of his thumb and forefinger. Begrudgingly, Fish pried open the elevator doors and trudged into the gallery, the inspector a pace behind.

Marcel was nowhere to be seen. A heavy sigh billowed from Fish's chest.

Rocky raked his claws against a battered sofa in the corner and Monty sniffed at a small maroon puddle of spilled wine on the floor.

"What are these, Picassos?" Toomey gestured at two paintings to his left, jabbing the air with his pen.

"No, that one's Marcel's. I think Stanley did the other one."

"Ah yeah, Marcel. He's the one whose name is on the lease. He around today?"

Fish thought of Marcel pacing on the roof, soliloquizing to his audience of skyscrapers and pigeons. He suddenly wished he hadn't tossed his phone off the Williamsburg Bridge so he could text Bennett to coax Marcel into drinking some coffee.

"I haven't seen him yet today but yeah, he might be in later," Fish lied.

"Mm-hmm . . . And what about this Stanley guy, is he an owner, too?"

"No, they're partners."

"Business partners but he's not on the lease?"

Toomey cocked a bushy eyebrow at Fish as though he'd caught him in a lie. He held the tip of his pen just above the clipboard in anticipation. It was a dagger held to Fish's throat.

"No, as in . . . they're together," said Fish, fumbling for the words.

Toomey paused a long moment before responding. "Oh, okay. I got it." His pen hand dropped to his side and that smirk reappeared beneath his mustache.

Toomey walked around to the fire exits, peered up the elevator shaft, pressed on the old windows, and tested a few outlets, jotting down notes on his clipboard all the while. While he was checking the smoke detectors, Fish stole into the kitchen. As fast as he could, he clambered up a ladder and stuffed a bundle of loose wires back underneath the insulation through which they'd dropped. He nearly fell off the ladder when the sound of the fire alarm tore through the silence of the gallery. Rocky and Monty shot under a sofa.

"Gotta test that," Officer Toomey said, checking a box on the bureaucratic form.

"Thanks for the warning," Fish muttered.

The inspector smiled but didn't look up. Bennett burst through the door, his mouth forming words but freezing when he saw the building inspector. Fish offered a silent, helpless shrug from behind Toomey. Bennett mimed tearing his hair out and mouthed an apology for being late. There were purplish circles under his eyes.

"Is Marcel still raving around upstairs?" Fish whispered, hearing the desperation in his voice.

"Yeah, kinda. Is he *drunk*? Even for Marcel that's . . . Jesus," hissed Bennett. "But he's in the studio. Nearly screamed when he heard that alarm. He thinks they're gonna tear it down, like, today. Beside himself."

From an anxious distance, they followed Toomey's lumbering frame around the gallery. Bennett dove under the desk to unplug an obscenely overloaded power strip before Toomey could notice. So many cords burst from its sockets that it looked like a beached squid. Fish stood with his back to the paint shelf, deftly sealing as many of the open flammable canisters as he could behind his back. Neither he nor Bennett was quite sure what constituted an infraction on the inspector's checklist.

When Toomey handed Fish a carbon copy sheet from the clipboard, the result of the inspection remained, for Fish, an inscrutable collection of lines and boxes and illegible markings. Toomey's parting words, however, were unambiguous.

"It's a nice space," he said, turning to walk up West Thirty-Ninth Street after Fish dropped him off at street level. "Old, though.

Hazardous. Enjoy it while you still can. I'd say you've got six months. Maybe less. Old building like this? I'd say it's gonna be one of the first to go once word comes down from the city."

As Toomey disappeared around the corner of Tenth Avenue, a dark shape careening through the air caught Fish's eye. He heard a sharp crash as it kamikazed into the street. Shards of dark glass were scattered across the pavement. Pigeons fluttered pathetically in all directions. A mutilated wine cork rolled towards Fish's feet. He looked up to the rooftop, and there was Marcel brandishing his middle finger like an Olympic torch, directing it towards the back of Toomey's gelatinous head.

● ● ●

E ver since he'd quit law school, Fish received less than a dozen emails each week. And even then, most of them were spam or articles from the *New York Times* that his mother would, for some reason, copy and paste into the body of the email whenever she wished to share some squash polenta recipe that was perfect for autumn or a profile of a youngish couple from Cleveland who'd been so, so lucky to find a two-bedroom in Park Slope that was within their two-million-dollar budget.

But tonight, when Fish settled down to his typewriter with a fresh bottle of Fernet-Branca (he'd read, in an article diligently copied from the *New York Times* and pasted into an email sent by his mother, that Matthew Gasda, who Fish hoped to one day rival, drank the stuff), he noticed a red icon indicating a new message in the inbox of his Gmail.

It was from Madame Meticulous. He hadn't heard from her in more than a month. But he hadn't forgotten their last conversation at the café in Alphabet City. A film of sweat glazed his palms like dew settling over a pasture. He wiped his hands on his pants and clicked the message open.

hi Fish

~friendship message~

my friend is throwing a rooftop party tonight. his parties are always killer and it's in bushwick so I thought of ya.

ps my texts aren't going through so I had to find your email on the yale law school website. didn't know you went to law school (!). did you get a new phone or something?

xx

Fish exhaled the breath he hadn't realized he'd been holding. He and Madame had left things on such strange, mostly bad terms that he had no idea what to make of this breezy invitation to a rooftop party. He tried to picture Madame Meticulous gyrating to some DJ's mash-up with the Manhattan skyline looming in the background. Would her belly be slightly swollen, he wondered? Poking out like a cantaloupe under one of her belly shirts? And would she still be drinking these days? The thoughts careened through his mind in bursts like starlings at dusk.

He took a long pull from the bottle of Fernet before typing out his reply. Then he deleted what little he'd written, Partiboy advising him to wait a few hours before replying so as not to appear overeager. He'd wait an hour or so, he decided. He used that hour to consume most of the bottle of Fernet. *Partiboy just wants to party, boy.*

Fish had grown so accustomed to stabbing at the typewriter that the laptop's slick, easily depressed buttons felt overly sensitive to his touch. He tried to match the breeziness of her message's tone. He thanked her casually and told her about how he'd moved to Spanish Harlem, which hadn't come up the last time they'd spoken. She must still think he lived in Bushwick, he realized. He thought about mentioning the pregnancy but decided against it. To await the answer to that question would put him in anxious limbo until she responded, and he recalled that she replied to texts at a glacial rate. He declined the invitation while leaving the door open to a potential future meet-up. There was something a little formal about emailing compared to texting, he felt, and a stiffness choked his words no matter how he rephrased them. He felt a little sick and a little relieved. He didn't acknowledge Madame's comments about law school or mention anything about his phone situation.

• • •

Fish passed the cigarette back to Bennett and he all but snatched it out of Fish's fingers. He'd run out of Juul pods one morning a few weeks back, and the unimaginable possibility of waiting until after work to feed his—and now Fish's too—nicotine habit had proved untenable. He'd slipped out to a corner bodega and bought a pack of cigarettes, and now it was all they smoked. It felt more fitting, somehow, to smoke cigarettes on the roof of the building instead of Juuling, which felt like dipping a toe into the derelict artist's lifestyle rather than a whole foot. It was windy on the terrace, and they huddled behind the robot sculpture to block the wind. A few of Jeff Koons' guildsmen, taking a break from monitoring the spray painting of massive balloon animal sculptures, were huddled in a corner across the terrace, using their blocky peacoats to light cigarettes of their own. Fish and Bennett agreed that Koons' guildsmen were cool.

While Fish had been looking forward to colder weather in the city, it had turned out to be far drearier an affair than he'd imagined. Though in the summer one could hardly make it thirty feet without inhaling a lungful of steaming piss-covered trash and soaking through freshly laundered shirts with the sweat accumulated from merely walking one block, at least his fingers didn't go numb each time he had to pull off his gloves with his teeth to fish a subway card or a set of keys out of his backpack.

"Think we're fucked?" Bennett asked.

A sharp gust whipped away the gray cloud passing through his chapped lips.

"Probably. I don't think Marcel's been paying rent. I bet he thinks it's not worth it at this point. Building coming down and all," Fish said.

Bennett passed him the cigarette. Pigeons ruffled their feathers and cooed along the iron bar that Stanley had built for them. Fish took a long drag and let the smoke seep out through his nostrils.

"Apparently Marcel bought Stanley a ring for ten grand."

"Jesus," scoffed Bennett. A hollow laugh that morphed into a cough erupted from his chest. He looked paler than ever; circles the shade of plum skin bagged in crescents under both eyes. "That's kinda nice though, isn't it?" he added, regaining his breath.

Fish shrugged. He'd always imagined that he'd get married one day, have a kid, do the whole thing. But the longer he lived in New York, the more ridiculous the idea sounded. Who had the time, he wondered? Or the money? And besides all those practicalities, who would want to give up their freedom like that? Because that's what it was, for Fish. He'd been giving in to his most selfish indulgences since moving to New York, had created a life and a self all his own.

And though the seasons had changed, the novelty of the city had yet to wear off. *Partiboy just wants to party, boy.*

He even had the first act of his play drafted. He wanted to stage it at the gallery, maybe sometime in the spring. It would be ultra-low budget. Actors could be sourced from Craigslist—dreamers looking to fill gaps in their resume and thus willing to work for free, people too earnest or too loyal to their craft to lie on their resume like most. If the building was still standing, he'd stage it right there in the gallery. Or out on the terrace, if the weather happened to cooperate. He'd advertise it in those underground print zines that he sometimes saw people with earrings reading on the L-train. Maybe a critic of some importance, someone who prided themselves on having their finger on the pulse of the city's underground theater scene, would happen to be in the audience, and then . . . Fish scarcely allowed himself to dream farther.

Bennett scuffed out the cigarette butt with the toe of his checkerboard Converse low-tops and they hunched against the wind as they walked across the terrace.

Once they were back inside, the tall French doors firmly shut, Fish asked, "Are you worried this place will shut down?"

"Why?" Bennett's voice was serious all of a sudden. "So, Marcel fucked up, who cares? You went to college. You'll be fine. You'll get another job." Fish detected a touch of resentment in Bennett's voice.

"You could've gone to college," Fish replied, and Bennett just shrugged and looked out the window. "But that's not the point."

"So, what's the point? Why do you care what happens to this place?"

It struck Fish that this was the most serious conversation they'd ever had—perhaps the only one. It was the longest they'd gone without rolling their eyes or devolving into impressions of Marcel and Stanley or light-humored chat about the peculiarities of their job.

"Think about it, man," Fish began, hearing a touch of excitement—or maybe desperation—in his voice. "We know Marcel isn't going to get his shit figured out by the end of the lease. But think about us, man! We're not going to find another job like this. We get to goof off and pursue our own shit on the side, meet interesting people . . . There's no other place like this."

"I feel like there's probably thousands of jobs like this in New York, dude. I mean, probably, like, half the people here don't work jobs—they work *day* jobs, you know? Work is just, like, fodder for conversation. In New York, I guess I mean."

Bennett stared at the ground as he spoke. He'd been working at the gallery since he was eighteen. It was the first job he'd ever had. He'd met Stanley when he'd stopped in the street—somewhere in the West Village—to compliment the lighting display Stanley had been affixing in the window of a costume shop. Sometimes Stanley took on odd jobs like that, something to flex the set design muscles he'd honed at FIT. Or just to get away from Marcel's mania for an afternoon. After talking for a while, Bennett had mentioned that he hadn't been able to get a job and that his savings were running out. He'd spent all his money on improv classes and was rationing his last jar of peanut butter with two-day-old bagels. Stanley had offered him a job on the spot.

"Think about what comes after this," Fish continued. "Sitting in some cubicle? Consulting? Marketing? Sales? Wearing one of those fucking, like, headsets with the little microphone thing?"

"Easy for you to say," Bennett said. "I'd probably end up washing dishes somewhere. Waiting tables at best. But shit, even that's competitive here."

Rocky and Monty peered at them from a nearby chair with expressions that looked, to Fish, a little like concern.

Chapter 8

At the corner of Seventh Avenue and Thirty-Ninth Street, Stanley pulled a crisp twenty-dollar bill out of his pocket. With Fish following dutifully behind him, he approached a middle-aged man wearing a threadbare bathrobe, torn khaki pants, and mittens. The man was collapsed against a bike rack outside of a bodega. The twenty-dollar bill joined a small family of coins at the bottom of the weathered blue coffee cup in the man's outstretched hands. He bowed his head slightly and his grizzled mouth began to form the words *thank you*.

"He'll be okay, right?" Stanley asked.

Though Stanley stood about a foot shorter than him, Fish had to rush to keep up. He barely broke stride as he negotiated crosswalk signals and slipped through crowded Manhattan sidewalks.

"Sure. Nice of you to give him that money. I feel bad; I never do that," Fish said.

"Oh, no. I meant Bennett. Have you talked to him?"

They'd just been trading conjectures about Bennett. He'd been missing for five days. No phone calls, no texts, nothing. Even for Bennett, who was persistently late and played hooky at least once a week—usually calling in sick because of a COVID scare that nearly always turned out to be a false alarm—missing this many days was worrisome. Fish had been to Bennett's apartment twice, knocking fruitlessly both times. He'd even called up Bennett's girlfriend,

Isabel. She'd met Bennett in an improv class at the Upright Citizen's Brigade, and was in the midst of finishing up her psychology degree at Hunter College. The call hadn't gone well. She'd whimpered a little, cried a little, and told Fish about how she'd wanted so badly for Bennett to go to college, in case the improv comedy thing didn't work out. Just for some *direction*. He'd booked a few auditions that had then dropped him when he'd failed to show up at the call time. She mentioned something about pills, but Fish hadn't pressed her for details. She'd actually been crying a lot.

"Not really. Isabel thinks he'll be okay, though."

Stanley nodded but Fish could see concern worrying deep lines on Stanley's angular face.

Rather than turning down Thirty-Ninth Street toward the gallery, Stanley kept walking. Fish followed at his heels. They kept walking south before turning up Twenty-Seventh Street and strolling down Fashion Avenue. It was around noon. Stanley bought Fish a slice of pizza and a Coke. Though winter was fast approaching, the weather was still just pleasant enough that they could eat outside on the Fashion Institute's courtyard benches. Students walked by toting large rectangular design pads. They wore herringbone jackets and gelled their hair at severe slants over their skulls, or else black jeans weighed down by several chains, their bleached hair falling in an angle over one eye. There were many unfashionable people, too, Fish noticed. From Times Square, Stanley said. A girl walked by wearing a cameo flight suit and stilettos followed by another woman wearing a full tuxedo.

"I used to be like that," Stanley said, watching the students trudge by on their way to class.

He'd graduated from FIT nearly three decades ago. He claimed he'd only applied because he'd wanted to meet other guys who were out and proud rather than the closeted farm boys he'd passed time with throughout his youth in a small depleted mill town way up the Hudson River. Once, as a student worker in the FIT Museum lighting department, he'd been tasked with asking Gianni Versace to please not smoke indoors. Versace had scoffed and continued smoking.

"Yeah? What changed?" Fish asked. He lit a cigarette as he spoke, and one for Stanley as well. Marcel would've gone ballistic if he knew.

Stanley laughed and shrugged, speaking only after a long, savored drag. "It gets exhausting. Trying so hard to stand out."

Stanley tore his crust up into small pieces and tossed them on the ground. Two fat pigeons waddled up and pecked at the bread chunks. As he watched them, Fish realized he had never noticed how the purple and green feathers around their throats glimmered like ascots when they moved. From a distance, they looked to be the same dusty-cement gray as the rest of the city, as though formed from the very materials of their environment.

• • •

Fish had started to feel like he ought to be eating healthier. Like he had in college. He was slimmer than ever, it was true. But he just felt gross. Half hungry, half bloated. He'd made it almost a week; salads for lunch, light dinners, easy on the carbs, no snacking between meals. But last night he'd broken. It started with something small, as it always did. The culprit, in this case, was the lone Snickers bar that remained at the bottom of the glass bowl leftover from Marcel's birthday party at the gallery. His birthday coincided with Halloween, so he always threw a party attended by a sparse collection of old queens from the neighborhood. Fish inhaled the Snickers before the door had even closed behind him, and, after a week of deprivation, his stomach yearned for more. Or, more precisely, his tongue, as an extension of his craving brain, wanted more.

At the first bodega he saw, he bought a package of chocolate chip cookies before he could think to stop himself. These he'd finished by the time he arrived at the new Hudson Yards subway station, eating them whole, one at a time. He matched the crunch of his teeth with his steps, their cheap, oversweet flavor triggering a twinge in the roots of his molars. On the train, he'd thought that maybe he could compensate by skipping dinner, start fresh tomorrow without too much regret. But then his devious brain chimed in, suggesting that if today was shot, if there was no hope of salvaging it, then he might as well make it a fuckup worth his while. *Partiboy just wants to party, boy.*

Immediately upon exiting the 6 train at One Hundred Sixteenth Street, he'd purchased—and subsequently devoured over the course of his walk home—three pastelitos de carne from Cuchifritos and a slice of pizza the size of a golf flag. The whole time that his jaws were masticating the savory pastries and the oil-drenched pepperonis, he was telling himself that this was just for tonight, that tomorrow he'd start over and this time, *this time*, he'd stick to it, because he knew, *he knew*, that he felt better when he didn't binge on crap like this. But *Partiboy just wants to party, boy.*

So because of his future virtue, he'd allowed himself a night of vice. He stopped at a rum bar and downed a few mojitos. Back at home, at night, Fish could only lie on his back and feel his stomach churn. He slept terribly—the sugars, dairy, alcohol, and regret pounding at the back of his head.

If I could just have this day back; if only that Snickers bar hadn't been lying so enticingly, so coquettishly at the bottom of that big glass bowl. Fish awoke with the sun and went for a run around Marcus Garvey Park for the first time in months. It was a chilly morning, and the sweat itched his skin beneath his heavy sweatshirt. He had a salad for lunch, a light dinner, and smoked cigarettes instead of snacking between meals.

· · ·

As winter's first severe chill settled over the city, Marcel began dressing as though an arctic storm were about to descend from the heavens. He wore a thick coat of imitation bear fur that he swore up and down was real. Deliberately hanging back a block behind, Fish watched Marcel amble slowly toward the gallery. From this distance, he looked like some hairy beast lumbering along Tenth Avenue. The Chewbacca of Hell's Kitchen. The Sasquatch of Manhattan. *Stanley must be up ahead somewhere*, Fish thought, *weaving through the crowd like a pinball, no doubt*. Stanley was too impatient to wait for Marcel, who was always pausing to appreciate some new mark of graffiti or talk to a young person with neon hair who looked like they might've just left a nightclub.

Fish caught up with Marcel when he paused at the corner of Little West Twelfth and Washington. He was staring up at a luxury condo complex being built on top of soot-blackened brick walls. It reminded Fish of when green plant shoots sprouted atop a tortoise's shell.

"Whatcha looking at?" Fish asked.

Marcel didn't even look back at Fish in surprise, responding as though they were already in mid conversation.

"This is new. I can't believe they're building on top of it." There was a faint anguish in his voice. He held a hand over his heart, his fur-clad shoulders slumped.

"What was it?"

Marcel didn't say anything, just kept staring up at the construction. A few guys in hard hats barked orders in Spanish to each other

from scaffolding pinioned against the building. They smoked cigarettes and beat their gloved hands together before picking up the
steel beams that had gone ice-cold in the morning chill.

"This is where Stanley and I met for the first time," Marcel finally replied.

For a moment Fish thought Marcel was crying, but it could've
just been from the sharp breeze catapulting off the Hudson. "What
was it?"

Marcel cast a slow glance over his shoulder as though seeing Fish
for the first time. After a moment, he smirked and looked back at the
building. "Depends what time you came."

"What do you mean?"

Still grinning, Marcel spread out his arms and turned in a circle. "All this used to be the Meatpacking District. Not so much
anymore, right? This was some butcher shop—I can't remember the
name now—but that was just during the day."

"Okay . . . And at night?"

He knew he had Fish now. He held Fish in suspense as long as
he could maintain the pregnant pause himself. The drama seemed
to warm him. His spray-tanned cheeks looked boyish and red. "At
night it was a gay leather bar called Pork. Get it?"

They laughed and continued walking toward the gallery. Fish
slowed his pace to match Marcel's unhurried lumber.

"That was twenty-eight years ago. Can you believe that? Of
course you can't. You're twenty-six, right? Thought so. You've never
known anyone—or any*thing*—for twenty-eight years."

Fish smiled and said nothing, knowing Marcel would keep
talking now that he had a captive audience.

"You should've seen this area back then. Dangerous! Oh, you
wouldn't believe it. Prostitutes on every corner. Drug dealers. Dogs
running around. Dogs! Can you believe that? Like an African

savanna or something. And none of these, these *buildings*, my god! And graffiti on everything. *Every*thing."

"You're talking like you miss it. Sounds pretty rough, though."

"Oh, no! No. It was incredible! This was the wild east! We had parties on the subways! You could never do any of that stuff now. Can't do anything anymore. The disco clubs . . . Does anyone listen to disco music anymore? No, of course not. You know, actually, I've got one for you. I've just thought of it."

"Let's hear it."

"There are no interesting people in nightclubs. There are only people on cocaine."

• • •

F ish collapsed onto the broken rolling chair behind the gallery's reception desk, not bothering to swipe away the cat hair as he used to. He and Partiboy had gone out last night. There was a movie theater called Syndicated in Bushwick that Fish had fallen in love with when he'd first begun reconceiving himself as the kind of guy that regularly patronized art house cinemas. Syndicated had been featuring a Wong Kar-wai marathon, and, recalling Madame Meticulous's lauding of the director's revolutionary style, Fish had gone three nights in a row, seeing *Chungking Express*, *2046*, and *As Tears Go By*. It was one of those theaters that sold cocktails and snacks at the seats, and Partiboy had indulged with vigor. *Partiboy just wants to party, boy.*

As usual, Partiboy was nowhere to be seen when the hangover the morning after crept its way into Fish's skull and solidified like rubber cement in the grooves of his cranium. No sooner had Fish closed his eyes and rested his head in his hands than a heavy fist began pounding on the door.

"Open up, Marcel! It's me."

Fish didn't recognize the voice, but it filled him with dread all the same. He sprang to the door and yanked it open. A man stood on the other side; his meaty fist still raised to knock. He was tall and bulky, like a quilt pulled tight over a ham hock. His arms were thick as cacti trunks, and he was balding but for a thresh of curly red hair that sprang off the sides of his head. Freckles covered his face and neck, blurred by his blotchy red skin.

"Hi, Marcel's not in. Can I help you?" It might as well have been the company slogan, whether or not Marcel was actually in the building.

The man snorted and glanced up the stairs. "What, is he hiding in his studio up there? I need to see him," wheezed the man.

He began to walk up the staircase and Fish lunged after him. The man took the stairs two at a time on his large rectangular feet.

"Sorry, who are you again? I've only been working here a few months," Fish stammered.

"Oh yeah? Figures. Marcel goes through employees like most people go through toilet paper. I'm Shane McCourt. I own the building."

They ascended the final flight of stairs, and McCourt shouldered his way through the steel door onto the roof. He barely broke stride, his elephantine legs surging across the roof to the elevator room. Fish couldn't catch him before he was pounding at the door again, his massive fist like a shot put at the end of his heavy arm.

"What's going on?" Fish finally managed, between ragged breaths.

"*What's going on?* Rent. Marcel's two months behind. Did he not tell you? He's fucking me over. Right, Marcel?" he yelled into the heavy steel door that hung akimbo from its frame. "Open up, Marcel! I hear that fucking music! You knew this was coming!"

The disco music that had been blaring from the studio's battered radio cut abruptly to silence.

• • •

M arcel couldn't stand still. He was pacing around the studio, picking up anything that wasn't nailed down—vases, the cats (who hissed and bared their teeth), keyboards—and putting them down again just as rapidly. He took his jacket off and put it back on. He never stopped talking.

"Well, Shane, I mean, come *on*! It's all just a little bit *ridiculous*, don't you think? You would agree with that, wouldn't you? I mean, I mean, when were you going to let me know about this?"

Shane stood in the middle of the room, rigid as a pillar. His eyes followed Marcel's sporadic movements. "What are you talking about, Marcel? It's rent. It happens every month. That's how it works."

"But the pandemic! You gave those hooligans downstairs a break last month, and don't you try to deny it, either . . . How short are we, anyway?"

"You're two months behind, you know that. And I know you've been dodging my calls and not responding to my emails. You know I had to come down here."

Shane's lips were fixed in a stern grimace. Marcel snapped his fingers and turned with a start, lunging toward a large self-portrait hanging from rusted nails on the brick wall. The nails were loose in the crumbling holes, clinging to the brick by their last striations. The oil paint was so thick and layered that a few of the patches seemed to stand up off the canvas, as though Marcel's visage was pushing into the room itself.

"Here, take this. It's worth between fifteen and twenty thousand, probably more. Those are conservative numbers. I hate conservatives, by the way . . ." Marcel trailed off, his mouth still jumping up and down as he stared imploringly at Shane.

Shane was impassive, his arms crossed over his chest like stale baguettes. "I don't want your paintings, Marcel."

Marcel tossed up his hands and began his frantic pacing again. "Well, you're going to regret that, I'll tell you that right now."

"Sure I will." Shane rolled his eyes. "What's the plan here, Marcel?"

"Oh, come on, Shane! How long have I known you? We've been here since your father owned the building!"

Shane scoffed. He seemed to bristle at the mention of his father. Fish had backed so far into the corner that his back was scraping against the brick wall.

"Yeah, everyone loved my father, right? My father almost lost the building because he was so friendly. I'm trying to run a business here, Marcel!"

"Give me another month. You know it's been slow, Shane. It's that fucking Hudson Yards development bullshit. Just one more month, okay? They're taking down the scaffolding on our block. People are going to be walking around here again. It's one month. Three weeks. Come on, Shane. Be a friend."

Marcel had stepped closer to Shane as he spoke, wringing his hands—not out of some pantomimed homage to a cartoonish beggar but because he seemed not to know where else to channel his nervous energy. He only came up to Shane's shoulder, even when rising and falling on his restless toes.

"No can do, Marcel. I've got those eminent domain pricks breathing down my neck, too, you know? Every month that my books show a loss of a profit is a decimal place to the left for them when they make their buyout offer. I've got to show them they're robbing me of something profitable here. And if you can't help me do that, I can't help you. Simple as that. I'll have to find a temporary tenant to take over your lease. Maybe one of those bullshit pop-up stores or something, I don't know."

Marcel straightened to his full height and stepped back, again throwing his hands in the air. "You vindictive little shit! You're the one doing the robbing around here! Where do you get off?"

Shane shrugged. He still hadn't moved from his spot in the middle of the cramped studio. His voice never wavered. "Hey, it's business, Marcel. Nothing personal, like they say."

Marcel came to a halt at the window. He stared out at the sharp new buildings surging up into the sky, columns of black and blue glass. He shook his head, staring.

"Fine. Fish, call Maureen. Let's figure this out." Marcel didn't turn around when he spoke. His fists clenched and unclenched at his sides.

Fish nodded and gave Shane a final, almost apologetic, almost blameful glance before stepping back out onto the roof. Shane was still standing, arms crossed in the middle of the studio, and Marcel was still shaking his head at the window as the door closed behind Fish.

• • •

Maureen burst through the door and ripped a violet feather boa off her shoulders and hurled it onto the desk. "All right. Where is he?" she hissed.

Her eyes were wild, wet, and jumpy like simmering beans. Fish pointed up and her voluptuous hips cranked like turnstiles as she marched to the roof. Cheeks red and her expansive chest heaving by the time she made it up the stairs, she flung open the door to the studio and pointed an accusing finger in Marcel's face.

"What did you do, mister?" she asked.

Marcel waved her finger away and retreated to the window. Shane was still standing, resolute, in the middle of the floor. An amused grin spread across his face as he watched Maureen's stocky legs march toward Marcel and her chubby finger punch into his chest.

"Oh, don't be so dramatic," Marcel said, throwing a dismissive gesture in her direction with a flip of his hand.

"What did you do?" she asked again.

Dramatic was the right word, Fish thought, watching her twist her face with Pacino-esque charisma. She'd seen everything on Broadway, though her favorite, she'd told Fish several times, was *Wicked*. But watching her stomp around the studio with Marcel gesticulating and babbling, it was easy to imagine the two of them taking up a residency of their own on an off-off-Broadway stage. Maureen chased Marcel in distraught circles around Shane, who watched them from the middle of the room with a bemused smile.

"It's been slow, you know that, Maureen," Marcel whined. He picked at the paint that had dried into a putty on the fibers of the paintbrushes, refusing to meet her piercing eyes.

"I know it's been slow—I'm your *fucking accountant*! But when were you going to tell me you were late on rent, huh?"

Maureen was the only one Fish had ever seen talk down to Marcel. Even Stanley was generally pretty obsequious, at most throwing up his hands and walking away in a huff. Fish suspected that working one day a week at the gallery fulfilled some theatrical need of Maureen's, a little taste of the riotous New York arts scene that she couldn't get in the monochrome cubicle where she worked the remainder of the week. Even now, she was not angry—not really. The chaos, Marcel's clichéd artistic unaccountability, satisfied some image she'd hoped to cultivate or maintain; of herself, of artists, of New York.

"I thought *you* took care of that!" Marcel yelped.

"I would if you gave me access to that account, but of course you won't because you know I'd stop you from spending ten grand on car trash to build into some robot for your patio!" Her voice had built into a shout by the end of the sentence.

"Have you seen the sculpture? It's coming along really well. Fantastic, actually. That reminds me—I need to call my welder to help me finish a few things . . . Fish, will you call Iris?"

"Enough!" yelled Maureen, slamming her hand down on the desk. "Show me the account."

Marcel looked from Maureen to Fish to Shane. Marcel narrowed his eyes back at Maureen. "Fine."

Marcel walked over to the computer in the corner—an old Macintosh from the '90s blanketed in a layer of dust. He curtsied sarcastically to Maureen as he passed her, and she raised a hand playfully as though to hit him. It took a long time for the computer to start up, making a whirring noise from somewhere deep in its blockish machinery.

Chapter 9

F ish and Becca got into a fight last night. They didn't fight much anymore, having pruned their relationship down to convenient, passionate, history-laden hookups whenever they both happened to be in the same city. Their sexual encounters were not unlike the stretched and faded T-shirts that one refuses to surrender to the trash, even after so many years. It was simply too comfortable. But when they did fight, it could be volcanic. So much went unsaid throughout their intermittent phone calls and occasional texts that their fights were like zits that burst of their own accord, the pressure building so that the slightest poke could cause an eruption of blood and puss.

Their arguments always left Fish feeling physically exhausted. It had been his fault, initially, he knew. But that was the kind of realization that became visible only after too many hurtful things had been said. At some point, the fights always morphed. One specific thing would light the fuse before the tinderbox exploded, the fight becoming about everything, as though they'd been saving up grievances in an account of some kind and now they'd decided to spend everything.

They'd had plans to meet for dinner at an Indian restaurant in SoHo, a place they'd been eager to try after it had received glowing reviews in the *New Yorker*. Becca was home in New Jersey for the birth of a nephew and had extended her trip for a one-night visit to

New York before returning to Philly. Fish had planned to go to the restaurant right after work. But around five o'clock, Marcel started pouring drinks. He poured with a heavy hand—vodka over ice with a Coca-Cola floater.

"Two drinks, never more! That's how you stay on top of it," Marcel slurred, sloshing vodka onto the countertop as he poured a fourth cocktail and pushed it towards Fish.

"Yeah, two of these, sure . . ."

"Two drinks, never more!"

They clinked the cold glasses too hard, their depth perceptions corrupted. The gallery was empty. Stanley had gone down to the garage to look for Dusty, an alley cat he'd taken to leaving little dishes of food out for. He hated when Marcel drank. The setting sun washed the empty gallery in a cognac-tinted light.

Partiboy just wants to party, boy.

Fish was already late by the time he'd stumbled out of the gallery. He walked all the way up Thirty-Ninth Street with just one arm in his jacket. Still without a phone, he had no way of contacting Becca to tell her he'd be late. He supposed he should've called the restaurant from the gallery phone. The subway had been a further challenge, jostling him into other passengers as he tried in vain to maintain balance. It also didn't help that it was one of those old trains, the ones with rust-orange seats and no digital display detailing the time or the next stop, so he'd had to crane his neck at each station to see where the hell he was. When he'd finally made it to the restaurant, Becca was waiting outside with her arms crossed over her chest. She threw her hands in the air when she saw him jogging up to her, his windbreaker flailing behind him as he continued his feeble attempts to thread his arm through the still-unoccupied sleeve.

"Well?"

"Sorry, work went a little late. And no phone right now, you know? But sorry, Becca." Fish shrugged helplessly.

Becca just stared him in the face. She could always tell. "Nice," was all she said.

"Look . . . I'm sorry, Becca. I lost track of time, okay?"

Fish could see anger flickering through her eyes. Without a word, she turned and started walking away down the street. Fish followed after her.

"Becca, come on, let's eat. I'm sorry! Let's not make this a big thing."

She halted and Fish almost crashed into her. His legs were functioning at a momentary delay.

"It is a *big thing*, Fisher! I was waiting an hour! They kept asking me if I wanted to keep the reservation! It was *humiliating*."

She was on the verge of tears. Fish stepped closer and put his hand on her shoulder. Becca shrugged it away.

"I know, I'm sorry. It's just . . . Marcel was pouring drinks, and you know how he is, how hard it is to get out of there."

"No! I don't know *how he is*!" she snapped, taking a step backward. "I've never met him! All I know is that I never know when you'll get out, and you can't tell me when you'll be free because you threw your phone in a *fucking river*, and it's impossible to make plans because you're too spineless to tell Marcel that you have to leave!"

That was the moment where the fight turned. It was no longer about his being late to the restaurant. That was simply the nest from which the hornets were now pouring forth.

"Wow. So that's how you see me now? Really? That's nice, Becca, thanks."

She scoffed and stomped down the steps to the subway. After a beat, Fish followed her. They said nothing to each other the entire ride back to Spanish Harlem. Neither of them spoke until the door closed on Fish's room. Once inside, it was impossible to hide in the claustrophobic space, with nothing but a bed between them. They couldn't help but look at one another, pushed to confrontation by the close walls. Becca dropped her scarf onto the bed and looked directly into Fish's eyes. When she did, Fish felt compelled to speak.

"Look, I wish I had a regular schedule like you. But I don't. And right now, this is how I make money, Becca."

"So get a new job! You have a college degree! You have connections! Go get a normal fucking job where your boss isn't paying you to listen to his fucking stories."

"That's not fair. I like working there."

"Why? Because it lets you feel like you're doing the *New York thing*? Working in an office would be selling out, right? I know how much you love saying you work at a gallery, getting drunk on Thursday afternoons, wearing pants with paint on them like you're a part of the fucking *scene* or something."

Fish was glad Klein was staying at Carmen's apartment for the evening. He and Becca got louder and louder like two advancing canons. They paced in the tight space, hurling their anger at each other in handfuls across the mattress. Becca told him he needed a therapist, and Fish told her she was acting like her mother, both blows stinging all the more because they were a little bit true. Eventually, Fish ended up leaving. He didn't even grab his jacket, but he barely felt the cold as he stomped down First Avenue.

He walked and walked. All the way to Central Park. He smoked a cigarette and stared up at the starless sky. The tobacco unwound the tension gripping his shoulders and back. His arms hung limp at his sides. The cigarette burned out, half smoked.

His toes had grown numb by the time Fish returned to his apartment. Becca was curled in a ball on the bed. Fish could see dry rivulets staining the parts of her cheeks that peeked through her huddled arms. He sat next to her and laid a hand on her shoulder. Without turning her face, she clasped his hand in hers. Her palm blanketed his cold fingers. The radiator clacked violently from the corner.

"Truce?"

"Truce."

• • •

Stanley called them "inspiration walks," and sometimes they'd log several miles in a single morning. They'd start in the Flower District, where he'd have Fish pause to smell petals or haggle over a bundle of ferns he was considering for the gallery terrace. Then they'd move on to the Garment District, where he'd have Fish run his fingers over silk, wool, cotton, and gossamer, and tell him how different it all used to be, how the districts were more than just a few shops. Working their way south, Fish had to rush to keep pace with Stanley, weighed down by the various purchases heaped in his arms. They'd spend a long time in the Lighting District, fiddling with different neon bulbs and strobing technicolor lanterns, flicking switches and watching the light spring to life in tinted globes. Stanley knew all the shopkeepers, everywhere they went, by name. He'd been patronizing their stores since he was a student at FIT. Fish often wondered if these stores, which were always shabbily maintained and ubiquitously understaffed, were kept alive solely by eccentric little men like Stanley, and how many of them could there be, even in New York? In the Rubber District, everything smelled like a tire burned out on the asphalt, and Stanley would stretch and pluck at the varied materials with his restless, inquisitive fingers.

By the time they worked their way down to SoHo, Fish's feet ached. But they couldn't stop. There was too much to smell, taste, touch, see, and hear. They paused along the sidewalk and bent their noses to the potted plants that shops had arranged near doors that had been tentatively cracked to let in the not-too-chilly breeze. It was a cool gray day, but Fish was sweating. They appraised window displays and discussed their merits and flaws in great depth, and Fish warmed each time Stanley would nod approvingly at his observations. Today they allowed themselves to be floored by an arrangement of blue papers folded into origami birds and strung across the window of a stationery store on Houston Street. A single branch bearing bright yellow blossoms rested on the floor of the display. It was subtle, suggestive, and elegant. Stanley marveled at it for a long moment.

"It's a dying art, window displays," he said softly, almost to himself. That was what he'd studied at FIT, when he'd first moved to New York after an art teacher had encouraged him to leave the upstate backwater where he'd been raised.

An Amazon delivery truck idled in front of an apartment building a block away as they crossed the street to check out an art installation housed in a brutalist cement hallway wedged between a garage and a French café. Green lights hung from rectangular bars that dangled from the ceiling and a haunting music of chimes and gongs thrummed from unseen speakers. A woman in a chair near the door handed Stanley a long feather and placed an arrowhead in Fish's palm. She had electric blue hair that bordered her pallid face in fluffy bursts like cotton candy. An oblong gold ring dangled from her septum and gauges stretched her earlobes. Her skin was the shade of mushroom stems. She told them the installation was meant to be a commentary on the exploitation of Native Americans. They handed back the feather and the arrowhead on their way out.

"I didn't get that *at all*, did you?" Stanley asked in a stage whisper on their way out the door.

"Way over my head," Fish said, relieved that he wouldn't have to concoct some deduction about the eerie, half-baked installation.

Stanley bought Fish a slice of pizza and one for a shoeless woman resting against a dumpster with her legs splayed out in front of her like a broken puppet. They'd been walking all morning, and Fish's feet were tired and his arms were beginning to tremble under the burden of ferns, bamboo, a few feet of gingham, and two hot pink floor lights. After lunch, Stanley hailed a cab. When they hit traffic on the West Side Highway, Stanley got impatient. He handed the cab driver a twenty and said he'd walk to his Forty-Ninth Street apartment from there.

"See you tomorrow, Fish," he said, winking and shutting the door. Fish watched him bob through the honking cars until he disappeared into the crowd streaming in both directions on Forty-Third Street.

After Stanley left, the cab driver made small talk, nudging the cab a few inches forward each time the traffic lurched into motion. He told Fish how the traffic kept getting worse, and how he lived in New Jersey because he couldn't afford to live in New York anymore. He said he liked driving a cab, though, meeting new people, being his own boss. He let Fish off at the gallery and Fish carried the haul upstairs. Tomorrow, Stanley would decide where everything should be placed, if he showed up. Stanley didn't particularly like working. He'd once told Fish that the first few years of his twenties had been spent moving from one sugar daddy to the next, accepting their hospitality at fancy townhouses in Amsterdam or Paris in exchange for the kind of companionship that Stanley didn't need to detail for Fish.

Marcel was painting upstairs, and Bennett was still missing. Fish poured himself a coffee and collapsed onto a retro yellow couch facing the window. Rocky arched his spine against Fish's leg. He dangled a finger to stroke along the cat's back, following the natural contours of his fur. Rocky froze, watching the pigeons flutter on the windowsill just beyond the glass with rapt attention. Fish stared, too, looking past them to the cacophonous traffic on the street below, the chaos that had enveloped him just moments ago.

Chapter 10

Fish was drunk at his desk again. The air outside was crisp, but the room felt stiflingly hot. The temperamental radiator seemed to have only two settings: off and tropical. Half the bottle of Fernet was gone. The blank page mocked him, reclining backward with its hips thrust forward in a cocksure stance as it lilted in the typewriter's scroll. Partiboy had encouraged him to eat a few blocks of the mushroom chocolates he'd stashed in the freezer because *Partiboy just wants to party, boy.*

But I'm not partying, dick, Fish replied. *I'm not partying anymore. I'm the introspective sort now. The kind of guy that lurks at the edges of the party drinking it all in, offering a few witty quips here and there. Not the douchebag who's first in line to keg stand. Not anymore.*

He'd expected to use the shroom chocolates—purchased from a smoke shop near Times Square that he'd taken to frequenting after work—for a concert or another night out in the East Village or something. For something outside his apartment, at least. But here he was, buzzed out of his mind in his bedroom, trying to harness the effects of the booze and the drugs into an art of some kind. He burped, tasting a bit of both, and started stabbing at the keys.

When exactly does one get to call themselves a writer? Or a playwright? After they've been published? After they've staged a shitty one-act in some Brooklyn basement? Or does it only count once it's their actual living? Like, they pay their rent out of the advances they reap from unpublished and unstaged stuff that they've got plans to finish. I'm not there yet, lord knows that much. I think I've been trying to do it backwards, a little bit. Like, reverse engineering the tortured artist. Getting wasted every night, experimenting with drugs. The whole Bright Lights, Big City *thing. Fuck, the whole Shakespeare thing, why not? Apparently they found pipes in his alleged backyard with traces of coca leaf in them. Who knows if that's true, but that dude was cruising on something. That's for goddamn sure.*

Last weekend, Carmen had organized a picnic in Central Park on an unseasonably warm November afternoon. It was framed as a casual hey-wouldn't-this-be-fun kind of get-together, but Fish suspected it was more of an official introduction, an inauguration of Klein as her new boyfriend. Like when Steve Jobs would don his trademark black turtleneck and reveal the latest iPhone generation.

At the picnic, she had referred to Fish as a playwright when introducing him to her friends. It had made him feel awkward. Like a loser, even. He had nothing to back up the claim, and they'd all— all of those guys in their Patagonia fleeces and those girls in their striped rompers—looked at him after she'd said that, waiting for him to take ownership of *Hamilton* or offer his take on *Waiting for Godot* or something. At least, that's how it had felt to Fish. He'd ended up saying, "Yeah, well, trying, at least . . ."

And they'd all nodded their heads with sincere interest and sympathetic smiles. In New York, Fish was finding, to know a failed playwright carried almost as much cachet at a cocktail party as knowing a successful, famous playwright.

Fuck it. Let's write a play, Partiboy. Brace yourselves, motherfuckers:

Postlapsaria, Connecticut

Act I, Scene 1

Dark stage. Suddenly, a floodlight on ADAM, suspended from wires. He floats awkwardly across the stage toward a refrigerator, inspecting his limbs as he goes. He is clothed in a retro outfit befitting the mid-century American businessman. He clutches the fridge door, and it opens, surprising him with its artificial light. He recoils. Gathering his courage, he returns to the fridge, slowly opening the door. Inside is a single, mouthwateringly perfect slice of apple pie. A sticky note clings to the plate on which the pie slice rests. It reads 'DO NOT EAT'. Adam reads the words aloud to himself.

ADAM
(Reading aloud)
Do not eat...

Fish collapsed back against the chair, dropping his hands into his lap.

Like, shit, is that anything? Feels meaningful, kinda. Oldest story in the world, right? Ah, fuck it. I'll work on it tomorrow. Or, wait, tomorrow's Friday, so I'll probably be going out . . . Maybe Saturday I'll have some time? If I'm not too hungover . . . Fuck it. I'm too drunk tonight, that's for sure.

•••

Fish loved living on First Avenue. It felt right for him to be able to look out his window onto the chronologically first major thoroughfare of the borough. Sometimes a herd of dirt bikers and ATV riders blasting music and gunning their engines would swarm the Shell station across the street, popping wheelies and hollering while people on the sidewalks stopped to watch. The route of the New York marathon went right past his apartment, too, miles of runners loping along First Avenue right there beneath his window.

...

In the summer, it was usually too hot to spend much time in the unventilated painting studio on top of the gallery. But by late autumn, once the sun's strength had eased to a pleasant dry warmth that seeped through the windows, Marcel would routinely recruit Fish (and Bennett, if he was around) up to the studio under the guise of appraising one of his new paintings, only to open a bottle of cheap vodka as soon as the iron door swung shut. Fish was sure Stanley knew what was going on, but Stanley preferred to argue with Marcel when they were back at their apartment on Forty-Ninth Street, where they'd lived for almost three decades. According to Marcel's hyperbolized tales of the first few years they'd lived there, the neighborhood had been rife with addicts, wild dogs, and lurid graffiti. One drug dealer had even, apparently, set up shop in an abandoned pharmacy, a flickering neon sign with the words *Drug Store* attracting clients like moths to a bulb. These days most of the neighborhood was populated by aging gay artists like themselves and, increasingly, yuppie thirty-somethings working remote jobs.

The late-afternoon sun beat through the old glass windows and filled the room with a stale warmth. Fish crouched on a barstool, moving only to bring the drink to his lips. Marcel didn't seem to notice the stuffiness of the enclosed space, pacing and raving as he did in every temperature. Beads of condensation streamed down their glasses and made honeycombs of wet rings on the paint-spattered picnic table. Fish got up to grab another Coke out of the mini fridge—Marcel had made the drinks far too strong, as usual, dumping vodka into the glasses as though he were filling a canteen with water ahead of a strenuous trek through the outback. Fish's joints felt loose as rubber in the throes of the late-afternoon buzz. He hadn't felt so drunk when he was planted on the stool. But now that he was standing, it felt as though the blood was whooshing from his head to his feet and back again, as if in an overturned hourglass. Turning, Fish stared out at the sherbet-colored sky glancing off the glass skyscrapers and gilding Weehawken's skyline in a honeyed tint. He felt mellow, content. As though he were exactly where he ought to be at this moment.

Fish began to sway his way back over to his stool at the picnic table when he noticed a small box sitting on a shelf above Marcel's desk. There was nothing particularly remarkable about the box, perhaps besides how perfectly square it was—the size and shape of a Rubik's Cube. It was a cardboard box, tightly sealed with some kind of industrial glue along all the edges. And when Fish picked it up, it felt much heavier than he'd anticipated. His hand, after a cumbersome delay in which Fish's muddled brain encouraged his fingers to wrap around the cube, held it up to eye level.

"What's this?"

It took a long time for Marcel to look up. He'd been doodling on the picnic table with a piece of charcoal and muttering quietly to himself about kicking Jeff Koons out of the building. When he finally looked up, he let out a high-pitched shout and leaped up from the picnic bench. The charcoal fell to the ground and burst into a puff of gray dust on the cement floor.

"Put that down! Don't touch that!"

He snatched the box out of Fish's palm and gingerly, with both hands, placed it back on the shelf over his desk. He furrowed his eyebrows at Fish. "Don't touch that," he said again.

Fish made a mental note to ask Bennett about it, whenever he resurfaced. He'd been absent again today, not that anybody but Fish noticed anymore.

"Sorry," Fish said. The word fell out of his mouth like a surrendered piece of chewing gum. For a moment they just stood there, staring at the box.

Marcel took a long slug from his glass. The ice rushed up to the rim and sent rivulets down his chin. He wiped them away with the sleeve of his eternally paint-stained T-shirt.

"What is it?" Fish asked again, unable to help himself.

Another long swig, more rivulets down his chin. It wasn't like Marcel to recuse himself from a pregnant pause. "Ashes," he said, after a while. "But we'll need another drink if I'm going to tell *this* story."

Partiboy just wants to party, boy.

Marcel sloppily dumped a handful of ice into Fish's glass and sloshed in enough vodka to make a Russian blush. Fish poured the rest of his Coke into the glass. It floated on top of the vodka like algae on a pond. The setting sun looked like the divot where a peach pit had recently laid its wrinkled head, all jagged edges of scarlet and tangerine. They sat back down at the picnic bench.

"Those are Hugh's ashes," Marcel began, dramatically pausing for a long sip.

Fish could sense that he was being cued to ask who Hugh was, so he played along. "Who's Hugh?"

Again, Fish had the sudden sensation that he was precisely where he belonged, precisely where he, the playwright, the beautiful fuckup, ought to find himself on a given Tuesday afternoon. He almost laughed when he thought of the stuffy, hushed library where he'd spent most of his time back at Yale, with all those jawlines and gunners, those haircuts, those douchebags, those suits. *Those poor fucks are probably there right now.* Fish smiled at the thought, and he pitied them in a sanctimonious kind of way.

Partiboy just wants to party, boy.

"Hugh," Marcel said, "was my ex. Before I met Stanley."

The air felt so uniquely still and silent in the room that Fish thought he could hear the bricks settling back on their haunches to listen to Marcel. Laconic dust particles floated in the sunlight streaming through the window.

"He was murdered." Big swig.

"Really?"

"Well, indirectly, I suppose." Marcel was droll, was Brando.

They both took long sips after that. Marcel was gearing up. Fish resisted the urge to check the time.

"We met in Los Angeles. Hollywood, actually. You didn't know I was in Hollywood, did you? You thought I was as much a part of this city as those gargoyles on the Chrysler Building, didn't you? I wanted to be an actor, you see. Oh, I was young! But I could never bring myself to speak someone else's words. You understand that, don't you?"

"Sure."

Marcel barely registered Fish's response before continuing. It was no longer a conversation. It was a soliloquy now. Marcel was listening to his own story too.

"Hugh, though . . ." he said. "Hugh was a brilliant composer. And handsome. I'm sure I have a picture . . . anyway, just picture a handsome guy; tan, dark hair, cheekbones, you get it. He composed symphonies. That's how we ended up in New York, actually. He'd received a commission from the philharmonic."

He stared out the window but held his glass in Fish's direction, hanging on to the rim with the tips of two fingers. Right on cue, Fish poured in another dash of vodka, and Marcel continued.

"We were walking up Sixth Avenue toward Broadway, going to see a play a friend of his was in. This was in 1973. Anyway, to make a long story short, this gang of assholes saw us holding hands and beat the hell out of us with golf clubs. Gentlemen, weren't they? It could have been baseball bats, I suppose. It was right there on Sixth Avenue, between Thirty-Eighth and Thirty-Ninth. Right up the street from here."

Marcel gestured over his shoulder with his glass, sending a small splash of vodka onto the floor. Fish couldn't think of anything to say to that so he just stared at Marcel, who continued staring out the window. Fish was conscious of his mouth hanging open just a little and quickly clamped it shut. "Jesus, Marcel . . ."

"I ended up okay. But Hugh . . . Hugh was never the same, Fish. That's what you have to realize. Never the same."

"What happened?"

"They got to his head. With the golf clubs. He never recovered. Not fully, anyway. He was a brilliant composer. His ear was his career! And they took that from him, Fish. They took his ear. He couldn't compose. Couldn't hear the notes quite right. You wouldn't know it from talking to him, necessarily. But he started drinking like you wouldn't believe. And the drugs . . . It's the only way he could stop whatever was hurting him inside. Can you see that? I tried to get him to stop—we all did. But he started dodging me, not coming home, going missing for days. Kidney failure. That's what got him in the end. In some squatter apartment down in SoHo. And not the SoHo you're picturing. It was basically a slum back then."

"So . . . those are his . . ."

Marcel drained his glass but kept it perched on his lip. He stared so intently into the cup that it looked as though he was using it as some kind of telescope, looking through the bottom of the glass to the street below. "Ashes," Marcel said finally.

The word floated up to the ceiling, evaporating into the dust particles.

"Damn, Marcel. That's heavy," Fish slurred.

Marcel nodded sagely. "That's when I started painting, too. I went back to the spot where it happened—the golf clubs and everything—and painted these colorful outlines of two bodies. Our two bodies. Right there on the street, like those body outlines you see on cop shows. Then I'd do it somewhere else a gay bashing had happened. I'd go to the spot and paint these beautiful, vibrant, technicolor outlines of the bodies. Fish, are you picturing it? I wish it was still there so I could show you . . ."

Marcel's voice trailed off and he stared at the ground. It looked as though he was going to drop the glass, balancing it by the rim on two fingers like that. Fish wanted to stand up to save it but he couldn't; his legs were glued to the stool. Stanley was on the patio below them, moving in abrupt bursts from one flowerpot to the next, pruning here, watering there. The sky settled into a faint ochre and a stripe of purple seeped across the horizon. The glass fell from Marcel's grasp and shattered upon the floor.

Second Trimester

Chapter 11

Purplish blisters capped the knuckles of Fish's smaller toes. He wore size twelve shoes when really he should've been wearing thirteens. But size thirteen shoes, to Fish's mind, were athlete's feet, and that was a plumage he'd molted. The Fish who'd worn size thirteen sneakers had clomped from classrooms where he sat with his knees splayed under his desk, forcing the rigid school chairs into a recline, and then toe-dragged the loose-laced shoes to the lunch room, where he'd eaten and eaten until a stack of plates the height of a toaster oven had gathered in front of him, a monument to his metabolism, and then on to the locker room, where the size thirteen feet had buttressed a mouth that hollered jokes at the pimpled heads pinned atop nascently muscular torsos and protein powder–fueled limbs atop other size thirteen feet. Jokes Fish cringed at now, thinking of them. And then the size thirteen feet bounded on muscled legs to practice and bent and exploded and pivoted. To live in New York was to walk, and walk, and walk, and his new feet, his new self, size twelve, wore blisters.

●●●

Fish was so tired that his flimsy yellow subway card felt heavy in his hand as he thrust it back down into the front pocket of his backpack. A friend of Klein's had offered him cocaine last night, and he'd accepted. He was not in the habit of turning down free drugs these days. And, of course, *Partiboy just wants to party, boy.* As it turned out, Partiboy loved cocaine. He'd ended up staying out with the finance bros all night, going from one bar to the next, snorting anthills of powder off the tip of his gallery key (it felt artsy and appropriate) in one bathroom stall after another, jumping each time an unseen hand pried at the bathroom doorknob.

Brushing the taste of tequila off his tongue this morning, he'd discovered a coiled tissue protruding from his left nostril. It was stained a rusty brown. He had no memory of implanting it the night before, and when he'd removed it, a fresh geyser of blood had burst down over his lips. The dollar coffee he was chugging out of the iconic amphora-inscribed blue paper cup paled in comparison to the horse-kick jolt of a cocaine stripe neatly snorted through a crisp bill rolled tightly into a rigid tube. With each turn or bob of his head as he ascended the steps to the gallery, Fish felt that his brain was lagging just a pace behind, clunking against his skull.

Even from downstairs, Fish could hear the metal saw screaming through car doors and engine chunks. He trudged doggedly upstairs, following the noise. The gallery was warm from the welded metal, and Fish took care to stay out of range of the sparks and cooling masses hunkering on the floor around the tall, thickly built man standing in the center of the room. He didn't notice Fish's presence until he lifted the heavy rectangular welding mask off his face to wipe the sweat streaming into his eyes.

"Iris, what's up, man?" Fish said.

"Hey kid," he said, winking at Fish from above the dark mutton chops affixed to his cheeks. His face was red, and sweat stained his white T-shirt.

"How's it coming?" Fish asked.

"Oh, you know Marcel. He'll have me back here in a month to give it wings or something," Iris said, chuckling.

"Don't suggest it—he'll have you do it."

"Oh, I know," Iris replied. "Another week and this will officially have been the longest business relationship I've ever retained. Four years. Can you believe that?"

"You've been working on that robot sculpture for four years?" Fish asked. "Damn, I had no idea."

"Marcel doesn't like to end things. Nothing final, you know? You'll figure that out. If you stick around."

"I'm starting to see that," Fish replied, thinking of the decades-old paintings that Marcel sometimes ripped from the walls and painted over with broad, uncompromising strokes. "I'm not planning on going anywhere. Unless they knock down the building, I guess."

"Heard about that. Huge bummer. By the way, there's a warehouse party tonight. Out in Ridgewood. A friend of mine is doing an art installation for it. I'll text you the address."

But it's a goddamn Monday! Fish thought. Then, naturally, Partiboy chimed in with his usual quip.

Iris was always inviting Fish to interesting, if self-consciously Brooklyn-y, events. And Fish always went—to the silent discos, the roller-skating happy hours, the boozy ghost tours, the microdosing bird-watching parties in Prospect Park, the pot-clouded vinyl-listening parties in East Williamsburg.

"Could you email it? I lost my phone."

Iris shrugged and nodded with another quick wink before disappearing behind the welder's mask again.

The truth was that Fish was enthralled by Iris, a man who had cobbled together a livelihood out of these fabrication and welding gigs, building a creative career through word of mouth and the quality of his work, plugged into New York's underground arts scene and respected by those that knew his work. To Fish, the graying mutton chops, the chain belt, the ripped dark wash jeans, the duct tape wallet, the flip phone, the Doc Martens boots, the whiskey-distiller-slash-tattoo-artist friends and the septum piercing that adorned Iris' persona were earned, justified. He was a hipster, to be sure, but with chasms of depth beneath the cliché surface. He was no phony.

Fire burst from the end of the welding torch as Iris set about fusing a fender to a clutch, forming what looked like a Frankensteinian arm. Fish watched him work until the fumes and heat started to make him feel lightheaded.

The gallery was as empty as ever. Fish poked through the cabinets until he came up with a few stale cookies, but he couldn't manage more than one bite before a mezcal-flavored burp threatened to evolve into a puke. *Well, that's no good.* He'd eaten nothing but a bodega chopped cheese sandwich in the past twenty-four hours. He tossed coins for Rocky to chase until he got bored and shuffled up the staircase, slowly, to the roof.

"Come look at this," Marcel said as Fish stepped into the studio.

Disco music blared from the staticky speakers. Marcel was sitting at the picnic bench and staring at a photograph, his eyes glazed. It looked like he'd been crying. The room smelled of wine corks and pot.

Taking a seat next to him, Fish saw that Marcel was holding a faded, sepia-toned photograph of horses and carriages and men in three-piece suits and bowler hats and women in petticoats walking on a dirt road lined with a few clapboard buildings.

"I always look at this photo," Marcel said. His voice was distant.

"Who are they?"

"That's the thing!" His voice took on an urgent tone. "It doesn't matter. They're all dead."

A moment passed in silence as they stared at the photo. It looked to be from the 1920s or '30s.

"I take comfort in it, don't you?" Marcel said after a while.

"Not really," said Fish. "You do?"

"I certainly do. Because, Fish, everyone in this photo is dead, right?"

"Right."

"Well, don't you find that comforting? There's probably, what, thirty people in this photo, no? Presumably, they all had problems, stress, and worries, and everything felt so crucial to them all the time. Undoubtedly, right? And now they're all dead, and everything moves on, and it's our turn to be all preoccupied with our lives. But the thing is, we'll die too, won't we?"

Fish nodded and held the picture, looking at the blurry, sallow faces strutting across the rectangular image.

"Do you know where that is? Can you tell?"

Fish shook his head and shrugged.

"Thirty-Ninth between Ten and Eleven! Can you believe that? It was *right here!*"

Together, they stared at the photograph some more. Fish handed it back to him. The sweat from his fingers was beginning to smudge the image's gloss.

Chapter 12

It turned out to be surprisingly easy to sneak into the New York Athletic Club. All Fish had to do was approach the glass door at the same instant as one of the members was exiting. The members were obvious to the acquainted eye. They were blazer-wearing men with Nike athletic bags draped over their purebred shoulders and shower-wet gray hair combed neatly across their presidential skulls. But the maneuver had to be performed casually, Fish knew, as though he'd just happened to walk up to the entrance at that moment.

Fish squared his jaw and nodded politely with a sort of half smile, and a man whose chin was enveloped in a cashmere scarf returned the nod and half smile and held the door open. This wordless exchange was the subtle, Scroll and Key–type of insider gesture in which the men (and Fish, at one time) trafficked. It was a privilege they'd worn in their skin since long before their Ivy League dormitories or summers on Martha's Vineyard. Generally speaking, that skin was white, their hair a sort of sandy brown, and their teeth blockish as gravestones. Their overtrust of the world was cohabitant with privilege, learned from a lifetime absent of threat and swaddled in leisure—which was why a young man of a certain look and a certain expression, toting a squash racket like a skeleton key, could march casually through the gates they so ardently kept.

The irony was that Fish had been going to such places his whole life, first tagging along with his dad and his brother to beat around a squash ball for an hour or two and then, when he was older, joining his friends at their country clubs for golf outings, lifting weights at their private gym facilities, or hitting on blond girls—they were always blond—at their private pools.

But today, Fish headed straight for the sauna that he knew would be nestled in a corner of the men's locker room. After a few more smiling nods and a confident, straight-shouldered gait he was there—and *it* was there, right where he'd expected it.

Fish found it funny. He'd been playing this darkly clad, skinny, cigarette-smoking character for so long now—half a year—that it felt strange to reinhabit the clothes, the stride, and the half grin of his former self. It puzzled him a little that he could slip so easily back into that mask—or was he removing a mask, he wondered? Fish didn't bother pondering the dichotomy. He hadn't once left the city since he'd fled New Haven, and he felt the need to take a little vacation from himself.

He snatched an ivory-colored towel off a tray in the hallway. It was warm from the laundry and smelled sweetly of lavender. A sign next to the sauna stated, in neatly stenciled letters, "NO PHONES BEYOND THIS POINT." *No problem there*, thought Fish. He turned the sauna temperature up as high as it would go, opened the door, and stepped into a wall of thick, oppressive heat. It stung the insides of his nostrils as he labored to inhale. His new cocaine habit was accompanied by a permanently congested nose, rubber cement boogers clinging like barnacles to the caverns of his nasal cavities. Steam poured off the coals in the steel box by the door like the smoke that billowed out of those first trains that had probably paved the way for some NYAC member's great-great-grandfather's inaugural membership to this heralded club and its wood-paneled lockers.

In one corner of the sauna, two older men with knobby knees and sunken, pale chests chatted about the Yankees. Fish took a seat in the corner farthest from their drooping, unabashedly uncovered ball sacks. He closed his eyes. Within minutes, beads of sweat were bursting from every inch of his flesh like cicadas hatching and emerging from the earth after a twenty-year hiatus. Fish relished each droplet that left his body, purging him of the coffee he drank too many cups of, the alcohol he'd been trying unsuccessfully to stop drinking on weeknights, the sugar and salt and calories he'd crammed down his throat more out of boredom than hunger, the drugs he loved to do only as long as they were being done, the effects never carrying on the appeal of the event, or even the appeal of the *notion* of the doing of drugs. More sweat, more sins draining through his skin. The cigarettes he couldn't quit and to which he had become addicted—a preposterous notion, now that he thought about it, that *he*, a former varsity athlete, had become addicted to cigarettes. He tried to revel in the inexplicability of it, the Nietzsche of it, the YOLO of it. But it didn't work this time. He just wanted to be the healthy, running, jumping springbok he used to be. At least for a weekend.

He stayed in the sauna far too long. His sodden limbs melted into the smoke-scented wood and his thoughts went blurry in the dim lighting. Only when he felt that he might begin to evaporate into the steam did he wobble out of the sauna. The two men continued chatting amiably. Fish took a cold shower. The chilled water seemed to remove layers off his body and after drying, he felt light as air, molted, newborn. Partiboy was silent, gone. Perhaps he was taking a vacation from himself for the weekend, too, Fish thought.

Fish was in the habit of scheduling doctor appointments every few months, even if he had no symptoms requiring the educated eye of an MD to diagnose. He'd always liked going to the doctor, even as a little kid. Getting measured and being told how tall he was, how healthy and strong. He liked to schedule them all on the same day—doctor, dentist, dermatologist, chiropractor. There was a feeling of productivity, even—or, perhaps, especially if—they told him he was just fine. He found something therapeutic in a person wearing a white coat and turquoise scrubs and holding a clipboard telling him that he was all right.

But today Fish's purpose was distinct: to avoid going bald. It was one of his greatest fears. And Marcel had made him irreparably conscious of it when he'd bemoaned his own loss of hair yesterday morning.

"Don't get old, Fish," he'd said. "Old just means getting fat, ugly, and bald. I hate the baldness. I can stand the ugliness—that's natural. And the fatness, well, you can do *some*thing about that, I suppose—I mean *I* don't, but *one* could. But I can't stand the baldness. The irreversibility of it. Can you see it? My hair was dark and thick like yours. But you don't believe me . . . I must have a picture—I modeled, you know . . ."

Fish would like to be the kind of man who bore it gracefully, shaving his scalp when the time came, succumbing with stoicism to inevitability, and presenting the revealed cap of his skull for public appraisal without inhibition or shame. And while he hadn't yet noticed any evidence of balding (he watched for any signs of his hairline's retreat by using a small mole on his forehead as a marker), he already felt as though he was not up to the challenge of baldness. Perhaps when he was a pentagenarian he would be able to bear it, but anything less and he feared that he would be counted among the men he saw who made him shudder: dense drapes of baleen curtaining their ears but with sparse desert grass quivering atop their domes, a thin, wispy presence that looked as though it might blow away at the slightest exhalation. Or worse, the men who turned to toupees, indoor hats, or plugs of lesser quality than Hollywood could provide.

Fish touched his finger gingerly to the top of his skull and slithered it through his hair—still damp from his shower at the club—as he entered the shop front on West Forty-Eighth Street, passing through a musty toy shop on his way upstairs to his first appointment. He'd managed to find a few doctors who accepted Obamacare, in which he'd enrolled in the fall—a fact which would have scandalized his parents, had they known.

"What you are doing here again?" Dr. Gregor Kurtsman held his hands out to his sides in surprise when he entered the examination room.

Fish smiled and shrugged back at him, the movement of his shoulders rustling the thin paper tunic the nurse had given him to wear.

"I see you, what, two month ago, no? I tell you then like I tell you now: you are okay. Young! Healthy! Strong man! I tell you this, no?"

To Fish's ears, Dr. Kurtsman's thick Ukrainian accent seemed to enhance the dissatisfaction in his words.

"I don't want to go bald," Fish said, pointing to his scalp as though to clarify.

Dr. Kurtsman rolled his eyes and set his clipboard down next to the sink. He squirted an antiseptic-smelling white foam into his hands, which were the color and size of two pork cutlets, and slapped them together with a forceful clap that snapped Fish to attention.

"Bald, eh? I just tell someone they have shingles, you know this? A very bad diagnosis for a person of advanced age."

"Oh, wow," Fish replied. "Were they bald?"

Again Dr. Kurtsman rolled his eyes. He took a step forward and bowed his large, round head towards Fish, regarding him over his wire-rimmed glasses with a reproachful look.

"You see this?" the doctor asked, pointing to the smooth, ba-gel-sized patch of skin crowning his skull. "I am bald. You see this?"

"I do, yes," Fish said. "I'd like for that not to happen to me, please."

"Is life! It happens to all men. It will happen to you, one day, too. And it is okay!" Dr. Kurtsman was nearly shouting. But this, Fish had learned, was just how he talked.

"No! Dr. Kurtsman, please!"

Fish found that his hands had come up near his face in protest, and Dr. Kurtsman quickly swatted them back down into Fish's lap with surprising force. The doctor removed his glasses, which had been forced to stretch to the limits of their cheap resistance in order to span his face, and rubbed the bridge of his nose.

"Look. Okay. Your father, he is bald?"

"No, not bald. Balding, I guess . . . But this isn't about him—"

Dr. Kurtsman held up a pork hand to stop the words flowing from Fish's lips. "How about mother's father? You grandpa, he is bald?"

Fish had to think about this for a moment, and he did so seri-ously, feeling it to be an important question.

"He died young . . . But he was balding, from what I can remem-ber of the pictures . . ."

"Okay, so maybe you go bald. It's okay. Is natural." Dr. Kurts-man shrugged and stretched the glasses back over his eyes.

"But I don't—" Fish began.

But Dr. Kurtsman picked up his clipboard and was halfway out the door before Fish could finish his sentence. "Listen, very busy. You healthy, okay? Bald is okay. Wear hat. See you next time."

Dr. Kurtsman gave Fish a brief, almost warm nod and exited the examination room.

The next two appointments were no more comforting than the first. His second was with a dermatologist in Chinatown. On the ground floor of the address he'd found on the internet, vendors selling dragon fruits, lychee, durian, and mangoes spilled out the door onto Canal Street. Each floor he ascended to get to the dermatology office made it seem less likely that the business would exist where the address claimed. The second floor appeared to be some kind of foreign bank, though Fish couldn't tell for certain, seeing only Chinese characters and glass windows through which notes and money were being passed, accompanied by respectful bows. On the third floor, small women with permed hairdos stood silently behind foldout tables, smiling and nodding to Fish as he passed, gesturing to the incense, sculptures of dragons and buddhas, wood carvings, colorful prints, and outdated electronics assembled in front of them. Fish double-checked the address and kept going upward. It was moments like this that he missed his iPhone. Turning a corner, however, he found himself transported into the sleek, clinical white aesthetic of the dermatology office. It could have been a doctor's office anywhere had it not been for the man hawking knock-off basketball sneakers just beyond the threshold, visible through the spotless glass door.

The dermatologist, a tall, elegant Taiwanese woman with perfect hair, teeth, and, naturally, skin, told him that balding was as natural as spring rain, but that he'd have some options—some very expensive options—to remedy his balding once it started. Fish's heart plummeted. Like Dr. Kurtsman, she spoke of balding as an eventuality rather than a possibility. Onto the next appointment.

The dentist told him he couldn't get a cleaning twice in a three-month period, so he kicked Fish out. And, when Fish asked, desperate from the failure of the first two appointments, and beginning to feel the effects of the mushroom chocolate he'd munched after his appointment in Chinatown (Partiboy had made a reappearance, unchanged—clearly *he* hadn't been to a sauna this morning), the dentist told Fish he couldn't help him with the balding. He laughed when he said it, running a hand through the coarse curled locks spilling off his head in all directions like a nurtured greenhouse vine.

•••

F ish was seated at the gallery desk, anxiously refreshing an inbox that never changed. He had hardly slept the night before. For some reason, his muse, who wasn't Partiboy but shared quite a few of Partiboy's proclivities, liked to strike at eleven at night, not dispensing with him until right around three in the morning. It was invigorating when it happened, filtering warmly through his veins like spiced cider on a chilly autumn day. But for all the frantic typing, his muse had only permitted him one stellar scene of ripe, resonant, unique, original, truly-Fishian back-and-forth dialogue between his principal characters before petering out into a drunken urge to reach an end point that would justify his slumping triumphantly into bed. Writing was a lousy existence, Fish was finding, like having homework all the time without any satisfying end in sight. For when it was finished—staged, lauded, beckoned onto off-Broadway and then to Broadway itself, he'd have to write something else, wouldn't he?

Fish heard Marcel's slipper-covered feet shuffling against the floor, disrupting the late-afternoon silence of the gallery. He collapsed into the chair next to Fish, spilling wine down the front of his shirt.

"Shit! Oh well," he said, flicking his hand as though to wave the matter away. The dark stain joined the constellation of paint splatters traversing his sleeves and chest. A blob of dry yellow paint had solidified at the roots of the forelock he was always pushing out of his face when he painted. "How'd we do today, Fish? Did we make some money? No, right? That's the story of today, isn't it?"

He slurped at his wineglass and licked his thumb where the wine had spilled onto his hand.

"Not bad," Fish said.

He debated whether to tell Marcel that only one individual had paid for entrance to the gallery today—a Dutch tourist who'd been looking for the Whitney and who had the manners to live with her mistake and stroll the gallery as though it had been her destination all along. One guest was more than they'd had in weeks—foot traffic had become abysmal once the temperature dipped below freezing. But Marcel was unpredictable when he was drunk, and Fish didn't have the energy for one of his tirades, so he said nothing.

"We're in the hole tens of thousands of dollars, according to Maureen, that witch. Oh, I'm terrible. I shouldn't say that. She's only doing her job . . . At least that ogre Shane didn't stop by. Isn't he awful?" Marcel asked.

"How long did he give us?" Fish ventured.

"Another six months. But I'm choosing to consider that a soft deadline," Marcel replied, shrugging. "Of course, he is threatening to sell the building to the city sooner rather than later. Can't blame him, I suppose. A payout for a teardown building is worth more than a drunk tenant that can't afford rent . . . At least we get to be the drunk tenants . . ."

"You seem pretty nonchalant about it," Fish said.

Marcel shrugged again and took another slurp of wine. "What can you do? Money talks. That's life, Fish. Consider it my final lesson for you." He winked and drained the glass.

"You built this place from nothing," Fish said. "It was an abandoned taxi garage when you started it. Doesn't that make you upset?"

Fish struggled to keep the indignance out of his voice, to sound like he was just a colleague making conversation.

"Oh, don't make me cry, Fish. I'm probably better off. Maybe Stanley and I will finally move down to South Beach like we always talk about."

Fish scoffed before he could suppress the noise from bursting out of his throat. It was true that Marcel often scrolled through Zillow listings, the palm trees and art deco patio furniture reflecting in his eyeglasses. But Fish had always thought this to be more of a wistful pastime than an actual endgame.

"Something to say, Fish? *Fisher*, that is?" Marcel cocked an eyebrow at him. His eyes swam in the tired depressions of his face.

"It's just," Fish began, but paused as soon as he started. He had to be tactful about what he said next. He chose his words like a mountain climber selecting their foothold.

"You're always saying how you have everything you want here. That you'd dreamed of this place since you were a kid. A place where every day was different and you could make the space entirely your own, where your imagination could run wild. You've got all that now! How could some retirement in *Florida* beat what you have *right now*?"

Marcel stared at Fish for a long moment and then nodded his head slowly. "So, you think I'm quitting, is that it? That if I go down and sell paintings on the boardwalk, it's what, some kind of defeat? I'm a loser now, is that it?"

"No! That's not what I'm saying," Fish interjected quickly. "Not at all, Marcel."

Marcel slumped in his chair, his chin resting against his chest. He stared at Fish from underneath his furrowed brow, his eyes narrow and his jaw working slowly in a lateral motion. "Well, tell me what to do then, Fish! You got thirty K lying around somewhere? And how about next month? That's the thing about months, Fish, they keep coming. I can hardly afford to pay you and Bennett as it is

. . . I suppose it's a good thing Bennett misses work so much, otherwise . . . Well, if you can't picture me anywhere else, *Fisher*, I've got news for you: neither can I! I mean, my god, my feet in flip-flops? That'd look like a . . . like a typewriter wearing thong underwear!"

Fish warmed at the passion he'd managed to coax out of his boss. Marcel sat up in his chair. Color returned to his eyes and his cheeks flushed. Strangely, Marcel's outburst relaxed Fish.

"I don't know what to do, Fish," Marcel said, when Fish failed to respond to the vivid image his boss had painted of his feet in rubber sandals.

Marcel stood and shuffled off to the kitchen, returning to the desk with the half-drunk bottle of wine and a second glass. Fish refreshed his inbox again. A new message appeared, and Fish's breath caught in his throat as he clicked it.

Chapter 13

The wet, slushy snow made Madame Meticulous's hair curl in bunches like grape clusters around her face. She had just returned from an exhibition in Toronto. A sleek rolling suitcase trailed behind her as she walked down Thirty-Ninth Street. Her gait was different. Not because of the ankle boot she'd been wearing last time he'd seen her, but because of the gentle swell of her belly, which she accommodated with one hand and slow, slightly splayed steps.

They exchanged a brief hug upon her arrival, and Fish felt the protrusion of her stomach pressing against him. She shook slushy droplets off her ankle-length parka as Fish piloted the elevator up to the gallery.

They did not speak of her pregnancy. On that matter, her email had been clear:

> so nice to hear from you Fish! as it happens, i'll be returning to the city this evening. i'd love to catch up! if it's ok, tho, i'd actually prefer that we don't talk about you-know-what? i'm still sorting the whole thing out in my head (and obvi with my therapist, haha) and i don't think i have the bandwidth for input just yet. If that sounds ok with u, an evening at the gallery sounds lovely! how about i pick up some dinner on the way? do you like thai? xx

Though Fish was still unsure why he'd yielded to a spontaneous urge to respond to her email that afternoon, he was aware of being thrilled to see her. He weighed the possibility that it might have had less to do with seeing Madame than the gallery itself. He wanted to share it with someone, especially as it felt the gallery was slipping away from him in slow motion. And he was lonely. Klein spent all his time with Carmen. Becca was knee-deep in textbooks in Philadelphia, cramming for another board exam. Bennett was gone. Fish had run out of cocaine earlier in the day, and the mellow depression that followed the empty baggie had made him miserable for companionship. And so he had responded to Madame's email.

Fish had worried that Marcel wouldn't leave in time for Madame's arrival. But the finishing of the wine bottle had signaled his departure—Fish having refreshed his own glass several times more than he would've liked in order to hasten Marcel's exit.

They sat at the island in the kitchen to eat the take-out Thai food Madame had picked up on her way from the train station. Fish had previously scattered cat treats across the room to keep Rocky and Monty from sticking their curious snouts into the steaming containers of pad thai. The chili oil coating the noodles made their lips buzz pleasantly as they listened to the wet globs of snow smacking against the gallery windows. They chatted amiably, laughing politely—and sometimes genuinely—here and there. She'd been busy with work stuff; he'd been preoccupied with the fate of the gallery. He asked about her new bas-reliefs; she asked about his play. After a while, it was as though the elephant in the room had ambled off into the darkened streets of Hell's Kitchen, disappearing into the winter storm. As he deposited the take-out containers into the recycling bin, Fish wondered if this was how it all could have been.

When the thunder started, they curled up on a couch and listened to the noise, bracing with each boom that hummed in their chests. They counted off the seconds between each blue match strike of lightning that pierced the sky, illuminating for an instant the black skyline facing down the storm.

They pushed back all the furniture and rode Razor scooters in circles around the expansive space, sipping drinks—a lemonade mocktail for Madame, a vodka tonic for Fish—and playing old Sinatra hits over the loudspeakers. Marcel and Stanley often rode the scooters to work in the summer, though they gathered dust under the gallery desk for the majority of the year. It struck Fish that this was the most fun he'd had in quite some time. Fish watched as Madame turned a wide circle, disappearing into a silhouette as she cruised past the gallery windows. Breathless, they met in the middle of the floor, nearly ramming into each other on the scooters. Fish caught Madame in his arms.

He tucked his hands up under the curtain of hair, her curls laying heavy on her narrow back. Her skin was sticky from the snow and her lips tasted of chili oil, pleasantly tempered by the iced lemonade that dangled from her hand.

Third Trimester

Chapter 14

Fish and Becca hadn't spoken in months, which was unusual for them. Even when they were at their most separated, they'd still send each other the occasional meme or a screenshot of something ridiculous—usually amusing texts from their respective parents—knowing that the other would appreciate it like nobody else could. But that last fight had been different. It had felt, to Fish, like the end of something.

But then, on a Friday night in April, a light spring rain peppering Fish's bedroom window, she'd called. Technically, she'd Zoom-called him. He still hadn't replaced the phone he'd jettisoned off the bridge. His Gmail tab registered a new message in the inbox. It was an invitation to join a Zoom call, its template and language familiar to anyone who had operated a computer throughout the COVID-19 pandemic.

Fish hesitated before clicking the link. A half-empty bottle of pinot noir sat next to the computer. He'd made more progress on the bottle than he had on his play that night, and the wine buzz had put him in a sleepy, self-pitying mood. He'd declined Klein's invitation to go out with the finance bros, citing the rain and the depressive aftereffects of the cocaine he'd vacuumed into his nose the night before.

It had been weeks since he'd touched his fingers to his laptop's keyboard. The typewriter had jammed one day, and Fish had neither the money nor the interest to get it fixed. Instead, it had been an excuse to shelf *Postlapsaria, Connecticut* for a while. Partiboy had taken the reins. Every shot, every cocktail, every puff off a joint, every casual romantic encounter, every snort off a key was chalked up to experience, leading to the kinds of nights that might eventually fuel a masterpiece. But after a hangover that seemed to last months, the pressure to renew his literary efforts returned. He'd begun to feel guilty about leading the life of a reprobate New York playwright without anything to show for it, though he knew he was the only one holding himself to account.

It was all he could do to even make it into work on time. Not that Marcel or Stanley noticed. The gallery hadn't had a visitor in weeks, and the building's destruction was beginning to feel imminent. Stanley's father had died after a long, demented struggle, and he'd gone upstate to be with his family and sort out the estate. Marcel was drinking and smoking away the days, moved to paint only rarely, on which occasions he would drag a massive canvas out onto the roof, strip naked and strike against the blank white expanse violently, slashing bright colors in a fury that left him coated in multicolored streaks from head to toe. He'd been complaining about a kidney stone for months, putting off the hospital visit in hopes that he might eventually pass it. Still no word from Bennett.

So, when Becca's Zoom invitation beckoned, Fish answered, happy for an excuse to cease his literary efforts for the night.

"Hey," she said. "Got a minute?"

She was sitting on her couch, which Fish had helped her lift and maneuver up the steep staircase to her third-floor apartment in Fishtown (the effort of which had occasioned another fight). Her lips were tinted scarlet, and she held a glass of red wine. Her hair was wet, as though she'd just taken a shower, and she wore an old T-shirt bearing the name of a soccer team she'd once played for.

"Sure," Fish said.

He held up his own glass and they gave each other a virtual cheers. Noticing the gaunt shadows painted into the crevices of his face, Fish adjusted the angle of his screen and fiddled with the lamp on his desk, which had little effect. He wasn't sure if it was Partiboy or himself occupying the right-hand side of the screen. He toggled the view so that Becca's face filled his screen, reducing his own visage to a small square the size of a butter pat in the top-right corner.

Becca wanted help editing a personal statement for her residency application. This made sense to Fish. She had recruited his English major background for such tasks in the past, though it had been a while. She was a strong, clear writer, but she did nothing halfway and was far too type-A to submit any assignment without first getting the input of someone she trusted.

"I could use a little help with my own writing, at the moment," Fish replied, glancing at the mediocre lines he'd been typing. He'd managed to unjam the keys but, wary of another jam, he'd been typing at a sloth's pace.

"I'm sure it's not that bad," said Becca. "Where's Klein?"

"Out. I didn't feel like it tonight. Can't really afford to keep up with those guys, anyway."

"You look tired," she said.

"Gee, thanks."

Becca laughed and he chuckled.

"Not how I meant it. I just mean . . . It's good to take a night off sometimes, right?"

"Sure, if getting drunk in my bedroom counts as a night off," he replied.

They didn't end up revising Becca's personal statement. Instead, they talked about their parents, their mutual friends, and laughed— belly laughed—at inside jokes and retellings of particularly funny scenes from *Nathan for You*, which they'd both recently binge-watched. They poured themselves another glass of their respective red wines, and then another. They reminisced about how they used to bring a camping tent to house parties in the summer, creating a shelter in backyards rather than gambling on finding a bed or a couch on which to pass out at the end of the night.

It felt familiar and pleasant, laughing together. Even the silent moments were comfortable. Fish had a sudden urge to leave New York, to take the next train to Philadelphia without packing a damn thing. He pictured himself knocking on Becca's door and burying his face in her neck, pulling her into his chest and collapsing onto the couch together, settling against each other's familiar bones and feeling each other's laughter through their chests as they watched *The Office* or *30 Rock* or some other show they'd seen a dozen times before. If Fish thought about it a little harder, he felt he could've cried.

• • •

Though he couldn't pinpoint exactly when it had happened, Fish was aware that he'd become addicted to cocaine. He was more surprised than ashamed by the realization. Cocaine addiction had always seemed, to Fish, like the kind of thing that happened to other people—B-list Hollywood actors, overworked restaurant managers who'd been in the game too long, rave chicks who'd gone to one Bonnaroo too many, white kids from the suburbs who'd lost their way. He supposed, regretfully, that he fell into the latter category.

One of Klein's finance bros had introduced him to a dealer with some "premium shit." Fish had never met the dealer, who went by Uncle Nemo and communicated only by telegram. Fish hadn't been aware that people still used telegrams, but there was a website where they could still be sent—simply plug in the message and the address of the recipient, pay the small fee, and a courier would deliver the message the same day. Without a phone, this mode of communication suited Fish. And he did enjoy the whimsy of communicating by so antiquated a method as telegram when such things as Zoom and FaceTime had evolved communication beyond even the imagination of *The Jetsons* cartoons he'd watched as a kid.

As with his alcohol consumption, what had begun as a weekend extravagance had become a weekday habit. *Partiboy just wants to party, boy.* The groove at the tip of his gallery key was clogged with densely packed white powder. He loved the way cocaine made him feel—alert, loquacious, confident, impenetrable. On cocaine, he was Batman. Bruce Wayne. The Dark Knight. The Christian Bale version, obviously. The hangovers were brutal, though. But luckily, the cause was the same as the cure. So, he'd fire off a telegram to Uncle Nemo and within a few hours, a black sedan with flashing hazards would appear in front of his apartment building or the gallery or whatever bar he happened to be at. He would casually seat himself in the passenger seat and a Middle Eastern guy about his age—never the same Middle Eastern guy but always a Middle Eastern guy—would hand him a small vial with a red cap, and he'd hand over a neatly folded wad of twenties before offering the guy a knucklebump and exiting the car as casually as he'd entered it.

Fish had almost quit a few months ago. He'd been at Mad Tropical, a Caribbean-themed rum bar and dance hall in Bushwick where he'd met up with Bennett and a few of his improv buddies (this was before Bennett had disappeared). Fish had stolen away into the establishment's grungy bathroom, its mirrors foggy and cracked, the walls plastered in colorful, peeling stickers advertising edgy social media accounts, online weed delivery services, hipster coffee shops and the like. Rummaging through his backpack, Fish discovered that his vial was missing from its usual place in the front pocket. He dumped his wallet and keys, various coins, a small notebook that he never used but carried around anyway, and a few pens into the sink. When at last his backpack was empty, the vial was nowhere to be found.

The several mojitos he'd imbibed made it difficult to retrace his steps. Bass lines throbbed through the walls of the bathroom and a drunken hand fumbled at the doorknob. Forcing himself to focus, he stared at himself in the cracked reflection of the mirror, as though willing the reflection to offer some clue, some hint as to where he'd left the precious goods. It was then that he noticed the brown rind crusting the underside of Partiboy's nostrils. It was hard to determine which nosebleed had been the cause of this stain. He rinsed his face off, blew his nose, and took a few wet gulps of water from the faucet.

It was at the gallery. Fish knew it, and it made his heart plummet into his stomach. If Marcel or Stanley found it . . . He hated to think about that. Would they think it was Bennett's, he wondered? Would they fire him? Amid these concerns was another one, a concern of almost equal weight: the night was young, and he had no cocaine. He left the bar without saying goodbye, taking the long subway ride back to Harlem and fretting over his own stupidity. His gums itched expectantly, and he ground his teeth for the relief that he had misplaced.

The next morning, he rose early after a fitful night of sleep. He went to the gallery an hour before his shift was slated to begin. It had been months since he'd shown up before noon. His heart beating, he unlocked the door and, relieved to find that Marcel and Stanley had not yet arrived, Fish made straight for the bathroom where he recalled doing his last bump. But the vial wasn't there. A fresh surge of worry twisted in his stomach. He debated leaving, going back home and avoiding the discomfort of a face-to-face interaction with Marcel or Stanley should they have discovered that he'd been consuming drugs—*hard* drugs—in their gallery.

He collapsed into the rolling chair at the reception desk. But when he settled his head in his hands, a small flash of red caught his eye. It was the vial! It perched neatly on top of the computer monitor. His instant relief turned to anguish again when he noticed the sticky note pinned under the vial. It bore Stanley's neat block lettering:

FISH—PLEASE BE CAREFUL. AND MORE DISCREET. WE DO NOT NEED TO DISCUSS FURTHER. –STANLEY

Fish read the terse message several times before crumpling it and tossing it into the wastebasket beneath the desk. He wanted to be relieved, but he felt only shame. He half wished that Stanley had yelled at him or something. The understanding, the concern, made him feel strangely uneasy about himself. He decided that cocaine might not be his drug. He'd leave it for a while—maybe forever.

He glanced at the clock. Marcel and Stanley wouldn't be in for another hour or so. Rocky and Monty curled around his shins, mewing to be fed. Wanting to feel useful, Fish emptied a can of unctuous brown chunks into the cats' bowls, and their mouths made small carnal noises as they chewed. Fish went to the bathroom and did a quick bump, and then another, telling himself he'd quit for good once he finished this batch.

• • •

Fish was biking through Domino Park in Williamsburg. He was playing hooky from work, which, with both Bennett and Stanley absent, was easier to do than ever. He felt a little bad about abandoning Marcel, but the tirades about the city knocking down the building and the vivid descriptions of the medical procedure to remove kidney stones had been wearing on Fish.

He'd had plans to meet up with a girl he'd met at a bar in the East Village last night. He'd been alone, doing his best to fill out a *New Yorker* crossword puzzle, the pages slightly damp from the gin and tonic he'd spilled on the table. She'd walked right up—a striking, narrow girl with long pink braids, a dimpled moon face, and coffee-colored eyes—and asked for his number. After recovering from his long explanation about how he didn't have a phone, she'd given him an address and he'd scribbled it down above the crossword puzzle. They'd ended up talking for a while at the bar. She worked in the digital content department for the *Wall Street Journal*, producing TikTok videos about personal finance tips. She claimed to be a descendant of a Ghanaian princess of some kind on her mother's side. But Fish had either misprinted the address or been stood up, because when he arrived at the bar in Williamsburg, the girl was nowhere to be found. He'd waited about an hour, drinking old-fashioneds until his fingers clumsily penned a tip he could hardly afford. After a final glance around the bar, he left.

It wasn't quite dark yet, and the late-April sun cast Brooklyn in a weak yellow light. He didn't want to go home just yet. Klein would be there with Carmen, cooking some elaborate dinner as he liked to do on Sundays, and if he walked in, they would feel compelled to invite him to join. Fish didn't feel like spoiling their evening. So, he hopped on a Citi Bike that someone had parked incorrectly in its dock—usually one needed an iPhone and an app to unlock the bike from its port—and began cruising slowly towards the East River, without any particular destination in mind. The wind was cool but pleasant, billowing his T-shirt. His drunken limbs pedaled laconically, feeling more fluid than they must have looked.

He was coasting along the boardwalk, using one hand to shield his eyes from the light glinting off the water and marveling at the

Williamsburg Bridge's grandiosity, the Manhattan skyline's expansiveness, when he saw something that made him falter, almost crash. It was Madame Meticulous, wasn't it? No, that couldn't be her, he thought. But then he recalled that she lived out here in Williamsburg, her resplendent bachelorette pad just a few blocks from the boardwalk. He hadn't seen her since their impromptu date at the gallery, back in the winter. She'd taken off for another exhibition in London shortly thereafter and had said she'd let him know when she was back in New York.

Fish slowed to a stop, watching. It was her. Definitely. He'd recognize that big bush of curly auburn hair anywhere, sprouting riotously from her petite frame like an overgrown dandelion ravaged by the wind. One of her small hands perched delicately atop the swell of her stomach. It was a much larger swell than the last time Fish had seen her.

Her other hand, the one that was not resting protectively, proudly atop her protruding belly, was intertwined with the hand of someone else—a man. He was tall—nearly as tall as Fish, if not taller—and handsome, in a hipster kind of way. He wore blocky glasses with clear frames and his strong jawline was peppered with stubble. His sandy blond hair was pulled back into a neat bun. With his non-hand-holding-hand he held a leash, at the end of which was a panting French bulldog the color and texture of suede. He and Madame Meticulous were laughing about something.

Fish watched them, frozen in place, as they strolled into the small dog park at the end of the pier. The little dog was released into the tumult of Labradors and Australian shepherds and Shiba Inus (it seemed that Williamsburg's dog owners shopped for purebreds only), and Madame Meticulous and Mystery Dude settled onto a bench. Mystery Dude draped his arm around Madame's shoulders, and she leaned her head into the crook of his neck.

The thought crossed Fish's mind that this might be the other man in question, the other possible impregnator. He was certainly acting as though he'd impregnated Madame Meticulous. But then, if that was how a potential impregnator acted, shouldn't he, Fish, be acting the same, he wondered? And did this mean that he was off the hook? *No, that sounds wrong*, he thought. But it was how he felt, just then. Though this was not the only feeling coursing through his veins. Jealousy was there, too. Part of him wished that he could be the one with his arm draped around Madame Meticulous, laughing with her about something, and watching a little dog with quietly proud eyes that might one day look upon a child with a similar, deeper feeling of connection.

Fish snuck a quick bump of cocaine off his gallery keys, hiding the act with his hands and a cocktail napkin. He then quickly pedaled in the opposite direction. He didn't stop until he was back in Harlem.

Chapter 15

After Bennett had been missing for over two months, Fish decided he'd go check Bennett's apartment again. He took the L train out to Bushwick. He'd been to Bennett's apartment a handful of times, usually for pregames before heading out to the funky bars and nightclubs in the neighborhood. This was the first time he'd been there during the daylight hours, and it felt odd, in a way. Like being drunk during the day, which Fish was.

He pressed the buzzer for Bennett's apartment but, like last time, there was no response. An image of Bennett passed out on the couch, a small orange bottle of pills clutched in his fingers, crossed his mind. Fish forced the image away. Just before he'd gone missing, Bennett had taken to snorting OxyContins and Percocets—his roommate had a prescription for chronic back pain and he shared the pills liberally. Whenever Bennett had offered Fish one of the small pills, he had declined. That was before he'd surrendered himself to cocaine, and snorting things had still scared him a little. Back then, he'd seen pills as something too intense, too out of character.

That felt like ages ago now. Time moved differently in New York, Fish was finding. The days were so jam-packed with anecdotes that while each day felt like a lifetime, the months slipped by in a blur. One did not run errands in New York, but, rather, completed little missions. On any given day, Fish might bear witness to the kinds of stories a small-towner would dine out on for weeks.

Fish supposed that was why so many writers and artists had passed through New York—for the daily inspiration that one hardly had to break a sweat to find.

When Bennett's buzzer failed, Fish punched at the other buttons until, finally, the door was unlocked by some unknown resident who was either too annoyed to allow the incessant buzzing to continue or who happened to be waiting on Chinese takeout or an Amazon package. Fish hurtled up the stairs to the fifth floor, out of breath by the time he reached Bennett's door. He rapped his knuckles against the door. No answer. Fish stood there awhile, knocking, pressing the doorbell. He pressed his ear to the door, but the apartment was silent on the other side. He didn't leave until a young Hispanic man pushing a stroller holding a small baby with pierced ears rounded the corner of the hallway. Fish helped the guy, who looked even younger than himself, to carry the stroller down the stairs.

• • •

F ish was writing more than ever. Not all of it was good—in fact, most of it was unreadable. But, he felt, in the chaotic discharges that poured out of his fingers—fueled by booze, nicotine, and, more often than not, cocaine—there were certain glimmers of latent talent, nuggets of quotable worth. Something about the depraved evenings (and sometimes afternoons and even mornings now) spent hunched over his typewriter, a bottle of half-drunk Fernet perched on the desk beside him, a cigarette dangling from his lower lip, and zebra stripes of cocaine arranged in neat rows on the cover of his passport, a scrolled twenty-dollar bill nestled under the shaggy locks cascading over his ears, felt wildly appropriate to Fish. This was *it*. Writing. Ingesting the intoxicants and unzipping his chest and simply allowing the words to pour forth. His play was almost complete.

He'd drafted and revised, drafted and revised, done the hard work. He saw himself, with some awareness of the stupidity of it, as the connective link between Samuel Beckett and Judd Apatow. Some Ginsberg references for the snoots, some dick jokes for the bros. Not overmuch of either component, though, Fish felt. More like a symbiotic blend of the high and the low. And whatever, anyway. Having been raised by snoots, Fish knew they would laugh at the dick jokes, too. Just like the bros. Because what were the snoots if not bros all grown up? And what were the snoots if not the class of Americans who'd had the luxury of a bro-y youth (SAT tutoring, lacrosse, opinion having, etc.) and who, because they had the pedigree and the wealth and the vacation time and the babysitters and the social media savvy to *be* appreciators of the arts, functioned as the de facto tastemakers of the mainstream? So Fish had tried to pander to them. A little here for the boomers, a little there for the millennials. Nothing for the zoomers (that is, Gen Z; Fish honestly had no clue what to make of them. They baffled him. Their freedom. Their radical self-acceptance.).

All he was missing was a final act. And the absence of it was giving him trouble, but he wasn't overly concerned about it. He could hardly believe he'd written (almost) a full play. He was becoming excited. He envisioned his words blurting from the mouths of struggling unpaid actors, noble and sincere in their innocence. He didn't remonstrate himself for dreaming this far ahead anymore. It was beginning to feel that possible, even though he'd shown the draft to nobody.

• • •

About two weeks after he'd seen her at Domino Park, Fish found an excuse to email Madame Meticulous. It had come in the form of a *New Yorker* article. He'd been a subscriber since last June, when he'd officially begun to consider himself a New York literary type, and, as such, the kind of guy who would read the *New Yorker* as he rode the subway. While flipping through the most current issue—he only ever read the fiction, the "Shouts and Murmurs," the restaurant review, and the cartoons—he'd seen a name he recognized. It was a review of Madame Meticulous's latest exhibition, housed at some small gallery in Chelsea. He pored over the review. It was a glowing account of a young female sculptor with promise, a young woman with the compunction and the cojones of her white male forebears. Fish followed the link to the online version of the article and then copy and pasted it into the body of an email response to Madame Meticulous, continuing the chain she'd begun when she'd invited him to the rooftop party in Bushwick.

Beneath the link to the article, he wrote: *Hey, Saw this review in this week's* New Yorker*—congrats!*

He signed his name and reread the message twice before hitting send. It was brief and friendly, carrying no odor of an attempt to reconnect—which was his intention, though of course he did want to reconnect with her. Ever since seeing her with Mystery Dude, he'd been thinking of little else other than what it might mean vis-à-vis his paternity situation. And what it might mean for *his* relationship with Madame Meticulous. Because he had a growing sense—a feeling that struck occasionally when he was sober and frequently when he was trashed or high—that he and Madame might have some kind of future together. The tortured playwright and the ascendant sculptor, New York's underground art scene's It Couple. They'd had fun together, had gotten along well, besides that one time . . . And, despite rarely being alone—always out at bars with friends and friends of friends or home with Klein and Carmen—Fish was lonely. Which, he supposed, was as it should be. Writing was solitary work.

Madame Meticulous's reply came almost instantly. Clearly, she had none of the qualms about appearing overeager that plagued Fish, which he took to be a good sign before resigning himself to the fact that maybe it was a bad sign, that she was so well-adjusted to her new Mystery Dude that a paltry congratulatory email from a not-so-recent former flame didn't warrant the delay of a carefully meditated response. It was a gracious reply, thanking him and inviting him to the exhibition's opening next weekend. Fish waited until the next morning to confirm that he would be there.

• • •

F ish picked at a ridge of crusted blue paint on the picnic table. He was drunk, which was often when such minute tasks seemed to deserve the full attention of his floating consciousness. Marcel was complaining about the procedure he'd be undergoing for his kidney stones the next week, describing the operation in graphic detail.

"You know what they do, don't you? They stick a slender instrument up into your urethra—that's your penis, Fish, your *penis*!—and snatch out the stone in this little net thing. Then they put in these stents. I'll be peeing blood—*blood*, Fish!—for a week. Until they remove the stents. Oh, it's too terrible. Someone is supposed to pick me up from the hospital. They don't let you leave alone, what with the anesthesia and such. I suppose that will have to be you . . ."

Marcel phrased this last bit as a statement, but he arched a somewhat embarrassed eyebrow at Fish as though it had been a question. Fish had hardly been paying attention, busily scraping at the crusted paint with his fingernail. The words hit him only a few moments after they'd been spoken, and it took him an extra second to register their import.

"Me?" he croaked. Conversations with Marcel rarely required much input from him, and when at last he spoke, his voice came out hoarse. Fish tried to temper the bafflement in his articulation with a quick cough.

"Well, yes," said Marcel. He was looking at Fish sadly. The silence grew pitiful, both men realizing at the same time that with Stanley gone upstate, Marcel had nobody else to meet him at the hospital other than the young man who'd been hired off Craigslist less than a year ago.

All too late, Fish tried to cover the embarrassment they both felt. "Of course, Marcel. I'll meet you there. No problem."

• • •

When Fish got home that day, there was a letter in his mailbox. There were rarely letters in his mailbox, save for the cards that his mom sent on every Catholic holiday. For a split second he thought it might be from Madame Meticulous, and his heart raced as he tore open the envelope. But it wasn't from Madame Meticulous. It was from Bennett, postmarked from Tucson, Arizona. Fish read it as he walked up the stairs to his apartment.

Yo Fish!

You sure are hard to get in touch with, you know that? I mean, throwing your phone off the Brooklyn Bridge?? Fucking ridiculous, dude. Seriously. But who am I to talk, right? They don't let us have phones in here. Hence the letter. I'm in this rehab place. Back home in Arizona. Guess you could've seen that one coming. Isabel said something to my parents, and they got worried, yada yada yada.

I guess I should be grateful to have someone so concerned about me they'd sell me out to my parents, right? We're still together, but she's not too happy with me, bro. I heard you gave her a call— thanks for that, man, truly. Anyway, I figured I'd reach out, just so you know I'm not dead. Maybe you were worried. And sorry for stranding you with Marcel and Stanley. Have they knocked down the building yet? Those guys have enough on their plate— they don't need me anymore, anyway. Not like I was doing much while I was there, huh? Probably for the best. Take care of yourself, homie. Maybe I'll make my way back to New York someday. I definitely can't stay in Tucson, that's for damn sure. Boring as fuck. Until next time, dude.

—Bennett

Fish stood at the top of the stairs and read the letter a few times through. He pictured Bennett in some shapeless hospital gown, surrounded by pale kids with raccoon eyes, their hands twitching. Bennett would be miserable in a place like that. At least they hadn't crushed his sense of humor—not yet, anyway. The letter hit Fish in a part of his chest that he hadn't felt before. He didn't drink that night. Didn't smoke, didn't trip, didn't snort. He typed out a few painful lines of dialogue (discovering that it was so much harder to release the lines when he was sober—like goose feathers slowly abandoning a pillow) and went to bed.

• • •

The exhibition was taking place in a broad, street-level venue in Chelsea with high ceilings, white walls, and large picture windows that stared out onto West Twenty-Third Street. Fish decided to walk there, the clipping from the *New Yorker* that bore the address folded neatly into his pocket.

He was cat-sitting for a Paramount executive—a former boss of Carmen's—and staying in the young exec's sixteenth-floor Chelsea apartment in Kheel Tower, across the street from the Museum at FIT. The chance to stay in the swanky studio apartment for a week, in addition to the five hundred dollars offered by the exec, had done little to entice Carmen—she had a handsome salary and a fancy apartment of her own. But when she'd offered it to Fish, he'd jumped at the opportunity. Not only would it mean he could walk to work for a week, but he needed the money. His cocaine habit had wreaked havoc on his checking account. And when he was coked up out at the bars, he was the first to brandish his credit card, buying rounds for everyone in earshot, thinking always that he'd deal with it later. But ditching his phone had meant ditching his Venmo account, so it was rare that he was adequately remunerated for his benevolence, and thus his savings account had shrunk to the kinds of numbers he'd been unhappy with even as a child when he'd first opened the account, depositing half of his weekly allowance into checking, the other half into savings. Even calling it a savings account seemed ironic to Fish at this point. As soon as he deposited some hopeful three-figure amount of his paycheck into the account, a seed that would one day bloom into financial stability, it seemed he was just as quickly transferring it back to his checking account and withdrawing it from the ATM at the laundromat near his apartment.

It was so quiet up there on the sixteenth floor. Absent the cat toys and the latent smell of kitty litter that permeated the apartment, it was as though the exec had hired a designer to craft the consummate yuppie bachelor pad. Guitars were pinned neatly to the walls. Books on personal finance, self-help, and novels—classics and lauded newcomers—spilled off the shelves of his bookcases and accumulated in hefty piles on the floor and along the windowsill, held in place by chunky glass business trophies. Framed portraits of world maps, artsy New York bar maps (color coded by dive bar, cocktail bar, etc.), framed *New Yorker* cartoons, a muted abstract oil painting, and candid photos from weddings and galas and international trips to Bangkok and Paris were hung neatly along the walls or pinned to the refrigerator with artsy little magnets. Below the wall-mounted TV was a VR headset, and the fridge was packed with Whole Foods–brand plant-based proteins. A set of expensive golf clubs rested in one corner and a well-stocked bar cart occupied another. The windows overlooked Hudson Yards' skyline, though from a different angle than that of the gallery.

And Partiboy loved it. Nearly every night of his stay, Fish had hosted a party at the apartment, basking in his friends' oohs and ahs as they exited the elevator that opened directly into the apartment and touring them around the space as though it were his own. Sometimes he would even wear one of the exec's shirts, which, despite looking rather plain to the eye, felt luxurious against his skin. After making a mental note of exactly where to replace the shirt once he'd laundered it, he would admire himself in the reflection of the windows at night before his guests arrived, imagining that the apartment, the shirts, the golf clubs, might have been his lot had he stuck with law school. Some nights, he and his friends—friends of Klein's or friends he'd met out at the bars, friends of friends, people he'd met at the gallery—never even left for the bars, simply drinking, snorting, and smoking in the apartment, the cat cowering under the king-sized bed, until the pale apricot light of sunrise began to seep across the skyline. *Partiboy just wants to party, boy.*

Fish had become effectively nocturnal. But he'd also, at moments, cut exactly the figure he'd imagined he'd become when he'd moved to New York. A little buzzed, a little stoned, right in that sweet spot before it all became a blabbering mess, when a fuzzy Talking Heads vinyl album was playing on a new record player that looked intentionally retro and he was leaning against the exec's bookshelf taking turns pointing at titles with some banking guy and they were just riffing—a little arrogantly—about what they'd gleaned about the author's purpose here or this or that character's arc, fibbing their way comfortably through the titles they were less familiar with, their confidence buoyed by the fact that they would never be called out by the other in so intimate a circumstance, looking forward to the next cigarette and pleasantly surprised at how long it had been since the last one, playing with the swollen leaves of the exec's succulent plant, at ease in the swanky apartment precisely because it was not his own, because he was far too real, too dark, too intellectual, too earring-having-without-making-a-big-deal-about-it-ing, too committed to his art to place value in such material things, but enough of all of those things to luck into a cat-sitting gig like this one. *Isn't that guy, that New York guy, exactly it?* he reflected. But that's all it was: a figure. If he'd watched himself doing all that, saying those things, on television, it would've felt more believable. As it was, he felt he was playing the role. Overthinking it, maybe, but performing it ably.

Madame's exhibition was sparsely attended by thin people in dark clothing, who rubbed their chins thoughtfully or strode with their hands clasped behind their backs as they moved from one piece to the next. Madame Meticulous was wearing these chunky leather boots that added nearly six inches to her height and a flowy canvas tunic of some kind that billowed out around her stomach, which was by now the size and shape of a volleyball. Fish noted with relief that Mystery Dude was nowhere to be seen.

Fish waited for Madame to finish chatting with two gallery attendees before making himself known. When she saw him, she smiled and embraced him in a gentle hug. Despite the height she gained from her outrageous footwear, her protruding stomach pressed up against Fish's hips.

"You came!" she said. She sounded genuinely delighted, which relieved Fish. He'd been debating with himself about whether or not her invitation had been sincere.

"This is incredible—honestly, it's beautiful work," Fish said. "You deserve that review."

And he meant it. He took a moment to drink in the large brutal shapes carved out of granite and illuminated dramatically by the overhead lights. He thought back to the first time they'd met.

"Thanks, Fish. I appreciate you coming down here to support. I've actually . . ." She trailed off and looked away before summoning her attention back to Fish. "I've actually been hoping for a chance to talk to you. I should've brought it up last time. At the gallery."

Fish felt an anxious, excited nerve twitch in his stomach.

"I've been wanting to apologize. About how our . . . *thing*, whatever you want to call it . . . about how we ended. I think I was reacting from a place of emotion more than reason. I could have been much clearer about my expectations from the beginning."

Fish recalled the lambasting he'd endured during that meeting with Madame, after their now infamous tumble down the stairs, where she'd torn him apart for his lack of caution, his fuckboy-ness. He was stunned by the apology. Particularly because he didn't feel she had all that much to apologize for. It took him a moment to respond.

"Oh . . . Well, thanks. Thank you. For saying that," he mumbled. "And I'm really sorry too. For, you know, my part in all that."

She waved his apology away with a flick of her small hand. "Water under the bridge. Honestly, pregnancy has put a lot of things into perspective for me. Grudges aren't worth holding onto. They don't serve anyone. I've talked it all through with my therapist. These days, I'm trying to put out only positive energy into the world." As she said this last part, she gave her stomach a satisfied pat.

"When are you due?" Fish asked.

It wasn't the question he was desperate to know, of course, but it felt like a way into that conversation. Madame's eyes scanned his face briefly before she answered.

"June. So, in a little over a month? Wow. It's gone by so fast."

She laughed and sighed at the same time. Fish thought of what a blur his past eight months had been and wondered if he'd been putting out positive energy into the world. *Partiboy just wants to party, boy.* He was glad he'd refrained from smoking the rest of the joint he'd found clutched in his fingers upon waking up an hour ago.

"And . . . are you seeing anyone, these days?" ventured Fish, tactfully, before blurting, "Because, you know, I'd be happy to be there, at the hospital or whatever, if, you know, you didn't want to, like, go alone or something . . ."

Again, she scanned his face. Then she took his large hand in both of hers and gave it a gentle squeeze.

"That's really sweet, Fish. Really. But actually . . . Well, I am seeing someone. He'll be there with me on the day," she said, adding, "I actually think you'd really like him."

Fish felt a cavern open in his stomach. "Well, clearly we have similar tastes," he joked.

Madame smiled and said, "That's funny."

"So, it is . . . I mean, he's the other . . ." Fish couldn't bring himself to finish the question. His sleep-addled mind was having difficulty sourcing tactful words.

"Candidate?" finished Madame Meticulous. This time she did laugh—a small staccato burst that leaped from her chest. "Yes, Fish.

He is both the potential father and the man that has elected to take this adventure with me."

Perhaps the hurt that Fish now felt showed on his face, because Madame squeezed his hand again. "You look tired, Fish. Thank you for coming by. I really appreciate it. It's good to see you. I mean that."

She gave Fish another hug, another soft smile. A woman with red-framed glasses and a severe bob pulled gently at Madame Meticulous's elbow. Madame smiled apologetically at Fish and turned away. Fish stuck around long enough to be polite, taking a few moments at each piece. As soon as a respectful amount of time had elapsed, he left the gallery, stopping at a liquor store on his way to Kheel Tower. He had to replace several of the expensive bottles of the exec's liquor that he and his friends had consumed over the course of the week. At some point he'd have to clean the place, too. Tomorrow would be his last day cat-sitting.

Chapter 16

Like a seasoned actress hitting her mark on day one of rehearsal, the first of May ended the weeks of pelting rain and winter-flavored gusts with a showstopping yellow sun dance that oozed across the horizon like a microwaved butter pat, dripping into lazy swoops beyond the skyline like well-used hammocks.

Fish had been expecting another dreary day. But by the time he'd biked across the topmost boundary of Central Park, along One Hundred Tenth Street (or Tito Puente Way, as it was known in his neighborhood), and parked at the docking station closest to Mount Sinai Morningside Hospital, his ill-advised long-sleeve knit T-shirt was drenched with sweat. Flapping his shirt away from his chest with a clinging hope that he might be able to air dry the dark splotches before entering the hospital, Fish regretted having had to beg Klein to unlock the Citi Bike for him. Up to this moment, Fish had been able to maintain his assertion that one did not need an iPhone in the modern world, and Klein had relished the opportunity—in a half-joking kind of way—to prove his roommate's stubbornness wrong. He'd been on Fish to get a new phone for weeks, thought he was nuts for ditching his phone. He was tired of being handed wads of bills and fistfuls of coins whenever it was Fish's turn to pay the Wi-Fi bill. Fish wished he'd just taken a cab; it would've spared him all kinds of ego fractures.

After a few misfires, Fish located the right building, and then the correct door. A surly Jamaican woman in orchid-print scrubs reprimanded him for not wearing a mask and ordered him to sit down in the waiting area until Marcel was brought down. Fish complied, digging a withered blue face mask out of the depths of his backpack. People hardly even wore them on the subway anymore. He affixed the fraying rectangle over the breathing parts of his face, secured the stretchy bands over his ears, and seated himself among the other people sentenced to purgatory. Like Fish, they craned their necks toward the vestibule each time the elevator doors opened onto the ground floor.

The other visitors languishing in the waiting area wore exactly two expressions: anxious or bored. The contortion of their respective faces depended, Fish presumed, on the severity of their loved ones' conditions or else the invasiveness of the operations taking place elsewhere in the sprawling hospital wing.

Fish wasn't sure that he looked anxious or bored so much as hungover and sweaty. It was almost as though he could feel the slack weight of his face hanging off his skull. A woman with a sleeping toddler resting akimbo on her lap sat in the chair to Fish's left, though he didn't notice her until she nudged him gently with her elbow. Looking up, he saw that she was proffering one of those small foldable tissues—the kind that come in the little rectangular packages that all moms seemed to carry in their purses. *Where the hell do they buy those things, anyway?* When Fish didn't respond right away, she gestured delicately toward her nose. He couldn't tell whether she was relying on hand gestures rather than speaking because of the sleeping toddler or because of the reverent hush of the waiting room. Then he felt the familiar, warm taste of blood coursing over his top lip. Peeling away his mask (which he now saw was stained with a maroon Rorschach, hence the woman's concern), he accepted the tissue, held it to his nostrils, pinched the bridge of his nose, and tilted his head back into what was now a familiar angle. He mouthed a *thank you* to the woman, but she didn't notice. She had returned to playing Fruit Ninja on her phone, slashing at careening watermelons and oranges with her thumb.

Just as the nosebleed was petering out into a manageable trickle, Fish heard his name called from across the room. He hadn't been able to watch the elevator doors from his semirecumbent position. Luckily, the hospital waiting room was one of the few public places where one could clumsily deal with an impromptu nosebleed without arousing undue suspicion. Probably the subway, too, Fish figured.

Snapping his head to the sound of his name, Fish saw Marcel charging unsteadily away from the nurse's guiding grasp. He was speaking at a volume that sounded indecently amplified in the semi-silent lobby.

"I'm fine, I'm fine! Fish? Have you seen . . . tall fellow, needs a haircut . . . Fish? Has an earring, which I *detest*, by the way . . . Fisher? Oh, Fish! There you are. There he is. Let's go, shall we?"

Weird, Fish thought. It was so odd to see Marcel outside of the gallery—like seeing one's teacher at the supermarket, where they were behaving, preposterously, like a human being. Despite Marcel's anesthetized gait, Fish had to rush to keep up with him. He felt himself blush as he signed off on a form for the surly receptionist and then pinballed out onto the street just in time to stop Marcel from walking into an oncoming bus. Fish hailed a taxi and Marcel brushed away his hands as he attempted to guide his boss into the passenger seat.

"Oh, stop it. Stop that! I'm no invalid. Of course, whoever that urologist was must've been a butcher before earning his medical degree because . . . well, I'll spare you the details, Fish. Suffice it to say,

I'll be avoiding erections like the plague for the foreseeable future. Not that Stanley is around. Upstate! Now! While I'm down here getting *procedures* done to my . . . which you'd think a husband would have a vested interest in, wouldn't you? I mean, *hell-o*? Well, anyway . . ."

An uncomfortable silence settled between them as the taxi meandered through the traffic of Columbus Avenue. Marcel grimaced at each bump or surprise lane change. Fish stared out the window, watching the stately facades of the Upper West Side slowly fade to stumps in the rearview mirror, replaced by the smoke shops, bodegas, hair salons, bars with rainbow flags flapping from doors and windows, tattoo parlors, and tenement buildings of Hell's Kitchen.

Fish wanted to be anywhere else, just then. For all the times he'd seen Marcel drunk and distraught, this self-aware undertone of embarrassment in his bluster was new—unsettlingly so. Marcel, too, stared out the window, perhaps just as baffled as to the circumstances that had led him to occupy this taxicab on the way home from the hospital with a tall fellow from Connecticut. Fish had never been sure how much of Marcel's raving, perpetually paranoid demeanor was performance and how much of it stemmed from a genuine inner turmoil. There in the taxicab, he felt he saw the mask slipping. Just a little, but enough. He counted down the street signs until they passed West Fiftieth.

The taxi pulled to a stop in front of Marcel's apartment building on West Forty-Ninth Street. Fish rummaged through Marcel's pockets for his keys and opened the door for him. Marcel waved him back out onto the stoop when Fish moved to help him up the brief staircase to the entrance.

"I can take it from here," Marcel said. He gave Fish a robotic nod and mumbled a thank you before hobbling up the stairs to his first-floor apartment.

It had felt so strange, Fish later reflected, because Marcel never mumbled anything.

A week later, exuding his typical bombast, Marcel revealed to Fish, between messy swigs of Ketel One over ice (Marcel anointed the cocktail "The People's Martini"), without a trace of embarrassment, that he'd wet his pants while crossing the threshold into his apartment.

From Marcel's apartment, Fish strolled to Central Park. He basked in the sun's nascent spring warmth, submitting himself to the rays that penetrated his skin and illuminated all the rooms of his body that had become stuffy and neglected for the duration of New York's long and petty winter. He thought about lighting up a joint but decided against it. He'd been so consistently fucked up for so long that conscious sobriety felt a little bit novel. Almost like a new kind of high.

• • •

F ish's fingers were dancing across his laptop's keyboard in the New York Public Library's reading room. The typewriter had jammed again but his muse had come earlier than usual today, striking in the late morning while he was still stuck at the gallery, dusting rarely viewed frames and nodding in the right places as Marcel soliloquized about his urinary troubles. Fish had figured out the ending of *Postlapsaria, Connecticut*. Or, at least, an idea for an ending. It had just sort of struck him out of nowhere, like the droppings of a pigeon (which, annoyingly, always seemed to fly *up* rather than *away* from oncoming feet on New York sidewalks). And ever since the idea had arrived in his brain, he'd been consumed by a restlessness, a physical itch that could only be scratched by reopening the Google Doc and hammering out the lines that were slipping like newts—lively, vigorous, peculiar—through his consciousness. It was an aching compulsion to write as he hadn't had in weeks.

His productivity had been waxing and waning like that, the ideas and words burbling up and out of him for a day or so before subsiding into a simmer of forced, clunky lines for several days or even weeks.

The fickleness of his muse was tremendously frustrating to Fish, particularly because his unimpressive liquidity had forced him to cut back on the cocaine, which had, to that point, proved to be quite the expediter for summoning the muse (if the muse could arrive before Partiboy, that is).

Now, sitting in the library, his lanky legs tucked under the long, stern wooden desks, with the overstuffed bookshelves staring down at him like disappointed parents, he searched the coffered ceiling and the luminous chandeliers for *just* the right word. *Just* the right phrase, the diction surgically deployed, that would capture the shallowness, the codedness of human speech while (simultaneously, somehow; Fish wished that someone would tell him just *how*) communicating the insurmountable gulf that separated Americans—separated humans(!)—from cohesive, definitive self-knowledge. A tall order, but nevertheless an order that Fish had demanded of himself and which he earnestly intended to fulfill. And *Partiboy just wants to party, boy.*

Partiboy, dude . . . I'm . . . Like, shit . . . I think I'm kind of, like, coming apart here, you know? Fragmenting, like. It's kinda like . . . You ever see one of those YouTube videos where an ice climber—you know, like, one of those crazy fucks with those wild crampon talons strapped to their boots and they're wielding those collapsible ice pickaxe thingies that they climb with? Like in that documentary I didn't want to watch but Becca did, so we watched it, and it was actually pretty cool? Well, Partiboy, not that you asked, but there's this thing called "dinner plating," where those nutjob adrenaline junkies smack their pickaxe thingy into, like, the ice shelf or whatever . . . and the ice they were relying on to support their weight . . . just, like, shatters into pieces. Like when you drop a dinner plate, you know? Oh, right . . . Well, sure. Yeah, well, of course you know about breaking kitchenware, Partiboy. I don't mean to patronize. I just mean that's how I feel. Like one of those ice shelf things that shatter when they shouldn't . . . No, what? No, man, you're not the climber in this metaphor. I don't know . . . Like I just fucking said, dude, I don't know! I don't know who the climber is. I'm just saying I'm the ice, okay? Christ, man . . . You're not a great listener, you know that?

Partiboy just wants to party, boy.

Knew you'd say that. Dickhead.

Fish took surreptitious sips of his doctored coffee, having spiked one of those iconic blue to-go cups—one of those ones with Greco-Roman designs lining the edges and the words "WE ARE HAPPY TO SERVE YOU" printed obsequiously across the middle and sold from vendor carts throughout Midtown—with a few fingers of Fernet-Branca. It tasted ghastly, though Fish had read that residents of the Southern Hemisphere—particularly the citizens of Argentina, Bolivia, and Uruguay, according to a half-assed Wikipedia search—improved their Coca-Colas with Fernet-Branca. So, Fish did not feel that he was sinking to complete tackiness by topping off his preferred caffeinated beverage. Rather, he was being positively cosmopolitan—or, at least, so said the overworked employees of his brain's rationalization factory.

Beverages were not permitted in the reading room, as an ancient, obese security guard in a preposterously large suit coldly informed him. So, he had to be sneaky about it. Of late, the booze had functioned like a speed dial, busting past the automated secretary and their inane, automated cheer and their maddeningly upbeat questions, and connecting Fish directly to the muse's extension after just a few rings.

Today, however, the words refused to come. *Better up the dosage,* thought Fish, taking another quick slug before setting the increasingly sodden paper cup back down onto the chair, nestling it protectively in the canyon between his thighs.

Partiboy just wants to party, boy.

Damn straight, Partiboy. But also, like, fuck off, man. Just for a little while. I'm trying finish this motherfucker, feel me?

"Fisher?"

Fish whipped his head in the direction of the whispering voice. Doing so forced him to confront both the fact and the extent of his drunkenness. It was barely noon. There was a man who appeared to be homeless snoozing in the chair across from him and a squirrely looking academic type with scruffy facial hair and big headphones to his left, furiously typing numbers into an Excel spreadsheet. The voice had come from somewhere over his right shoulder. Fish twisted into an uncomfortable position in the wooden chair to look behind him.

"Hey! Oh, so it *is* you. I thought so, but I wasn't sure. I was like, wait, is that *Fisher*? And then you turned around and I was like, okay, yeah, that's *definitely* Fisher, L-O-L. Your hair's so long! How are you? How are things?"

It was Phoebe Johansen, and she'd actually said the letters *L* and *O* and *L* aloud just then. The shocked expression that had glanced across her face like a lopsided kite when he'd turned around quickly dissolved into a preppy smile. They'd taken a few classes together in law school (Torts and Property Law, Fish recalled with a grimace). They had even had a few semiflirtatious study dates in the Yale Law library. She wore her straight, well-brushed hair in a severe bun at the crown of her head, the exquisitely furled bump sitting primly atop her skull like a tee ball. She had that radiant Scandinavian skin that was like yellow lamplight. Despite her mousy, anxious temperament (she had a noticeable habit of defaulting to awkward self-deprecation when silences stretched beyond a few seconds), she was built like a mythic Amazon, all shoulders and limbs—the fruits of her college swimming career.

Fish recalled a rumor he'd heard. One of his law school roommates had mentioned something about how Phoebe would wake up at five every morning to swim at the campus pool before classes. This fact was considered to be germane evidence supporting the meaty, too-specific-not-to-be-true basis of the rumor, which held that Phoebe Johansen struggled with an acute case of obsessive-compulsive disorder. As in, she'd been diagnosed with OCD by a licensed doctor. She was not one of those people who, half joking, half faux-apologetic and fully looking for a cheap laugh when mired in the semi-awkwardness of group projects, announced their OCD as a breezy, catch-all explanation for the pains they took to perfectly, *perfectly* align headings and subheadings along the red guidelines that the Google Slides templates provided for such people.

Phoebe's affliction, according to the rumor, was so severe that she was liable to have some kind of breakdown if she didn't swim *precisely* fifty laps every morning. It had happened once, according to her gossipy roommate, when the pool was closed for Indigenous Peoples' Day even though the weekly emailed newsletter (*News Haven*, it was clunkily entitled) had said it would be open. As the story went, she'd torn a fistful of hair from her scalp and cried loudly in a public place (it was either the dining hall or the law students' lounge, Fish couldn't remember).

Yale Law was a small, selective program. Everyone knew (and cataloged, Fish had often suspected) the doings of everyone else. The Yale Law program—maybe all law programs—were petri dishes under a microscope, while New York City (Fish now philosophized, with more than a little self-satisfaction at the conclusion he'd deduced—especially considering how drunk he was) was a glorious, riotous jumble of cells meiosis-ing and mitosis-ing in a beautiful, hectic frenzy that refused to be pinned beneath some elementary magnifying device—which is to say, the city (*THE City! Capital letters all the way*) refused to be comprehended, reveling instead in its bewildering, tantalizing incoherence.

Phoebe finished the first semester at the top of the class. The study dates that she and Fish would sometimes casually arrange typically functioned as desperate attempts by Fish to understand material he had not read while she pantomimed exasperation at his charmingly boyish lack of preparation. He'd finished the first semester at basically the bottom of the class (he'd only surpassed a kid who had, tragically, committed suicide halfway through the semester). And he hadn't made it to the end of the second semester to learn where he might've ranked, though he knew it would have been equally unimpressive. Phoebe had essentially been the closest thing he'd had to a friend during his brief stint in law school. His roommates spent all their time studying, discussing upcoming tests, and then dissecting the tests in minute detail immediately afterwards, tactfully phrasing their assertions and conjectures toward the slim possibility that they could be wrong about this or that. But Fish knew they were all getting As and knew that they all knew he was barely scraping by. It made things too awkward for a mutually respectful friendship to blossom. They would abruptly cease discussing their grades whenever he'd cross through the living room, where they held their nightly self-congratulatory salons. But Phoebe had always been patient and kind, laughing at his jokes and gently encouraging him to apply himself *just a little bit harder* and he'd be fine, totally fine.

And yet, though it had only been about a year since he'd last seen her, Fish felt like he was bumping into someone he'd gone to elementary school with, or a friend of his mom's to whom he'd have to behave like a nice young man.

Fish gathered his jaw and his eyes back into their respective neutral positions before responding. He decided, semiconsciously, to play it casual. *Partiboy just wants to party, boy.*

"Oh, shit, Phoebe? Hey! Damn. What, uh . . . what's up? What brings you here?" he stammered, matching her whispered tone, and nearly knocking over the coffee cup as he stood to give her an awkward hug.

The security guard gave him a stern look and he returned an apologetic smile, shoving the nearly empty cup into his backpack. It wasn't until he sat back down that he smelled the booze on his own breath. If Phoebe had noticed, she was too polite to say anything.

"Doing some research for a tort I'm working on. And they've got the archives here, so . . . And I was getting pretty sick of the Yale law library, L-O-L. Needed a change of scenery, you know? I'm one of those people who need, like, a perfect environment to study."

"Yeah, I get that," replied Fish, glancing gloomily around the reading room.

For (it felt like, to Fish) the trillionth time, he wished he had some cocaine. Just a pinch. Just enough to swipe against his gums. *God, wouldn't that be fantastic, Partiboy?* But Partiboy was gone. He didn't do libraries. Not his scene.

"Right," Phoebe replied, with a little sighing laugh, "I guess *you* get that. So, I mean, have you, like, been in New York this whole time? We weren't sure where you went. And, as you'll recall, the administration tells us next to *nothing*, L-O-L . . . We just came into class for that test . . . What was it, property law? Yeah, must've been, because I remember the schedule was adjusted because we came back from Memorial Day weekend on a Tuesday rather than . . . Well, anyway, we came into class and you just . . . well, you weren't there! We were all a little concerned, actually. Anyway, it's good to see that you're, you know, alive, L-O-L."

A nervous tremor thrilled through her voice as she spoke. Fish wished he hadn't skipped the cigarette break he'd been delaying. He'd been planning on rewarding himself with a smoke sesh once he'd strung together a few decent lines. Thinking of his last day in New Haven sent a sudden, inadequately buried surge of shame up through his chest and into his throat. He felt himself blushing. Silence filled the space between them and stretched just a little.

"Sorry, I know I ramble," Phoebe said, fiddling with her backpack straps.

Fish had been in the library, cramming for the property law test. It was not going well. He'd skipped the class enough times to earn a stern warning email from the dean. But, at some point, the library clock ticking toward test time, his eyes had refused to ingest even one more word of the punishingly small typeface in the aggressively drab, leather-bound textbook. Then his hand had refused to flip the page.

"Yep, ha. I'm alive. That property law test, right . . . Yeah, I guess that's the one that did me in. I just kinda burned out, I guess you could say. They told—do you remember this?—they told us," Fish began, flummoxed by the words that came spilling out of his mouth, overriding his cognition. "At the beginning, you know? During that orientation thing? They told us that ten percent of the class would drop out or fail out by the end of the year. Remember? But nobody really thinks it's gonna be them, right?" Fish tried a laugh, but it came out more like a sigh. "Well, I guess I'm one of those guys. L-O-L."

It wasn't Fish's fault that he hadn't studied for that property law test. Not entirely, he felt. He granted himself that much grace. As it happened, he'd spent Memorial Day weekend (a three-day holiday that was denuded of its implicit relief by the massively consequential property law exam he'd have to take on the following Tuesday) in Manhattan. He'd been visiting the 9/11 Memorial—his first time seeing it in person. His parents had driven in from Connecticut, and they'd all spent the weekend in a swanky hotel in SoHo.

It had been the five-year anniversary of his brother's death. Five years had felt like enough of a benchmark number to warrant a somewhat more special memorial than their annual take-out dinner from Shake Shack, which had been his brother's favorite restaurant. Plus, they'd never been to the 9/11 Memorial. Maybe, Fish remembered thinking, it was still too soon. Fish's mom had wept silently, and his dad had stoically rubbed her back, his eyes misting up a little and his voice catching in his throat in that way that dads cry.

"Are you writing something?" Phoebe asked, changing the subject in that seamless, innocuous way that would probably make her a great lawyer.

Staring down into those endless square pits at the memorial, the water rushing down down down into a dark infinity, Fish had felt the gravity of the tragedy, the loss, the catastrophe. But he hadn't felt any particularly personal connection to it. The war had been going on for fifteen years by the time his brother died.

The most tragic part of losing his brother, if Fish really thought about it, was that it had happened when it did. They were both in their twenties, which is the age when brothers start to see each other as adults, discussing their childhood and their parents with the only other person who could speak to the specifics of that shared experience.

His brother was four years older than him. Their respective recollections of 9/11 were the hazy memories of childhood. His brother claimed to remember seeing the second plane collide with the tower on television. The billowing smoke. Fish just had a vague memory of his class being dismissed early and his parents acting strange, watching the news in the middle of the day. Fish thought maybe he'd feel something more potent—maybe he'd even cry—if he were to go to Kabul to see the spot where the IED had blown up his brother's vehicle. Maybe there'd be a crater or something.

"Oh, not really, no. It's just, like . . . Well, I'm kinda playing around with this idea I had for a play," Fish finally replied.

His hand moved instinctively to drag the cursor toward the *X* at the top right corner of the Google Doc, but he stopped himself from pulling such a cowardly move. Even so, the words sounded lame tumbling out of his mouth. *Way to play it casual, dude. Partiboy just wants to party, boy. Oh, great. Look who finally decided to show up. Fantastic. Hooray. Hey Partiboy, be real with me a sec: is muse, like, mad at me or something?*

Partiboy just wants to party, boy.

Fish's brain was stewed and salad-tossed. If he excelled at any-thing, it was stubbornly rationalizing his decisions until he *himself* believed his intentions to be true and good. But with Phoebe tow-ering over him, his back twisted strangely against the rigid chair, he was at a loss. Phoebe was nearing the end of her L2 year. There was a light at the end of her tunnel. Her life—*real* life—would be starting soon. Just starting.

Fish's inner self winced. His brain's rationalization factory was abandoned (he served as foreman-slash-liaison to Fish's outer self). The rationalization factory workers were on strike. They demanded usable material. Said that one can't make grape juice with kumquats. *Kumquats? Really?* Claimed they hadn't had a decent night's sleep in months because of all the overtime they'd been working.

Benevolently, Fish acknowledged their demands. His was, to be sure, a rather absurd case, which Phoebe Johansen, through no fault of her own, was now prosecuting simply by her presence. Fish broke immediately, wilting under her cross-examination before it had even started. He gave it all up. Ratted on himself. Sang like a bird. Named names (there were just two, his own and Partiboy). Claimed to be both the patsy and the puppeteer.

Phoebe's presence, this phantom from his law school stint, a lifetime ago, addressed a jury of Fish's peers. The case was as good as won as far as the prosecution—that is, Phoebe's presence—was concerned. The trial was just a formality. Grandstanding. Showmanship. Gravy.

Inner Fish's lawyer, a frumpy public defendant (Inner Fish had been too ashamed to call his parents for help), rifled anxiously through his manila folders. He was sweating through his cheap suit. His toupee sat askew on his skull like a beret. It was his first case. He'd earned his law degree online from a since-discredited institution.

Consider the facts, began Phoebe Phantom:

To have left Yale Law School to type out a sophomoric play in a public library next to a man whose numerous misfortunes included smelling like a football locker room at a poorly funded high school after a character-building practice in the rain. To have left Yale Law School to get addicted to one substance after the next. To have left Yale Law School to possibly impregnate a cute sculptor whom the accused had sorta fallen for and who'd since moved on with her life. With another guy. Mystery Dude. To have left Yale Law School—and all it promised!—just to do that awkward sidewalk dance, whereby he and some oncoming stranger selected the same direction and then made the same adjustment and nearly bumped into each other again, only to both readjust to the same opposite direction and, impossibly, nearly collide *again*, a third time, before, finally, figuring it out and cruising past each other and putting the encounter out of their minds forever as though the brief dance had never occurred. To have left Yale Law School to hitch himself to a failing art gallery in a building that would soon be reduced to rubble and to an artist who was such a spectacularly deluded failure that he had to be picked up from the hospital for his kidney stone procedure by the only employee of his who wasn't in rehab in Arizona.

What Fish did recall feeling, there at the 9/11 Memorial, was his sense of wonder at New York City itself, the Manhattanites and tourists flooding past him on their way to or from interesting places as they emerged from the subway stations and crossed through the plaza. The city's riotous skyline beckoned Fish from the rearview mirror as they'd driven home to Connecticut, stopping at the Shake Shack in Darien before dropping him off in New Haven, where he knew, as soon as he seated himself at a corner table in the library, un-studied pages staring up at him from the desk, that he would not—could not—stay. Not when New York with its unfettering promise of a fresh start, of a life comprised of extraordinary days—doing interesting things and meeting interesting people—was only a brief train ride away.

His brother had died at twenty-five years old. Fish was a year older than his brother would ever be. *And what did he have to show for it besides a semester and a half of law school credits and a shelf cluttered with lacrosse trophies?* he'd pondered. So he'd slapped the book closed and left the library, left campus, packed up his apart-ment, sent an apologetic letter to the dean (who never responded), sacrificed his security deposit to end his lease prematurely, DM'd a drummer named Jeremy about the room in Bushwick he'd been offering to sublet on Facebook, agreed to sell his car to a Muslim dude in the Bronx who was planning on quitting his job to drive for DoorDash rather than get the COVID vaccine that his com-pany was now mandating, and, finally, drove back home to break the news to his parents, who had been baffled and more than a little upset by his reckless impulsivity.

But Fish had to give them credit—they'd adjusted themselves to the news relatively quickly, agreeing that Fish was not, ultimately, the lawyering type. His brother was, though, with his *summa cum laude* degree from Dartmouth. When he'd joined the military, everyone figured he had political ambitions. He'd planned on going to law school after his first tour, which was where Fish got the idea to go to law school himself. Doing his best to match his footprints to those his brother had left in his wake, as Fish had always done.

His brother never talked about wanting to run for office, but Fish knew the aspiration was there. It was there in the way he scanned several newspapers every morning over coffee, a pen in hand. It was there in the way he'd always been so comfortable speaking to adults. In the way he parted his hair. In the way he always listened, quietly and sincerely, before saying anything.

Nor was Fish a hedge fund type, or a part-time real estate agent type, like his dad and mom were, respectively, giving them little choice but to support whatever their son showed an interest in, something—*anything*—that might excite him towards a career of some kind. His dad had long ago given up hope that his sons would follow in his footsteps and embrace a Wall Street career. Every morning when their dad was leaving for work, Fish's brother would say, "So long, pop. Those hedges aren't gonna fund themselves."

And everyone would chuckle there at the breakfast table and their dad would grin ruefully on his way out the door. And while Fish's parents were concerned about his moving to the city without a job in hand, they seemed to be genuinely excited when they drove him and Becca to the train station, his biggest suitcase clunking in the trunk of his father's Cadillac.

When the train made a turn and the Manhattan skyline filled his window, Fish had never felt so unencumbered, so unscheduled—no lacrosse practice, no SAT prep, no morning team lift, no classes—in his life.

The notion that he'd lost that idealized wonder about the city crossed his mind. He wasn't sure if the thought should make him sad or, maybe, sort of proud to have become another cynical New Yorker. It had been almost a year, but he didn't feel like he'd earned the right to encamp himself with the latter party just yet.

"Neat! What's it about?" Phoebe asked, with what sounded like sincere interest.

"Well . . . The fall of man, I guess . . ." muttered Fish.

But then they received a severe shushing from the security guard and a few peeved glances from their fellow library patrons, so Phoebe smiled, gave him a loose, weird, puppet-arms hug, and left. Fish waited a few minutes before slamming his laptop shut and leaving the library himself.

Chapter 17

Fish hadn't been expecting to spend the entire day at the gallery. Really, he'd just stopped by to slip upstairs, snag his paycheck, and then head back to Johnny's Bar in the West Village to finish writing his play. He was so damn close to finishing it. He really just needed one day of buckled down, no-nonsense, honest-to-goodness writing to finish the motherfucker—with assistance from a few cheap gin and tonics. It was a compromise he'd made with Partiboy. Fish had wanted to go to a drip coffee bar, but alas, this being a Friday and payday and all, they had decided a bar would be better.

But instead, Fish ended up staying at the gallery for the whole day. Partiboy was delighted by the change of plans—Fish wound up getting much drunker than he'd intended. *Partiboy just wants to party, boy.* When he'd grabbed his paycheck from the gallery mailbox, there had been a nondescript envelope—addressed to the gallery—nestled just behind it. It was odd, because the gallery rarely received mail other than Fish's weekly paycheck, save for the occasional Chinese take-out menus and glossy credit card offers.

When he saw that the envelope was from a government entity—New York City's eminent domain authority—he'd felt his heart throb in his chest, and he'd sprinted up the stairs to the gallery. He'd left his keys in the bathroom at Johnny's Bar the night before, trading key bumps with an actor—an understudy for Lysander in Shakespeare in the Park's production of *A Midsummer Night's*

Dream—which was the other reason he'd been hoping to return to the bar.

Fish slipped his hand behind the portrait of Rocky and Monty, found the spare key, flung the door open, and collapsed onto the nearest couch. His sweating palms softened the neat creases of the envelope. He checked over his shoulder to make sure Marcel wasn't around. Probably painting upstairs, as he always seemed to be these days. He was more prolific than ever, churning out canvases as fast as a griddle cook flipped pancakes. Some of them were actually pretty good, too, Fish thought.

The letter was brief and governmental, not one word linked to the next without the explicit approval of a humorless lawyer. It was as though the words themselves were wearing drab gray suits and sensible loafers. But Fish's eyes tore across the page as though it were a spy novel building to a climax. He had to read it three times to be sure the gut punch he'd felt upon the first read wasn't a gross miscomprehension.

Eminent domain was being executed. They had exactly one month to vacate the building. They would be given a modest relocation fee, which they were free to appeal for a larger amount in court. Marcel had already talked through the inadequacy of this measure. No judge was going to give money to a failing art gallery. And when Officer Toomey, the building inspector, had returned with an appraiser, business hadn't been so bad. Had the appraiser looked at their disastrous accounting books now, the business would hardly be valued at half as much as the relocation fee presumed. So that was it.

Fish debated showing the letter to Marcel. He knew he would have to eventually. Girding himself, he walked upstairs to the painting studio to deliver the grim news. Marcel took it pretty much exactly as Fish had expected.

"Well, now, isn't that fantastic? Four decades in the arts, beauti-fying what was once the *anus* of this borough, Fish, the *anus*! I class up the joint and they pull a sleazy piss-in-the-punch-bowl move like this. Cowards. Sending me a letter like I'm some kind of . . . some kind of . . . pioneer! All they see is numbers, Fish. Don't ever for-get that. You're an artist, too. What was it? A novel? A play, right, yes, of course. Fish the *dramaturg*. Well, in the end, someone with a corner office is going to reduce you to a number. And let me tell you something, Fish: that number, no matter what it is, will never be enough."

Though Fish was reasonably scared of what Marcel might do once the soliloquy ended, it did warm him a little to be called an artist. Of course, it was Marcel bestowing that title on him, and . . . Well, maybe he, too, would not be appreciated until he was too dead to know the difference. A moment later, Marcel was pouring vodka and Coca-Cola into two glasses, thrusting one into Fish's chest and splashing all over the painting studio, launching into his most epic tirade to date. He castigated, in no uncertain terms, the city, the philistines, the homophobes, the developers, the yuppies, his generation, Fish's generation, Ronald Reagan, the *New Yorker* and the *New York Times*, Rudy Giuliani, Fox News, Donald Trump, the homeless, those who overlooked the homeless, the subway system, Florida, his land-lord, Marlon Brando (though he did note that the famously charismatic actor did, for a time, live on his block on West For-ty-Ninth Street), Texas, feminists, the McDonald's restaurant chain, rats, Jeff Koons, Florida again, and Times Square.

It was his swan song, and the more he drank, the faster it spewed out of him, as though his very bones were purging the animosity for these people and entities and places from their pores. When he'd finished, drunk and spent, he collapsed down onto his haunches to stroke Monty and Rocky, who'd been swirling about his ankles as he paced frantically around the studio.

After Marcel's long outburst had petered out into a slurring, mumbled combination of beep-bopped, scatted manifesto and cooing baby talk to the cats, Fish found that he felt oddly calm. It was as though Marcel had expended all the outrage about the building's destruction, leaving none for Fish. He'd miss the paychecks, naturally, and the fact that he rarely had to come in to work to earn them. Mostly he'd miss the romance of it, what the gallery did for the character he'd crafted. It was like the final touch to the costume, working at a place like this, and it was a keystone of sorts, the only element of the persona that had any real weight, a full physical building with unwanted art pieces hanging at haughty angles upon the walls, granting credibility to the rest of the guise. Fish hated to lose that. Now, he felt, he was just another asshole on a barstool talking about the play he was working on.

For a few days afterward, Marcel threw himself into a ferocious grassroots campaign, calling old contacts from his political activism days (most of whom had died of AIDS, the original clarion call for their activism), everyone he knew in the press (one guy, who'd retired twelve years ago), and the other businesses slated for destruction (who had all been preparing for this eventuality for months, if not years). Stanley came back to the city to lend an ear to Marcel's frequent, violent outbursts over the course of those few days, and Fish actually came into work on the weekend (much to Partiboy's chagrin), staying the full day to either help Marcel craft pleading emails or simply to get drunk and commiserate with him (which Partiboy abided).

After a week or so, Stanley had gotten Marcel to come around to the idea of an early retirement. They were tired. If each day in New York was equivalent to a lifetime anywhere else, then a lifetime in New York was exhausting. They hatched a plan to use the relocation money to buy a house for themselves up-state, near Stanley's family, perhaps somewhere a little outside the artists' enclave of Beacon, New York. Technically the money was earmarked for the establishment of a new business, but who was to say a little house with a few paintings hanging on its walls wasn't a quaint little countryside gallery, they reasoned. By the end of the following week, they even seemed a little excited about the idea.

• • •

Oh, Partiboy was in rare form on the night that Fish finished his play. Once Marcel had given up the righteous fight of keeping the gallery open, Fish hadn't felt much need to continue going into work. With his days free and his final paycheck in hand, *Postlapsaria, Connecticut* became his sole occupation. Well, that and the cocaine, cocktails, cigarettes, and mushroom chocolates that he poured into himself like gasoline into a race car. Sometimes Partiboy answered the call, but when the muse picked up rather than apathetically allowing the call to go to voicemail, Fish typed. He wrote and rewrote, drafted and erased, edited and wrote again. His fingers hammered the keyboard, chasing the end of the play, chasing that elusive "BLACKOUT" like a cheetah hurtling across the savanna in pursuit of a tiring antelope. It was a game of matching precise words to precise feelings. And thus, one day in the middle of May, he finished. He scrolled up and down through the lengthy document, staring lovingly at his creation. Upon typing out those final words and holding the thickish sheaf of papers in his hands, he felt as though he'd lost ten pounds. Scoring a tie-breaking lacrosse goal had never felt this good.

He still had half a vial of Uncle Nemo's good stuff left by the time he'd finished, the other half coursing through his veins. His jaw working back and forth like a factory machine, his lips beginning to chap from incessant licking, his gums pleasantly, chemically numb from the refuse he'd been rubbing over them as he wrote, Fish knew he had to celebrate. *Partiboy just wants to party, boy.* Klein was out of town, introducing Carmen to his parents back home in Rhode Island. But no matter. Klein had become increasingly unwilling to join Fish on his raucous nights out, always citing plans with Carmen or a need for sleep that Fish ignored, staying up until sunrise and sleeping all day with a regularity that would have impressed a raccoon. Plus, Klein was still a little miffed at Fish because a few nights back, Fish had gotten himself locked on the roof of the apartment building when he'd gone up there to smoke a joint. He'd been too stoned to use the fire escape to get down, and so, after firing off a desperate email from the laptop Fish had taken to carrying around should a writerly inspiration strike, Klein had Ubered back from Carmen's place to rescue him. Fish had ponied up thirty dollars for the Uber, but still, he'd kind of spoiled Klein's night with Carmen.

So, Fish fired off an email to Psycho B. The subject line read, in all caps, "WHERE R U DUDE LETS PARTY." He flagged the message as important before hitting send. Partiboy bounced up and down on the balls of his feet, awaiting a response. It came almost instantly—Psycho B was anal like that, pushing email notifications to his phone. They agreed to meet at Mad Tropical, where Psycho B was already several Bud Lights and a few key bumps deep. Willfully forgetting his lacking funds, Fish took a cab from Spanish Harlem all the way out to Bushwick. The cabbie's credit card reader wasn't working, and Fish was too keyed up to sit around in the backseat waiting for the machine to restart. He thrust a fifty-dollar bill at the driver and all but sprinted into the bar.

A shirtless man with a nipple piercing was manning the bar. Fish struck up a conversation about said piercing, presenting the ornament dangling from his own ear as an icebreaker. Fish had been to enough bars enough times to know that establishing rapport with the bartender early in the night, while he still had the mental faculties to muster a not-insane persona, would be crucial when thirst occurred later in the night when the bar was more packed.

Psycho B was on the dance floor, moving his limbs in strange, jellyfish-like undulations. He cackled when he saw Fish, dapping him up and pulling him into a tight bro hug. Psycho B was yelling something into his ear, but it was too loud to talk—or hear. The DJ was a nerdy looking Hispanic dude with a goatee and a flat-brimmed LA Dodgers baseball hat. He played remixed '80s tracks, the soaring vocals and bopping rhythms giving way to dubstep drops that made everyone in the crowded room gyrate frenetically. As always, Psycho B traveled with a small crowd. Girls in belly shirts with gems pasted at almond-shaped angles around their eyes and dudes who, like Psycho B, had recently expatriated from Boston but hadn't stopped dressing like they lived in Southie—polo shirts, dark slacks, backwards baseball caps. A girl with a mullet asked Psycho B's roommate if he was a Mormon, yelling the question, and they all had a laugh about that. Fish felt the molecules in his body lifting out of his skin, connecting to the music, the movements, and the hazy purple lighting that refracted at mesmerizing angles off of the disco ball hanging from the ceiling.

Partiboy just wants to party, boy. Partiboy just wants to party, boy. Partiboy just wants to party, boy. And Fish relinquished himself to Partiboy. He'd finished the play he'd been slaving over for the better part of a year. There it was, in its entirety. Stashed in a neat pile on his desk and ready to be unleashed on the world.

Around 2 a.m., a consensus was reached and they stumbled to

Elsewhere, the music still throbbing in their ears as they passed taco trucks in the street and walls bearing spectacular displays of graffiti. Someone—a very benevolent someone—fronted the cover charge and they were each given wristbands and stamps. Fish bought a round of gin and tonics that he couldn't afford but would worry about tomorrow. This was followed by more cocaine in bathroom stalls with faulty locks that required one to lean up against the door while snorting small white mounds off of keys in order to have anything close to privacy, surreptitious handoffs on the dance floor and knowing smiles once the most recent drug abuser returned to the group. Losing and finding each other in the club's labyrinthian assortment of dance halls.

Eventually, last call came and they were ushered into the street. Psycho B overheard two girls smoking cigarettes talking about an after-party in Ridgewood and got the address. An Uber was summoned by another benevolent someone—or perhaps it was the same benevolent someone, Fish couldn't tell. A raucous Uber ride, Psycho B commandeering the aux cord and blasting leaked Travis Scott tracks from his SoundCloud app.

But when they arrived at the supposed after-party address, a quiet suburban street on the barrier between Brooklyn and Queens, the brick duplexes lining the blocks were silent. Another Uber pulled up, and they commiserated with the young strangers that stepped out of the car about having been duped. Fish was getting tired, and even Partiboy was flagging. They'd run out of coke, and a pale gray sun was beginning to poke its head up over the horizon. Without saying a word of goodbye, Fish trudged to the L-train stop. He fell asleep on the train, waking up in Times Square only when a man in an MTA uniform prodded him gently on the shoulder. Fish stumbled outside onto West Forty-Second Street, the light from the elevated screens nearly blinding him, hailed the first cab he saw, and slurred the address of his intended destination to the driver. The ride felt short—too short even for the chemical distortions of time brought on by drugs and sleep deprivation. Stepping out of the cab, Fish realized he had given the cab driver the address of the gallery.

Without really thinking about it, he wandered up the stairs. The place was silent. Marcel and Stanley were probably still asleep on Forty-Ninth Street. There had been a half-hearted attempt to remove the paintings in preparation for the building's imminent destruction, and the naked patches of wall made the gallery feel even larger. But most of the paintings were still affixed at uneven angles to the nails drilled haphazardly into the painted brick walls.

Of course, thought Fish. *It's perfect. I'll put on my play. Here. The night before the building is destroyed.* The idea took root in his soul, buoying his steps as he trudged toward the subway station in the warming morning light.

Chapter 18

When Klein informed Fish, sort of accidentally, that Becca had a new boyfriend, Fish was surprised by how stung he felt.

"Look at this chode," Klein said, chuckling and holding up his iPhone for Fish's appraisal.

It was an Instagram photo of Becca wearing a white coat, wrapping her arms around a handsome Asian dude, who was also wearing a white coat. She was beaming in this candid "omg I can't believe you're taking a picture!" type of way, staring directly at the camera—directly at Fish—and the dude was looking handsomely off to the side, showcasing a jawline as sharp as an ice skate. The caption read: "When your eyes lock across the cadaver . . . #InstaOfish."

Fish didn't think the guy looked like a chode. He looked like a winner. He looked like how Fish had used to look in pictures, strapping, broad-chested, confident, clean-shaven, healthy. Husband material. Fish pictured them buying plants for some two-bedroom apartment in an up-and-coming neighborhood of a second-tier city, making pasta with noodles they bought fresh from some farmer's market. It wasn't as though Becca were cheating on him, though it felt a little bit like that to Fish. He'd presumed—wrongly, he now realized—that their watches were in sync, and that they would, ultimately, end up together. Probably. That's how he'd been thinking about it, at least. To the extent that he'd been thinking about it at all. Clearly, she'd reset her watch at some point. He handed the phone back to Klein.

"Oh, cool, look at that," Fish replied, he hoped casually.

Fish waited an appropriate amount of time before retiring to his bedroom to watch a few episodes of *The Office* that he'd seen a million times. He laughed at the jokes, even though he knew them all by heart. He didn't care. It felt familiar, comfortable.

• • •

F ish was stunned by how many actors were willing to work for free. His play had only five roles—Adam (Lead), Eve (Lead), Jainkoa (Supporting), Lou (Supporting), and Mike (Supporting)—but his Craigslist post advertising a call for audition submissions received over a hundred respondents. Within an hour, his Gmail inbox was flooded with headshots, resumes, and video reels. He couldn't believe the response.

It was becoming so real. His play was *actually* going to be staged by *real* New York actors—or, at least, wannabe actors. But this was fitting, he felt, as he was nothing if not a wannabe playwright. With the help of Klein (who he deputized as his casting director) and a twelve pack of Modelo beer, he pored over the submissions, narrowing down the applicants one by one. Phone calls were made (using Klein's phone), and the roles were cast.

In *Postlapsaria, Connecticut*, Adam was a bachelor in his midthirties, who'd conquered Wall Street at a young age and left the city for the suburbs, having inherited a palatial country house and a riotous garden in Connecticut from a distant relative, complete with a greenhouse. Eve, also single and in her thirties, was a botanist from the city that appeared one day—hired by the house's previous owner—to identify the strange plants growing in the greenhouse and to advise Adam about how best to care for the estate's lush garden. God, in *Postlapsaria, Connecticut*, took the form of the house's caretaker, an old Basque man who went by Jainkoa. Satan was adapted into the character of Lou, a shifty plumber that showed up to the estate unannounced, purportedly to take a look at the garden's irrigation system. And Mike, a facsimile of Saint Michael, was the stern but friendly neighbor who lived in the estate across the lake and served as president of Postlapsaria's homeowner's association.

The first rehearsal took place in Fish's apartment. The actors were eager and charismatic, most of them new to the city and from places like Iowa and Pennsylvania. A handsome waiter named Zeke had taken on the role of Adam. He had recently moved to the city from Los Angeles, having become fed up with competing against Tik-Tok influencers for even the smallest roles in short films. Zeke was against all that, and Fish recognized a kindred spirit. Eve was to be played by a recent Tisch grad named Josephine. She was by far the strongest actor in the cast, and Fish was shocked that she'd agreed to take on the part. She spoke of the character's *motivations* and made these weird guttural noises to warm up her voice before each rehearsal. Sometimes she spoke strange Dr. Seussical lyrics aloud to herself:

"Red leather, yellow leather. Red leather, yellow leather. Unique, New York. Unique, New York."

Fish was amazed at the way they listened whenever he gave some direction on a line reading or offered an alternative schema for blocking the scene. They asked insightful questions about his "vision." They smoked cigarettes in between scenes and went out for mojitos and tacos after rehearsal, discussing their favorite movies, their apartment situations, what their parents thought about their life choices, what had made them want to be actors. A few of them already had their lines memorized. And by the end of the week, rehearsing every night at Fish's apartment, they were all off book.

With the help of Klein and the actors, the play was advertised across various social media feeds. Because he had divorced himself from such things, Fish took pains to advertise the play in the most underground ways he could imagine. He posted it on Craigslist, contributed it to the weekly "nonsense New York" email newsletter, submitted it to Brooklyn's neighborhood zines, and pasted flyers to the walls of subway stations. The flyers, which he'd designed to look edgy and serious, shunned colors and exclamation points in hopes of piquing intrigue with the subtlety of the information and the telegram-type font, a clarion call to hipster artsy types who fancied themselves appreciators of New York's anti-yuppie arts scene. The flyers read as follows:

POSTLAPSARIA, CONNECTICUT

A play in five acts

Written & Directed by:

Fish

When: May 31st, 9PM

Where: The Temporary Contemporary Gallery

528 W. 39th Street, 3rd Floor

New York, NY

Ring buzzer for freight elevator upon arrival.

One show only. The building will be destroyed on
June 1st.

FREE

Fish stared pridefully at the advertisement, vacillating minute
to minute between a gripping paranoia that nobody would show up
and an equally potent fear that the turnout would be huge.

• • •

On opening night (which, of course, was also closing night), the
turnout was somewhere in the middle of his frets. Nearly all of
the couches, chairs, and love seats that he'd dragged into the middle of the gallery floor were filled, and a few ambivalent attendees
stood at the back, unsure, just yet, whether they'd be staying for the
duration of this very clearly low-budget play. Marcel and Stanley
had helped him design the set. Ferns, trees in clay pots, flowers,
and hanging vines had been dragged from the terrace into the gallery, arranged to form a mock Eden. Stanley directed the overhead
lights away from the paintings and down onto a small stage that
had been borrowed from Josephine, who used it for her one-woman
show (entitled "I Am The Egg Woman"). Refreshments consisting of
boxed wine and bodega plantain chips were served from the kitchen
counter.

Fish waited with the actors behind one of Marcel's largest paintings, which had been repurposed as an improvised wall. He'd hardly
slept the night before, thoughts of disaster coursing past his eyelids—nobody showing up, a lambasting review that ended his career
before it even started, an actor forgetting their lines, a light falling
from the ceiling and braining an audience member.

Peering out from behind the painting, he glanced at the audience. Fish had basked in their awe as they were taken up in the freight elevator, offering brief comments about the paintings lining the elevator shaft and milking the drama of opening the old iron doors onto the gleaming white space of the gallery. A constellation of warmly lit windows from the Hudson Yards skyscrapers was visible beyond the terrace. The audience was primarily populated by people around Fish's age wearing beanies and fiddling with their septum piercings. A few faces he recognized—there was Iris, sipping wine out of a plastic cup and running his hand over his mutton chops as he chatted with his Carhartt-clad friends. There was Klein, passing a joint to one of his overdressed finance bros, his arm draped over Carmen's shoulders. There was Psycho B, his coked-up leg thrumming a tattoo into the floor and cackling at something with his small herd of compatriots. Marcel and Stanley occupied a love seat in the front row, Rocky and Monty purring on their laps.

And there was Madame Meticulous! He hadn't seen her arrive— she must've taken the stairs. She fanned herself with a *Bon Appétit* magazine, reclined in a chair with her bulbous tummy splaying her thin legs out to the sides. The sight of her here, in the gallery where they'd first met, brought a fresh wave of self-doubt to his stomach. Now a real artist, an artist who'd been featured in the fucking *New Yorker*, would be appraising his work. She'd seen Fish naked, and yet he'd never felt more vulnerable.

Then Mystery Dude appeared, a cup of red wine in one hand and a napkin full of plantain chips for Madame Meticulous in the other. She gave him a weary smile and he kissed her on the cheek, leaving a small red stain on her satin skin. Fish thought it was kind of a dick move that he'd drink when she couldn't. He wondered if he would drink if it had been him, instead of

Mystery Dude, there at her side. He would've at least given sobriety a try, he thought.

The lights dimmed, the audience hushed, and Fish refilled his wine cup for the third time. Drained it. *Partiboy just wants—No, shut up, not now.* He took a breath and walked out from behind the canvas and stepped gingerly up onto the stage. His friends in the audience led a cheer and a raucous—as yet unwarranted—burst of applause echoed throughout the gallery.

"Encore!" shouted Psycho B.

Fish held up his hands—which he realized were shaking a little—to quiet the audience. He clasped them behind his back as he spoke. He felt his knuckles going white.

"Hi everyone. Um, yeah, so . . . I'm Fish. And, uh, thanks for coming tonight! I really appreciate it, and I know our actors—who are honestly, like, super talented, by the way—I know they really appreciate it, too. Um, yeah, and so before we begin, I just want to thank Marcel and Stanley real quick. This is their gallery, and this is the last night this building will be here. So . . . so, yeah, thanks for, you know, making it a special night."

Marcel half-stood and gave a brief Queen Elizabeth II wave to the audience and everyone applauded loudly. Stanley dabbed at his eyes with a fluorescent pocket square and Marcel clutched his chest dramatically and mouthed *thank you* in Fish's direction. As the applause for Marcel and Stanley simmered into silence, Fish found himself locking eyes with Madame Meticulous. She gave him a little half smile and a thumbs up with the hand that was not supporting her stomach.

"Okay! Well, uh, I think there's some more wine around here unless Psycho B drank it all already."

Polite laughter.

"Fire exits are over there-ish, and . . . well, obviously turn off your cell phones, please—don't be a dick. Um, yeah . . . I guess that's pretty much it, so . . . enjoy the play!"

Fish gave a final wave and walked on wobbly legs back behind the painting. The actors patted him on the back, and he gave each of their hands a final, supportive squeeze.

Zeke, transformed into Adam, stepped out onto the stage, pausing in the center of a pool of light. Fish had decided, in the end, not to go through with his whole antigravity winch idea. It was too complicated, too expensive. Adam glanced a little curiously, a little nervously around the staged kitchen. Working up some nerve, he opened the refrigerator. There was the single slice of apple pie, which Carmen had baked the night before.

> ADAM
> (Reading aloud from the sticky note attached to the pie plate)
> Do not eat…

Fish allowed himself a breath. *Here we go . . .*

The first act ended without incident. *So far, so good.* Fish's heart thrummed in his chest as the play, *his* play, unfolded before the audience.

> EVE
> There is one plant I wasn't able to identify …
> It's an apple tree, that much is clear. But it's
> a genus I've never encountered before.

> ADAM
> How strange.

> EVE

Indeed. I've taken the liberty of instructing
Lou not to water it too much until I've deduced
the species, its needs and so forth.

ADAM

Sorry, who?

EVE

Lou—the plumber? Perhaps you haven't met. Charming fellow. Says the previous tenant loved to
make pies from the windfall apples.

ADAM

Is that so...
(Gesturing to a goldfish in a bowl)
Say, do you suppose this goldfish looks like a
Matthew? Matt for short, obviously. Or maybe a
Peter?

EVE

Why complicate it? Just call it Goldfish.

ADAM

But Goldie, for short, right?

EVE

I don't see why not.

Fish risked a glance at the audience, tearing his eyes from the
stage. They were smiling, watching. Psycho B's foot thrummed contentedly against the floor. Exeunt. Begin act three.

ADAM

Eat it?

EVE

Sure, why not?

ADAM

Because it's just been sitting in this fridge for
who knows how long!

EVE

(shrugging)
Lou says it's the best apple pie he's ever had.

ADAM

Yeah?

EVE

Yeah.

ADAM

But…

EVE

But what? I'm starving, what's the big deal? It
doesn't count as a date if we fuck without eating
something, you know…

ADAM

Ha. Right. Right. It's just that … Well … You
know Jainkoa?

                    EVE
That creepy guy who lurks around the garden?
Yes, I've had the misfortune of making his ac-
                  quaintance.

                   ADAM
Right, well … It's just … Well, he says I
            shouldn't eat the pie.

                    EVE
                  (beat)
Ah, I see … And you're, what, scared?

                   ADAM
No, not scared, exactly …

Right around the end of the fourth act, Fish heard a hushed
commotion coming from the audience. His eyes had been glued
to the stage, entranced by the actors, the words he'd been hammering and tinkering with for months leaving their mouths and
living, briefly, in the air. He couldn't be sure (he was far too
invested), but he thought it was going rather well. Everyone was
remembering their lines and articulating them clearly and with
feeling. The blocking they'd devised looked natural and unhurried, and the set looked great. Stanley had a friend who worked
on Broadway, and she'd supplied costumes. It all looked, all
sounded, all felt—just great.

                    LOU
What's the worst that could happen? It's a slice
            of pie, for godsakes!

The commotion grew louder, more urgent. Fish heard chair legs scraping gently against the painted cement floors and hushed gasps that grew louder.

"Someone call 911!" someone shouted.

The actors faltered.

                         ADAM
    Enough of this Yoda bullshit, dude. What's the
            big deal? What happens if we—

More chairs scraping. Adam distracted. Not scripted. Whispers becoming shouts.

                         ADAM
          If we take a bite of the pie?

                       JAINKOA
    If there is one piece of advice that I implore
              you to … uh, Fish?

Fish whipped his head toward the commotion, peering out from behind the painting and scanning the darkened audience for the source.

"Already on it! It's fine! Sorry for the interruption, everyone." It was Mystery Dude, holding an iPhone to his ear (in blatant disregard to the phones off rule, Fish noted).

"Why are you apologizing? Get me *the fuck* out of here!" hissed Madame Meticulous.

Fish had never heard her sound so angry before, had never seen her placid face contorted with such emotion. After a beat, he realized he'd been frozen in place, watching the scene unfold as though it were a continuation of the play. Much of the audience appeared to be thinking along the same lines, gazing with rapt attention from the stage to Madame Meticulous and back to the stage, considering whether this experimental touch added or detracted from the decorum of *Postlapsaria, Connecticut*. Fish leaped into action, rushing to Madame Meticulous's side, and helping Mystery Dude, who had her other arm, guide her into the elevator. The actors stared, dumbfounded, at Fish, at each other, at the audience.

"Are you okay? What happened? Are you hurt?" Fish asked, the words streaming out of his mouth.

"She's fine. Her water just broke," said Mystery Dude.

"I am most certainly *not* fine!" snapped Madame. "And I refuse to have my baby in a creepy old elevator in Hell's Kitchen."

Mystery Dude rolled his eyes at Fish over the top of Madame's head. Fish ignored him, hated him.

"No offense, Fish," added Madame Meticulous, her voice softer, between quick breaths and winces of pain that screwed her face up into a pinched almond. "And it's a lovely play. Really lovely. I guess this little fucker wants me to miss the fifth act. He or she or *they* is a week early."

"But hopefully a *he*," joked Mystery Dude.

A withering glance from Madame Meticulous deleted the grin from his face.

"Thanks," was all Fish could manage to say.

He piloted the elevator down to the street, opening the doors just as a screaming ambulance was pulling to a halt in front of the building. Mystery Dude and two EMTs with buzz cuts helped Madame onto a gurney in the back of the ambulance. Mystery Dude reached out to shake Fish's hand. Fish grasped it, feeling his rubbery arm being pumped up and down twice. Then Mystery Dude gave him an exasperated look that suggested something like, "well, here we go," and climbed into the back of the ambulance next to Madame Meticulous. The heavy doors slammed shut and Fish watched until the flashing lights disappeared down Tenth Avenue. A junkie poked her mousy head from a weathered camping tent on the sidewalk and asked him what time it was. Fish didn't have a watch or a phone, but when he said "ten-ish" the junkie shrugged and disappeared back into the tent. Fish took the elevator back up to the gallery.

Upon exiting the elevator, hands in pockets, eyes on the ground, imagining Madame Meticulous being sped off to the hospital in the back of that ambulance, Mystery Dude telling her everything would be fine, it took Fish a few steps before he realized that the audience was staring at him. He stared back, unsure what to say.

"Encore!" Psycho B shouted again, breaking the silence.

The audience cheered and the actors beckoned Fish up onto the stage. After a few false starts, he managed to speak.

"Everything's cool. Her water broke, but she's on her way to Mount Sinai now."

Again, the audience cheered. Fish noticed that all of the wine boxes were now empty, and a cloud of pot smoke hung thick in the air. Perhaps the audience would be stupefied into thinking the play was halfway decent. The actors picked up where they'd left off, continuing as though nothing had happened. A surge of pride filled Fish's chest as he watched them finish the performance.

MIKE
There was one rule—literally just one! And you
broke it. Nice going. Fucking idiots.

•••

Fish smoked a cigarette on the roof of the gallery. The skyscrapers showed dark against the ghostly predawn sky. Not quite night, not quite day. The audience was long gone, traipsing out of the elevator a little buzzed and conversing about the play and their plans for the evening.

A few people had told him they'd loved it, and that had felt nice. The actors had hugged him and left, promising to stay in touch and asking him to keep them in mind for future projects. Marcel and Stanley had given him a tearful hug and he'd bent to stroke Rocky and Monty for probably the last time. Marcel and Stanley walked home hand in hand without looking back at the gallery, the cats mounted on their shoulders like pirates' parrots. Klein and Psycho B had invited him out, but he'd declined, making an excuse about needing to clean up the stage.

But he didn't have to clean up the stage. The building was scheduled to be knocked down by a great wrecking ball in a matter of hours. Already he could see men in neon vests and hard hats assembling on the sidewalk below, smoking cigarettes and drinking coffee out of Styrofoam cups. In the end, Marcel and Stanley hadn't bothered removing the rest of the paintings from the walls. They'd be destroyed with the building.

Fish felt strangely drained. He'd spent almost a year working on the play: editing it, casting it, staging it, and everything. He'd done the damn thing. Poured everything he had into it. So, Fish was stunned to discover how fleeting the sense of accomplishment was. Questions shot through his mind, and he felt uneasy. He'd written and staged a play—and yet, did this make him a playwright? Nobody was paying him to write. So, what next? Would it always be like this? Finish one project and immediately look to the next? Keep hoping that something—anything—would somehow break through to the critics or the mainstream audience? Keep toiling over his typewriter for . . . for *what* exactly? Himself?

Fish wasn't sure he had it in him. The neglected cigarette singed his fingers, and he flicked it away across the roof. The butt burst into a brief, glowing orange plume before simmering into invisibility in the gray light.

As the sun broke through the morning fog, the West Side illuminated in a brilliant copper glow, Fish watched the tall wrecking ball making its ponderous way down West Thirty-Ninth Street. The thought of staying planted, right there on the roof, as the wrecking ball came swinging towards the building, flitted quickly through Fish's consciousness. It was hardly a serious thought. But his heart bent toward the romance of it—succumbing to the wrecking ball like the paintings on the walls, a tortured playwright committing passive suicide after the premiere and only performance of his one play.

The wrecking ball was getting closer. *I ought to get moving.* It was a preposterous machine, a boxy cockpit with a giraffe-like neck and what looked like a massive bowling ball locked in place three-fourths of the way up the neck. It looked medieval. A brutal way to destroy a thing.

Fish crept slowly down the stairs to the gallery. He entered the elevator for the last time, took a final glance at the gallery, and tried to reminisce on his year there. He came up a little blank, the memories blurring together in a jumble of vodka-drunk afternoons and bleary-eyed hungover mornings. Though his own set of gallery keys swung from the carabiner on his belt loop, he grabbed the spare key from behind the cat portrait in the stairwell and pocketed it. Perhaps he'd come across the key months, years, or decades from now and it would stir something in his memory. An image. Or some random quote from Marcel. Maybe just a feeling of some kind.

He piloted the elevator down to the street for the last time, leaving the heavy doors open, the paintings decorating the elevator shaft on display for whoever might walk by. While the repeated phone calls to 311 had gone unheeded, the rumbling approach of the wrecking ball was enough to break through the junkies' stupor. Their wild, frantic limbs gathered their encampment into a shopping cart in a frenzy of activity, panic rattling their eyes.

Fish walked up Thirty-Ninth Street, passing the wrecking ball as it crossed Tenth Avenue.

Birth

Chapter 19

And Fish kept walking. Through the warm gas fumes that linger in the air around the Port Authority. Past the blaring screens of Times Square, the dingy blocks eerily empty but for two prostitutes perched on a pair of docked Citi Bikes, smoking cigarettes. The light from a Taco Bell advertisement gilded their fishnets each time they lazily pumped their knees against the pedals of the stationary bikes. Fish stared straight ahead as he walked by, feeling their eyes follow. One whispered something to the other and they erupted into a fit of laughter. As Fish passed a grimy alcove, the sound of bare feet scraping softly against the sidewalk announced the presence of a skeletal figure ensconced in the shadows. Fish kept walking uptown. For several blocks he didn't see another soul, until there was a taxi driver urinating into a storm drain. The sun had begun its daily ascent, washing the sky in a cement gray. Around the upper limits of Hell's Kitchen, he saw a drag queen setting out carafes of ice water on little tables housed in one of those outdoor enclosures that restaurants had erected during the pandemic.

At West Sixty-Fifth Street, he cut into Central Park. Bikers in tight neon jerseys and smooth, meringue-shaped helmets whooshed past him on their skinny-tired bikes, leaving a gust of exhaled breath in their wake. Fish could no longer imagine having that kind of energy, the kind that got you out of bed at five in the morning and in a full-body sweat by six. He used to have that kind of energy. He could hardly believe that at one point in his life, that had been him pumping out reps with his teammates in those predawn hours in the university gymnasium. One of the bikers plowed right into a pigeon that had been too late in taking wing from the oncoming wheels. The biker wobbled, nearly falling over, before swatting the pigeon away from his handlebars. The pigeon pinwheeled briefly through the air before catching itself and fluttering off to rejoin its flock. Fish stopped walking to watch the pigeon. Blown about by the world, dodging disaster a beat too late, exhausted, and covered in city soot. The pigeon disappeared behind a tree. Fish resumed his peripatetic route.

He hadn't slept last night. Hadn't even gone home. His eyelids felt dry as parchment, his tongue too large for his mouth. After a while, he realized his feet were taking him north, up to Morningside Heights. His somnambulant legs carried him out of the park. A few students wearing JanSport backpacks and crew neck sweaters ambled out of the Columbia University library, rubbing their eyes against the harsh morning light. Fish wondered if they'd been cramming for some test or pulling an all-nighter to finish a term paper or something. He supposed their semester must be coming to an end soon. He would've been finishing his L2 year. He had new regrets now, but he knew in his bones that leaving the law program had not been a mistake. For better or worse, he'd done what he'd come to New York to do—had, more or less, sounded his barbaric yawp over the roofs of the world. It had not been easy.

Fish had been to Mount Sinai Morningside only once before, to retrieve Marcel after his kidney stone procedure. The hospital was hard to miss—a sprawling collection of glass buildings juxtaposed against its neighbor, the Cathedral Church of St. John the Divine. As last time, it took Fish a few tries to locate the right building, the one that housed the maternity ward. He gave Madame Meticulous's name—her real name—to the receptionist.

"And how do you know the mother?" the receptionist asked. She regarded Fish dubiously over the top of her Duane Reade eyeglasses.

"I'm the father," he croaked. It may not have been a lie. His voice felt as though it hadn't been used in weeks.

The receptionist had him sign a form, checked his ID and vaccination card, took his temperature with this little *Star Wars* gun-looking thing, and told him the room number and how to get there, reminding him to put on a mask, please.

One of the bands on his mask snapped as soon as he pulled it over his ears in the elevator. He left it dangling from one ear, to show some effort. He knocked at door 4C, and a man's voice called out, "Come in!"

Oh, great, thought Fish. *Fucking Mystery Dude.*

But when he entered, Mystery Dude was nowhere to be seen. The voice belonged to a doctor, a tall bent man with a kindly face and hair the color of sugar. He was standing next to the hospital bed with a clipboard in his hands. A stethoscope dangled around his neck. Madame Meticulous was propped up at a forty-five-degree angle in the bed, wearing a soft pink gown and clutching a pillow to her chest. She had a dazed, apprehensive look on her face, though she didn't appear to be all that shocked by Fish's surprise appearance.

"Oh, you're not my PA," said the doctor, adding a soft chuckle.

"No. . . I'm Fish."

"That's . . . What an interesting name," the doctor replied, smiling.

"Could we get a minute, please?"

Madame Meticulous had spoken so quietly that it took the doctor a moment to register her request.

"Of course. I'll check in on you in a bit. Ring if you need anything." The doctor placed a tender hand on Madame's shoulder, smiled again at Fish, and left the room.

Fish and Madame Meticulous stared at each other for a moment. Fish broke eye contact first, directing his gaze to the window. One of St. John's spires stared back at him. Fish searched for something to say, but realized he wasn't sure why he'd come here. Finally, mercifully, Madame spoke.

"I was going to ask what you're doing here, but I guess I know," she said.

"Oh?"

"You want to know if Auguste was yours, right?"

"Auguste?" Fish asked.

"As in Rodin. The sculptor?"

"Right." Fish wasn't sure what to do with his hands, so he shoved them in his pockets. His skin was clammy and his clothes felt too loose here, too tight there.

"How'd the play end up? Sorry if I derailed things a little bit," she said.

"Oh, no, it was totally fine. You don't have to apologize," he said. "And thanks for coming, by the way. Means a lot."

"You came to my exhibition opening, remember?"

"Right, yeah . . . So where's—"

But Fish's question was cut short by a gentle sob that escaped from somewhere in Madame's chest. She looked away, out the window. The spire stared back, its solidity an unspoken indictment of flesh's impermanence. A teardrop teetered at the corner of her eye.

Fish took a step closer to the bed. Madame regarded him briefly before smiling and wiping her eyes.

"You're not a dad, Fish," sighed Madame Meticulous. "I don't know if that's a disappointment or a relief, but it's the truth."

A "huh" slithered out from Fish's throat, seeping through his chapped lips. Then silence. Madame's gaze drifted back to the window. Fish cleared his throat.

"So, where's the other guy? The dad, I mean. The guy at the play."

"Ugh," groaned Madame Meticulous. "He was pissing me off,

anyway. Unhelpful. I suppose he was anxious about all this too . . . I don't think he expected . . . *Neither* of us expected . . . Well, anyway, I sent him out for coffee. I haven't had a coffee in nine months, can you believe that?"

Fish pictured Mystery Dude walking into the room, two Starbucks coffees in his hands and a butter-damp bag of scones pinched in his fingers. Would he punch Fish? Tell him to fuck off? Yell? Fish felt his knees creak under the weight of his body.

"Oh, so . . . It was a . . . "

"A stillbirth, you can say it," Madame interrupted, pasting on a weary grin as red splotches colored her cheeks. "More common than you'd think, apparently."

Fish's feet were rooted in place. He couldn't shake the feeling that he'd come here to do *something*, though he wasn't sure what. Nausea constricted his stomach, and he felt an acrid film coating his teeth. He was finding it necessary to remind himself to breathe.

It had been there. This thing that had been fucking with the gravity of his consciousness, no matter how many drugs he did or cocktails he downed. It had been there. For nine months. He was surprised to find himself worrying that he'd miss it, that weight. He'd grown so used to its presence, clouding every thought of the future such that he'd been forced to live very nearly in the present. Nine months of that.

His thoughts, trickling wearily through his consciousness, grew in strength and volume until the dam burst, flooding his skull. Fish suddenly felt very awake. Madame picked at a callus on her palm. He pictured her bent over a hunk of marble, chiseling with great concentration as she worked the stone into her own vision. He kicked himself for how quickly—how *instantaneously*—his mind had jumped to what the news of the lost child would mean *for him*. He couldn't imagine how Madame Meticulous had dealt with it—*would* deal with it. Maybe forever. She'd been thinking of herself as two people. All that time. It had been there. *Fuck.*

"God, I'm sorry. That's . . ." stammered Fish. "I should go, yeah? I feel like an *asshole* . . . Fuck, I don't know why I—"

"No, stay, Fish. Please. It's all right, honestly. Sit down. Did you sleep last night? You look like hell—no offense. Not that I can judge . . ." she said, forcing a chuckle and gesturing to a chair next to the bed.

"But what about—"

"It's fine. Really. Please, sit with me," she said. She took his hand and pulled him gently down into a chair beside the bed. This was the husband chair, Fish figured. "I think it was sweet of you to come, actually. I think."

Fish could hardly speak. Thoughts were being relayed to his mouth, but the runners kept dropping the damn baton.

"You look beautiful, actually," Fish said, finally, sitting down and dragging the chair into a conversational angle. He'd meant it, but it sounded corny as hell.

"Oh, shut up," she said with a laugh. After a moment, Fish laughed too.

They ended up talking for more than an hour. They talked through their first impressions of one another, mocking each other's perceptions and misperceptions. They discussed the untimely ending of their relationship. They apologized to each other and spoke frankly about how they ought to have gone about things, what should've been said and when. After a while, the conversation lulled. They were both staring out the window.

"Hey," ventured Fish, "how long ago did he go out for coffee? I can run out for some if—"

"Last night," said Madame Meticulous, not meeting Fish's eyes. "There's a Starbucks across the street. I don't expect he'll be returning." Though she uttered these words in her usual matter-of-fact manner, her voice cracked a little as she spoke. After a long pause, she inhaled and smiled up at Fish.

"Oh," said Fish. "Sorry, I didn't mean . . ."

"It's fine. We were fighting a lot. I think he was looking for a good excuse to bail, honestly. I suppose it's easier, this way . . ."

Her voice trailed off, and Fish took her hand. A sense of chivalry, of purpose, suddenly suffused his bones. This was it, he thought. This was how his year in New York would end. This was his next chapter. Yes, *this* was the direction his life would take. He and Madame Meticulous would be one of those young handsome couples who strolled around Park Slope on weekends, coming from or going to cozy little brunch spots and making excuses not to hang out with friends because honestly their favorite thing was just staying home and watching Netflix together.

"You know, maybe I could . . . Maybe we could—" Fish began, but Madame Meticulous cut him off.

"Fish," she said, looking him directly in the eye. "I know you're trying to do the white knight thing here. It's sweet—honestly, it is. But I think . . . You've got to get your own shit figured out before you get back involved in mine, you know?"

When Fish said nothing, she went on. "I'm moving back home to San Francisco. Just for a little while. To be close to my mom. She was all excited about being a grandma . . . I think I just need a little break. Know what I mean?"

"Sure, I get that," Fish said, the words deflating as they bypassed his teeth.

Madame Meticulous smiled at him again. Not condescendingly, but with a sort of wise, knowing expression. When he stood to leave, Madame Meticulous stretched out one arm and pulled him down into a hug. He kissed her on the cheek. She smelled like soap, but her skin tasted salty. In that moment, he wanted nothing more than to nestle up next to her on that hospital bed, prop her head up in the crook of his arm, and talk about how it all would be.

Leaving the hospital, he felt empty again, like he had up on the roof of the art gallery. It was nearly noon. Though the streets were bathed in the sun's early summer warmth, a chill passed through his bones each time he crossed through the long shadows cast by St. John's spires. Fish caught the 1 train down to the West Village and walked straight to Johnny's Bar.

Chapter 20

Finally, the bathroom stopped spinning. Fish had no idea what time it was. He picked his head up from the toilet bowl, using his sleeve to wipe a crusty substance from his lips. From what he could recall, it had been one of those puking situations where he had wondered at what point, exactly, he ought to be concerned enough to go to the hospital. He pictured himself being wheeled in on a gurney, vomit staining his T-shirt, just as Madame Meticulous was leaving, bypassing each other in the hospital lobby.

Using the toilet as an anchor, he pulled himself to his feet. He noticed his toothbrush by the mirror, which was a good sign—he'd made it back home, at least. He had no memory of the final commute that had brought him, miraculously, back to Spanish Harlem. After Johnny's Bar, he'd bought a homeless man—who'd had a lump on his forehead the size of an egg, Fish remembered now—a box of cereal and a quart of milk in exchange for his Citi Bike. He'd asked the man about the lump and the man, who looked to be about sixty but could've been twenty years older or younger than that, explained that it was a fatty tissue growth that would have to be removed, but that he was holding off on taking care of it until he could get his knees replaced, as they were his medical priority at the moment.

Then Fish had pedaled off in the direction of the Lower East Side. He stopped only when he came to a low cement wall overlooking the East River. Tourists milled about Seaport, laughing over cheeseburgers on outdoor patios and pointing up at buildings and into shop windows. Fish took a seat at the first bar he saw—an outdoor imitation bungalow serving overpriced rum cocktails. He had several of these and worked casually, drunkenly on this week's *New Yorker* crossword puzzle. He made very little progress, and the tiki stool became uncomfortable. He grimaced as he paid the tab before deciding that he would not allow financial constraints to infect his consciousness that day. He stopped at the first smoke shop he saw, bongs arranged in neat rows in the foggy window and a tobacco pipe replacing the first *S* in the Smoke Shop sign. He purchased a mushroom chocolate bar, and wolfed half of it down—more out of hunger than any desire to zoot his mind into outer space, though this was a happy consequence. He couldn't remember when or what his last meal had been.

Strolling along Ludlow Street, he noticed that Metrograph Theater was playing *Chinatown*. He took a few puffs of a joint and wandered into the theater, purchasing a ticket and sitting all the way in the back. It was one of those movies he'd had on a mental list forever, recommended to him dozens of times by dozens of people, but had never gotten around to seeing. Whether it was the hallucinogens or the drama of the film itself, Fish was captivated from start to finish. The movie ended. He returned to his wandering.

It had started to rain, so he ducked into a 7-Eleven and purchased an umbrella. It blew apart after a few blocks. Fish let the drizzle spatter him as he walked, trying to shift his mindset to consciously enjoy the soft, wet pellets dappling his face. Again his courseless course was halted by the water, the Williamsburg Bridge looming grandly a few blocks away as bikers and runners huffed up the dramatic ascent over the East River. Fish noticed a bar a block down the road called Parkside Lounge. He couldn't see where the park was that it was supposed to be beside, but he wanted a drink and to get out of the rain—despite his best efforts, he couldn't, that afternoon, retrain his brain into enjoying something unpleasant.

It was a dingy dive—his favorite kind of place. Partiboy's favorite kind of place. It was dark and loud '80s rock blasted from unseen speakers as swirling, multicolored, polka dot lights streamed in revolutions around the bar. A stocky, badass chick was playing pool with a scruffy dude in jeans—beating him easily, from what Fish could tell—and a few regulars engaged the attractive bartender in slurred conversation.

Fish took up a chair at the other end of the bar. He flopped open his crossword puzzle and ordered a gin and tonic from the bartender, who, up close, was indeed very attractive. After two more gin and tonics he felt himself fading. He ought to go home, he knew. It was nearly midnight. He was exhausted. The bartender—her name was Liv—let him borrow her phone. Fish sent Uncle Nemo a telegram requesting a gram of the good stuff. Liv said she'd watch his magazine while he stepped out to use an ATM. Fish thought he caught a flirtatious flicker passing through her eyes as she spoke.

When Fish saw the familiar black sedan with flashing hazards pull to a stop a little ways down East Houston Street, he walked quickly to the vehicle and took a seat in the passenger seat. The driver, a young Middle Eastern dude with sharply manicured stubble, was on the phone with a woman. He motioned for Fish to be silent. Fish complied and listened as the driver explained to the speakerphone woman—she sounded like a girlfriend—that he was at the gym as he traded Fish a small vial of white powder in exchange for the neat fold of twenty-dollar bills in Fish's palm, winking at Fish and offering him a knucklebump as he made his silent departure. Fish went back into the bar and did a quick key bump in the grimy bathroom before settling his tab.

Someone had finished his crossword puzzle. Liv winked at him as he left but Fish was too hopped up to articulate any smooth lines. He left a generous tip. It turned out to be pretty easy to leave generous tips when money was temporarily detached from the reality of one's finances. On a whim, he stepped into a palmistry shop advertising readings for twenty bucks a pop. He'd always wondered how these places afforded rent—were *that many* people really desperate enough? Deluded enough? Drunk enough?

A little bell tinkled as he entered and a barefoot Indian woman in flowy crimson clothes silently beckoned him to sit in the plush seat across from her. She tucked her legs up in a pretzel beneath her and Fish hunched forward on his knees.

"Think of two wishes but speak only one of them out loud," she said.

This took Fish awhile, debating between telling the truth and skirting it, wary of how much to give away and trying to maintain a balance between buying into the spontaneity of the psychic session while retaining enough cynicism to sniff out a charlatan. His first wish was easily determined. After a long pause, he spoke the second wish aloud. The psychic had never at any point pressured him to hurry up with his answer. She had a placid expression and dark, searching eyes.

"I wish to be content." He liked the sound of that. It was both ambiguous and specific. He was excited to hear what the psychic would say.

"Hold out your hands," she gently commanded.

Fish complied, and she immediately began the reading, tracing the lines of his palms with the soft point of her index finger.

"You have a very strong life line. You have much passion. You are creative. In a past life, you were a writer. I can see that clearly. You are filled with doubt."

Fish thrilled at what she'd said about being a writer in his past life and missed most of what she'd said after that. She released his hands and settled Fish in her gaze, a neutral expression on her face.

"So," she said, opening her palms to him before settling them over her stomach, "What do you think of all that?"

Again Fish deliberated before speaking. None of it came out as enlightened as he'd hoped.

"It's crazy you said that thing about being a writer in my past life or whatever. I *am* a writer. Or, like, I'm trying to be. I don't know what to do next, though, you know? Like, I feel like I'm waiting for something to happen to me, or someone to reach out or something, and then I'll, like, suddenly have a writing career, you know? I feel like I have no, like, autonomy over it. Like, at all. I just wrote this play, and I staged it and everything and now it's over and I'm not sure what happens next or why I even did all that in the first place. If that makes sense?"

The psychic nodded sagely before speaking. "You must stay the course. Do not waver. Your passion forbids it. You must continue writing. But you must first become centered. Your mind is at odds with your soul. You must unite them. This is imperative."

Fish nodded, drinking in her words. He felt better already. The mushrooms, alcohol, cocaine, and nicotine were still flowing through his bloodstream, warming his numb extremities. He felt oddly lighter, as though he'd relieved himself of a heavy bag of groceries carted ten blocks and up several flights of stairs.

"Wow. Thank you. So much," he said, standing to leave.

"If you would like guidance in this journey—and this I very strongly suggest—I offer my services for personal guidance for a one-time fee of no more than two hundred and seventy dollars. You needn't answer now but consider it. Consider it very seriously. I believe that within eight sessions you will be able to break through this blockade of self-doubt."

She handed Fish a purple pamphlet advertising the rates of her services. This broke the spell a little bit for Fish; psychic enlightenment condensed into an à la carte menu.

"Thanks," he said, standing to leave. "Maybe some other time. Thanks, though. I enjoyed this. Really."

She nodded once more and waved as he exited the shop, the door tinkling again. Any possibility of calling it a night and heading home had left his consciousness. The rain had stopped. The streets were cool and perfumed with a damp sweetness.

It had been about an hour, so far as he could tell (time tended to distort into a surreal blur whenever he did coke or mushrooms, and mixing the two, well, forget about it), since he'd last curbed his appetite with a bump of cocaine. So, he stopped in at a little bistro on Orchard Street. He ordered a steak and four martinis, which he drank quickly between visits to the bathroom for quick snorts from the vial. At the table, he read the *New Yorker* issue's weekly "Shouts and Murmurs" and fiction installments, retaining very little of either. The waitress was a Rubenesque chick with face tattoos and a shaved head, and she was super cool with his lone wolf vibe. That's how it felt to Fish, at least. Maybe the massive bill he was running up with those martinis had something to do with her benevolent aura. He hardly touched the steak.

After the bistro, he found himself returning to Parkside Lounge, taking up the same seat he'd occupied earlier. To his delight, Liv, with her aquamarine eyes and dark curly hair, was still there— would probably be there until the bar closed around 4:00 a.m.

"Forget something?" she asked, already pouring a gin and tonic.

"Can I ask you an honest question and give you an honest statement?" Fish said.

"Sure," Liv said, adding a jocular shrug and leaning over the bar on her elbows.

She was less than a foot from his nose, and Fish felt her warmth emanating onto his face. The cocaine, like coal poured into a steam engine's furnace, motored his jaws into action.

"Are we flirting?" he asked.

"Yes, I think so," she said. "What's the honest statement?"

"I came back here to flirt with you some more," he said. He smiled in a way that he hoped was disarming, but his lips were struggling to catch up to his mind.

She laughed and jotted her number down on the back of a receipt. "Oh, wait, you don't have a phone!" she said. "Who the fuck doesn't have a phone, anyway?"

Fish shrugged. They made plans to hang out after her shift ended.

A guy sitting a few seats down from Fish struck up a conversation about books, having overheard something about Fish being a writer. He was more into Tolkien and George R.R. Martin–type stuff, and he had some choice words for the creators of *Game of Thrones*. But Fish was fucked up enough to enjoy batting around a conversation with the guy, whose name was Gabe. Gabe was in his mid-forties, affable, a chef, South Polynesian on his dad's side, scraggily goateed, his arms decorated in dark, angular tribal tattoos.

To kill some time until his date with Liv, Fish followed Gabe to his apartment, which was around the corner from the bar, as he'd proudly explained. He was a regular. Gabe's living situation was temporary, he said, but he'd also said he'd been living there for nearly two years. He slept on an air mattress that sagged beside a queen-sized bed in the studio apartment. The queen of the queen-sized bed was his roommate, a girl he'd used to hook up with but who now had this boyfriend, but sometimes she cheated on said boyfriend with Gabe, and Gabe was in love with the roommate, but she didn't reciprocate these feelings so it was a sort of awkward, sexy situation, he explained. They smoked a joint and snorted little anthills of cocaine off the roommate's makeup mirror until the vial was empty.

Gabe's roommate had a dachshund puppy that she'd bought during COVID but which she couldn't really care for once her office job went back to being in-person rather than remote. Hence Gabe's presence—he was currently unemployed, but he lived rent free so long as he took care of the puppy. Fish held the puppy in his arms, and it squirmed and teethed playfully on his hands, and Fish was too messed up to notice the raised chain of little red welts it left over his knuckles. Sometime after four, Gabe's phone buzzed and he answered it. It was Liv (so he really was a regular, Fish thought), calling to ask for Fish back. Fish left Gabe's apartment, giving him a drunken hug and making a promise to hang out again soon, which, even in his fucked-up state, he seriously doubted.

He met up with Liv at a twenty-four-hour diner that she liked to hit up after her shift ended and they learned a little about each other. She said she was polyamorous and pansexual, and she was in an open relationship with a boyfriend. She lived in Bed-Stuy. She played the drums. She was a year older than Fish and a Pisces. She said it made sense that Fish was a Virgo. These were the only details Fish would retain the next day. They made out while she waited for a cab. He kissed her neck, and she told him to hold his horses. She smiled, told him to stop by the bar again sometime, told him to get some sleep, kissed him on the cheek, and left in the cab.

The sun was coming up. Fish was struck suddenly by a notion that he would be late for work. It was a Sunday—or it had been when he'd started drinking. He walk-sprinted all the way to the West Side, pausing at a souvenir shop in Times Square to buy a new shirt—one of those kitschy, cliché "I heart NY" T-shirts with a big red heart replacing the second word—to wear instead of his current T-shirt, which smelled of dive bar cigarette smoke, pot, and sweat.

Rushing, he ripped off his T-shirt, thrust it into the depths of his backpack, and yanked the new shirt over his head as he jogged down West Thirty-Ninth Street, unsure how late he was—or if he was late at all. The sun had just risen but his sense of time had become so distorted that he couldn't trust any of time's physical signs. The T-shirt felt cheap and boxy, billowing around his wiry frame.

He at last came to a stop at 528 West Thirty-Ninth Street. But that was after he'd walked by it a few times, thinking he'd missed it. Then, finally, it hit him: it was gone. A small part of him had known this the whole time, but this small part had been out-shouted by the cacophony of his thoughts. The building was demolished. It had been leveled into a rubble-strewn lot surrounded by a chain-link fence. Fish pressed his face up against the fence, staring for a while.

• • •

And somehow he'd made it back to his apartment. A calcified slice of pepperoni pizza rested on the edge of the sink, uneaten. Fish looked in the mirror. A thin white crust caked the underside of his nose like the finishing touch on a confection, stained a little pink at the edges from some nosebleed that he couldn't recall. He was still wearing that stupid souvenir shop T-shirt. And there was Partiboy, staring back at him.

Partiboy just wants to party, boy.
We already did that. Can't you tell?
Partiboy just wants to party, boy.
Course he does.
Partiboy just wants to party, boy.
Anyone ever tell you you have a tendency to repeat yourself?
Partiboy just wants to party, boy. Partiboy just wants to drink. Partiboy just wants to smoke. And snort and yell and laugh and tune in and

tune out, boy. Partiboy never wants to sleep again. Partiboy loves that splintering feeling when the strobe lights flash in time with the electronic music at the clubs. Partiboy just wants to come apart, boy. Partiboy just wants to dissolve into a million pieces and float around the coolest blocks in the city, boy. Partiboy just wants to be interesting, boy. Partiboy just wants YOU to be interesting, boy. And hasn't Partiboy done that, boy? You have a few stories under your belt now, don't you, boy? Partiboy gives you the best reality, boy, and you type them up into the best stories, don't you, boy? And who do you have to thank for that, boy? Partiboy, boy. Because Partiboy just wants to party, boy.

Fish stared in shock at Partiboy. Without bothering to brush his teeth or wipe the mess from his nose, he stumbled to his bedroom. He picked the typewriter up from his desk. Cajoled his limbs into bearing its weight down the stairs, out into the street. Dumped it into a trash bin on the corner of One Hundred Seventeenth Street and First Avenue. Trudged back upstairs to his apartment. Collapsed onto his bed.

Slept and slept.

• • •

F ish awoke to his body convulsing from a heaving cough. Sunlight beamed through his bedroom window, cooking his sheets. He kicked the covers away from his legs, feeling a dry crust of salt coating his skin. His nose felt as though it had been stuffed with calcified putty. Another cough erupted from his chest, forcing him to sit up against his pillows until the hacking fit subsided. He wasn't sure what time it was, or even what day.

Standing, his legs wobbled beneath him, and with the ungainly strides of a newborn giraffe, Fish made his way to the bathroom. He tossed the pizza slice in the garbage and took a long shower, inhaling the steam gratefully and surrendering himself to the torrent of hot water as it blasted the grime from his skin. He wondered briefly if Madame Meticulous would still be at the hospital. He wiped the steam from the bathroom mirror. There he was.

Ravenous, he bought an everything bagel from a café on the corner, its sliced faces coated in an inch of cream cheese and laden with thick slabs of smoked salmon. He devoured it messily on the subway, riding the 6 train all the way to Brooklyn Bridge-City Hall, the train line's terminal stop. Snippets of German, Spanish, Russian, and Italian fluttered at his ear as he walked through the herd of tourists milling about The Battery's grassy lawns. He bought a coffee from a street vendor, feeling its warmth against his palm through the flimsy blue paper cup. Untangling himself from the smiling, pointing crowds, he came to a stop at Manhattan's southern tip.

Sunlight glimmered in the ripples of the Hudson River, and a cool breeze flitted through his hair. From the way the sun peered out in orange bursts from behind the skyscrapers, Fish could tell it was some time in the late afternoon. He realized with pleasure that he had nowhere to be. When a Japanese family vacated a park bench overlooking the river, Fish plunked himself down against the weathered wooden planks. Sipping his coffee, he stared out at the water. Seagulls squawked petulantly as they beat the air overhead. The Staten Island ferry chugged unhurriedly under the Statue of Liberty's triumphal figure. Fish stared at the statue for a while. It looked small from this distance—small enough to fit in his pocket. He remained on the bench until the last flickers of dusk were extinguished by encroaching night. He felt the city at his back, a swell of riotous energy. Whether that energy was pushing him out toward the water or grasping at his shoulders to yank him back into its chaotic core, he could not tell. With a final glance at Lady Liberty, Fish strolled back toward the subway station.

Upon returning to his apartment, Fish noticed that the typewriter had been plucked from the top of the trash bin. Good riddance, he thought. Let it be some other quixotic rambler's burden. A flood of relief gushed over him. He was not a writer—he knew that now. But maybe he could be a New Yorker. And that would be enough.

About the Author

Fletcher Michael is a writer and actor based in Brooklyn, New York. He is the founder of Infinite Monkey Theater Company, through which he writes, directs, and produces full-length plays and sketch comedy shows. *Sidewalk Dance* is his third novel, following *Glass Bottle Season* (Keylight Books, 2023) and *Vulture* (Rebel Satori Press, 2022). For more information about past, current, and upcoming projects, check out fletcherisuptosomething.com.